# PRAISE FOR *HOW LUCKY YOU ARE*

"A nuanced, heartfelt debut, *How Lucky You Are* artfully honors the importance of dear old friends. I can't wait to read more from Kristyn Kusek Lewis."

—Allie Larkin, author of *Stay* and *Why Can't I Be You*

"[A] strong debut."

—*Publishers Weekly*

"In this wise and compulsively readable debut, Lewis follows three thirtysomething female friends and tackles even the heaviest of subjects with a restrained and self-assured hand, avoiding sentimentality while displaying an impressive emotional range. I could smell the doughnut muffins, taste the margaritas, and feel each high and low right along with the delightful characters. If you've ever had a best friend or been a best friend, this is a book for you."

—Meg Mitchell Moore, author of *The Arrivals* and *So Far Away*

"*How Lucky You Are* is a moving, thoughtful story about what happens when friends become family and stay close despite all odds. It's an honest, empathetic novel of love, commitment, and female friendship with characters I didn't want to let go."

—Meredith Goldstein, author of *The Singles* and Love Letters columnist at the *Boston Globe*

## ALSO BY KRISTYN KUSEK LEWIS

*How Lucky You Are*

# Save Me

*Kristyn Kusek Lewis*

GRAND CENTRAL
PUBLISHING

NEW YORK    BOSTON

Grand Central Publishing
Hachette Book Group
1290 Avenue of the Americas
New York, NY 10104

www.HachetteBookGroup.com

Printed in the United States of America

RRD-C

First Edition: December 2014
10 9 8 7 6 5 4 3 2 1

Grand Central Publishing is a division of Hachette Book Group, Inc.
The Grand Central Publishing name and logo is a trademark of Hachette Book Group, Inc.

The Hachette Speakers Bureau provides a wide range of authors for speaking events. To find out more, go to www.hachettespeakersbureau.com or call (866) 376-6591.

The publisher is not responsible for websites (or their content) that are not owned by the publisher.

Library of Congress Cataloging-in-Publication Data
Lewis, Kristyn Kusek.
  Save me / Kristyn Kusek Lewis. — First edition.
      pages cm
  ISBN 978-1-4555-7223-6 (paperback)—ISBN 978-1-4555-7222-9 (ebook)
1. Life change events—Fiction. 2. Self-realization in women—Fiction.
3. Marriage—Fiction. I. Title.
  PS3612.E9655S28 2015
  813'.6—dc23
                                    2014016032

*For Jay*

**Macbeth:** Canst thou not minister to a mind diseas'd,
Pluck from the memory a rooted sorrow,
Raze out the written troubles of the brain,
And with some sweet oblivious antidote
Cleanse the stuff'd bosom of the perilous stuff
Which weighs upon the heart?

**Doctor:** Therein the patient
Must minister to himself.

—WILLIAM SHAKESPEARE, *Macbeth*


You can never know the truth of anyone's marriage, including your own.

—NORA EPHRON, *I Remember Nothing*

# Save Me

# CHAPTER ONE

The cancer is back. I'm sure of it. What else could explain why I haven't heard from him?

I called Owen's cell twice in the hour I sat at the airport in Philadelphia and once before that, from my hotel. *Be patient, Daphne,* I think. I pull the newspaper out of my bag and try to flip through it but I can't focus. The words are slippery. My eyes jump from headline to headline. *New campaign finance legislation introduced. Silver screen legend dead at the age of ninety-six. Strong storms expected in the Midwest.*

The flight attendant gets on the intercom to tell us that we're beginning our descent into Raleigh–Durham. *Two different places,* I think. I don't know why it irritates me so much every time I hear it, but it does. People don't live in *Raleigh–Durham* any more than they do in *New York–New Jersey* or *San Francisco–San Jose.* Two. Different. Places. I fold the paper in my lap and close my eyes. *He's just busy,* I say to myself like a mantra—*he's just busy, just busy. No news isn't always bad news.* Minutes later, the plane's wheels hit the ground and I pull the phone from my bag. No messages. I call him again. No answer.

I shove the newspaper into my bag. The woman next to me—skinny, smelling faintly of coffee and the mint gum she's been chewing since takeoff—is sitting obediently with her hands clasped over her lap, her eyes pinned on the seat belt sign, waiting for it to ding and tell her it's okay to get up. I look out the window and tell myself to stop overreacting—*he's just busy*—and remind myself to breathe.

It's normal for Owen and me to ignore each other's messages during the workday, but this day is different. Kevin, who's fourteen and one of his favorite patients (really his favorite patient, not that he'd admit to having one) is getting the results of his latest scan. Owen's done everything he can to treat the leukemia, all of the traditional methods and then a clinical trial. The test is due back today. *If the blood work still shows evidence...* I stand up in my seat and smile at the woman next to me, who's still frozen in her seat even though the people three rows up are starting to get off the plane.

I could tell that he was anxious when we spoke last night, him at home and me in my room in Philadelphia, where I was staying for an annual medical conference I always dread. I hesitated whether to even bring up his birthday, which is today, because I knew he wouldn't want to acknowledge it if Kevin's scan was bad. *Are you nervous?* I finally asked. He cleared his throat and muttered that he was. When he didn't elaborate, I changed the subject, saying that I'd pick up takeout from his favorite Mexican place and that we could just eat it whenever he got home. He said that sounded fine (his code for that he didn't really care) and then asked how my talk had gone. I made a bad joke about there being a drunken rush for my autograph at the cocktail reception, and he laughed politely.

I told him that I loved him. I wished him luck. I said good night.

Three hours later, I look out our kitchen window at the sun setting behind the pine trees that line the edge of our property. I know that I am lucky to have such problems, but I can't help feeling like there's something wrong with the fact that it's seven p.m. and I still haven't spoken to my husband on his birthday. I picture him in one of the hospital conference rooms with Kevin and his parents, whom I've never met, of course, but whom I feel like I know well. I picture the boy's mother with a crumpled tissue in her hand. I picture the boy, his thin frame lost in an oversized Duke sweatshirt (he was a fan long before his health brought him here for care), and I sit down on the wood floor next to Blue, the Newfoundland we adopted two years ago. Our pre-baby baby, I joked. I scratch the top of her head and wonder how soon he'll be back, whether I should put the takeout in the oven to warm it up.

I decide to set the table at least, placing Owen's present in the middle like a centerpiece. Inside the box is a gift certificate for the two of us to go on a paddling trip later this spring on the Outer Banks, which, despite the fact that we've lived in North Carolina for ten years, is a place we've never been. I was able to make a reservation with a touring company without specifying a date, which is good, since pinning down a weekend when Owen can take off work is never easy.

It will be good for us. Canoeing is our thing—sort of. Owen even proposed on a canoe six years ago, which, now that I think about it, might actually be the last time I held an oar in my hands, but it's part of our history. We met when we were twelve years old, at summer camp in western Massachusetts, and our friendship began on the day that we sat across from each other in an old metal boat on the lake. Though it was almost twenty-five years ago, I still remember how it felt to be there, my skin seeming to glow from the summertime film of dirt and sweat that I can feel just thinking about it. Owen and I were buddies, that's the very best way I can describe it. We compared bug bites, raced each other during Capture the Flag, and sang the goofy songs that the counselors taught us to pass the time during hikes ("Fried ham, fried ham, cheese and bologna..."). He called me Daph and I let him, even though I had recently decided that because I was almost a teenager—*twelve and a half, almost an adult, really*—that I would answer only to Daphne.

The following summer, we shared a tentative slow dance at the August banquet and then we kissed. It was quick and sweet and meant that the one photograph that I had of him, in a dirty T-shirt and the soccer shorts we all wore that summer, was granted a permanent spot in the front of the Velcro wallet that I'd started carrying in my book bag. We wrote letters throughout the fall. My family lived outside of Boston, and he was farther west, near Springfield. He doodled at the bottom of the spiral notebook pages where he signed his name—blocky graffiti letters, *Owen + Daph*. Of course, we were in middle school, so by Christmas break, the letters were sporadic on both of our parts. That spring, my father's job got us transferred to Northern Virginia. Owen became a memory, and a good one.

Thirteen years later, I was standing in line at a sandwich place on Ninth Street just before the start of my residency when I noticed a handsome guy with a mop of wavy dark hair wearing the very same Duke tee that I'd bought for myself at a bookshop hours earlier. When our eyes met, he squinted, and then he shook his head in disbelief. "This is going to sound really weird, but did we go to summer camp together?" he asked, abandoning the guy who was reaching across the counter to hand him his turkey on rye. "Are you Daph? Daphne Mitchell?"

He was about to start his residency, too.

We found a bench somewhere and ate our lunch. Mustard spilled down my shirt and we both pretended not to notice. We moved on to afternoon beers in a dark pub where somebody kept playing Joni Mitchell on the jukebox and we discovered after a few drinks that we both remembered the words to "Fried Ham." The next week, we found time in our packed orientation schedules to share a walk across campus, and under the archway of an old stone building, we had our second kiss, all those years since the first.

*What were the chances that we'd both end up here? In Durham, North Carolina? After all of these years?* We kept saying it, over and over again, to each other, to our parents, to anyone who asked how we met. There was eventually an apartment together, and five years ago, a wedding, and now the farmhouse, which we fell in love with last fall despite its iffy foundation and the cracks in its windows. It is slowly coming together. Everything is falling into place.


Nine o'clock.

The laundry is folded. The floors are swept. I am answering emails and halfheartedly watching a TV cooking competition when I see Owen's headlights finally bouncing up the long driveway. I close my laptop and head into the kitchen, where I pull one of his favorite IPAs out of the six-pack that I bought on my way home from the airport. I'm pulling the top off of the bottle when he comes in the side door. He looks exhausted.

"Hey." I smile. Blue beats me to him and I gently nudge her away with my knee so that I can wrap my arms around him. I press my head to his chest and he kisses my cheek. "How was your day?" I ask.

"I'm sorry I didn't call," he says, his lips vibrating on the top of my head as he speaks. "I had my phone on silent all day."

"It's okay," I say, running my hand up and down his back. *The news isn't good.* "I'm guessing that you don't want to celebrate?"

"Actually," he says, taking the beer from my hand, "Actually, the scan was good."

"What?" I take a step back and put my hands to my face. "He was clear?"

Owen smiles. God, he looks so tired. He nods. "Crystal clear."

"Owen! That's such good news!" I squeal. "We need to celebrate! His family must be so happy. Have you been with them all day?" I don't want to dampen the mood but I can't help but ask: "What took you so long to get home?"

He walks to the kitchen table, where he puts down his beer and runs a finger along the top of the box that holds his present.

My stomach flutters. I don't want to fight tonight. Lately we've been arguing a lot. Well, not arguing, but bickering, picking at each other, starting little fires about nothing—whose turn it is to pick up the dry cleaning, the way he refuses to rinse the peanut butter off a knife before he puts it in the dishwasher. I've stalled on having the talk we need to have though I know why it's happening. I want to have a baby. Owen's still not ready. We've been talking about it for months—or, more accurately, *I've* been talking about it. A few days ago, just before my trip, I brought it up again, reminding Owen that I am turning thirty-seven in a matter of weeks. Thirty-seven! He brushed it off, in the way that he always does, and the tension's been building ever since. I could feel it every time we talked while I was on my trip.

"Daph," he says, turning to me.

"I'm sorry," I start. "I know that things haven't been great. But it's your birthday and—"

"Daph, please." He runs his hands through his hair. "We need to talk."

"Owen, come on. It's your *birthday*," I say again. "And we have great news about Kevin. The other stuff can wait." I go to him and start to put my arms around him again but his body goes stiff. He's never brushed me away before. "Owen?"

He rubs his palms up and down his face and then I watch the way his eyes survey the room. He starts to say something but then he stops.

"Owen, what is it?"

"Daph, I..." He looks at me for several seconds before he speaks again. "Daphne, I met someone."

Wait. *What?*

"Daphne, there's someone else."

# CHAPTER TWO

How could anyone know Owen Monahan like I do? His dark hair has been graying at his temples for years. His eyes are the same shape and silvery green color as his mother's. His favorite candy is Snickers, and when I remember, I stock bags of the fun-size bars in our freezer. He is a lifelong Red Sox fan, and the ticket stub from his first game at Fenway, where Bruce Hurst pitched, has been in a frame on his dresser for as long as I've known him. He is afraid of spiders but not of blood scans, reduced white cell counts, or poking around a person's body for tumors. I know his hands—the scar on his third knuckle (an oyster-shucking mishap), raggedy hangnails. I know that he doesn't dance, even after several drinks. He uses a black office-supply binder clip instead of a money clip or wallet. He watches old comedies like *Airplane!* when he's stressed. He worries that his father isn't proud of him.

We have roots, a history.

"What do you mean, *someone else?*" I can taste the bile in the back of my throat. "What do you *mean*, Owen?" The room is spinning.

He shakes his head as if this isn't going how he'd expected it to go. *How did he expect it to go?* "Let's sit down," he says.

I collapse into the left side of the sofa, my usual spot. *Twenty minutes ago, I was emailing Annie, inviting her and Jack to dinner next week.* Owen sits down next to me—right next to me, in the center of the couch—and I recoil as if he is a stranger and not the person I love more than anyone or anything on earth. He pulls back, giving me space.

"Tell me," I say, my ears ringing. "Tell me what you mean." I'm certain we can both hear my heart pounding.

As he starts to speak, tears well in my eyes and the room goes blurry.

"I don't know how to say it, Daph," he's says. He won't look at me. He's talking into his lap. It's all so clinical, the way that he reveals the details.

It happened in January. He met her at the hospital. She's a social worker in his division.

"So right after Christmas, then?" I say, my voice rising with each word. "After we went up to my parents' house and invited your parents to join us and the six of us sat around my mother's dining room table, eating pie and talking about whether we should hire someone to tile the guest bathroom? I assume you'd met her, your…relationship had started?" My skin is tingling. I feel like I'm going to be sick.

"I-it's not like that," he stutters.

"What's her name?" I say, barely able to catch my breath.

"Bridget."

"How long?"

"What?"

"How long have you been seeing her?" I wail. My voice is shaking so much. My heart is beating in my ears.

"I'm not *seeing* her, Daphne. I just—"

"You just slept with her." When the words come out of my mouth, the reality of what's happened really hits me. I grab a handful of his sleeve and start shaking him. "Owen, how could you?" *How is this possible? How is this happening?* "Owen, how? *How?*"

"I know, Daphne, I know," he says, his voice soft, as if it will cushion the blow. He circles his fingers around my wrists, attempting to calm me, and I snatch my hands away.

"*You know?*" I wail. "You don't know how this feels! I can't believe this!" I press my hands to my face, as if by not seeing him, I can make the whole thing go away. "How could you do this, Owen?"

"I'm so sorry."

When I look up at him, he's shaking his head like he's the one who's been hurt.

"And she knows about me? Your *wife?*" I'm sobbing. I use my sleeve to wipe my nose.

He rubs his hands over his mouth.

"Owen, answer me!"

"She knows about you," he says through his fingers.

*I can't believe this. How? How is there a she? I don't understand what this means, why he's confessing it now, but I can't bear another second of it. Not now.*

"Get out," I say. "I need you to leave the house right now."

"Daphne, can we—"

"Go, Owen!" I say, fighting to keep my voice steady as I stand and point toward the door. "Get out now."


For a long time after I hear his car reverse down our long gravel driveway, I just sit there on the couch. Surely this isn't real. How could Owen—*my* Owen—cheat? Owen is not a cheater. He's my husband, my best friend, the person who makes sure the doors are locked before we go to bed at night. He is upright, beloved by his patients and their families, the better one out of the two of us who rolls his eyes at me when I gossip. He is steady, solid, my north star, the thing I can always count on. There is no way that Owen would do this.

Sometime around midnight, I consider calling my mother. I'm sure she's up watching Letterman as always, but this will kill her. Owen is the son she never had—she literally tells him that, squeezing his shoulders. When we visit, she bakes his favorite brownies and checks with us beforehand to find out what type of cereal is his current preference. She leaves him voicemails. *You don't need to call me back—I'm just calling to say hello!* On the rare occasion when I vent to her about some argument we're having, she'll say, in her antiquated stand-by-your-man sort of way, "Oh, honey, Owen works so hard, cut him some slack." As if being an internist at a cutting-edge medical practice is just something I do to pass the time until Owen gets home from the hospital. I suppose that's easy to forget now, given Owen's heroic cancer slaying. I suppose a lot of things are easy to forget, but not the events of this night.

I think about calling Lucy, my younger sister. I start to call Annie, my best friend. Instead, I stumble to the bathroom and I vomit, through the sobs, over and over again, because the only person who could make me feel better right now is my husband, and on so many levels, I don't know where he is.

# CHAPTER THREE

It is so unoriginal.

She's twenty-six, ten years younger than me.

*Bridget Batton.* That's her name. It's sickening. It sounds like the name of a bobble-headed local TV weather girl. Not even— it sounds like the name of a bobble-headed local TV weather girl in the dumbed-down comedies that Owen loves. I wish that she was a weather girl, or a silly actress, or a department store perfume spritzer, or a professional cheerleader, or anything other than what she is, which is a social worker at the hospital who counsels the pediatric cancer patients whom Owen treats. You would think that someone whose career is based on compassion wouldn't sleep with other women's husbands, but I guess the Mother Teresa parallel only goes so far.

I held out all night from looking her up online, knowing how badly it would hurt me, but on my way into work this morning, as I was standing bleary-eyed at the coffee shop where I picked up an extra-strong espresso drink, I gave myself permission to do it. The second I came into the office, I sat down at my desk, still wearing my coat, and pulled up the Web page for Owen's department. *So that's her,* I thought, analyzing her orthodontically perfect smile, her high cheekbones, the long straight brown hair not so unlike my own. *This is the woman who had sex with my husband.*

The Google search was severely productive. Bridget Batton got her master's in social work at Columbia University, which, according to the *US News & World Report* website, is one of the top-ranked programs in the country. Like Owen (and unlike me) she does triathlons, and her online race results show that she's accustomed to placing in the top ten for her category (which is the impossibly young sounding 25–29 age group). She is originally from Austin, Texas. I have always secretly despised women from Texas because every single one I've ever met has had long, long hair and long, long legs and a teeny-tiny Barbie doll wardrobe. Bridget is not an exception. In a sorority photo I found online, she's wearing a minidress and cowboy boots and actually pulling it off.

But that's not the worst image. There's another one of her, this one from a 2009 edition of a local New Jersey newspaper, and in it, she has her arm around a sweet-looking, bald thirteen-year-old boy. The article details the boy's ongoing leukemia treatment and how Bridget, his counselor, helps him get through his thrice-weekly chemotherapy by reading *Harry Potter* with him, quizzing him before his Spanish tests, and even getting his favorite athlete, a receiver for the New York Giants, to surprise him at the hospital. The author of the article seems to be nominating her for sainthood, and reading it, I forget for a minute that the woman whom the boy's mother declares is "a godsend, a lifesaver" is also the woman who my husband…I feel sick. How can a person like her do the thing that she's done? How could Owen?

Without thinking, I pick up my phone and start to call him. I need him to tell me that this was an awful joke and that a marching band and a television camera are going to barrel into my office any minute now and reveal that this was all a prank and we've won a Caribbean vacation. His voicemail comes on—the generic message, nothing too personal, which is probably a good thing. Hearing his voice might kill me.

I glance at the clock—it's 7:45. Is he at work? At a hotel? Curled up in bed, running a finger along her shoulder? But he said it was just one time. I press the button to end the call. What is there to say?

There's a knock on my door—*ba-dum-dum*. Annie's knock.

"Come in." Phlegm catches in my voice as I say it.

"Good morning!" she sings, and then, "Oh, God." She closes the door behind her.

I rub my fingertips under my eyes. I was able to pull on some work clothes and brush my teeth before I left home but that's as far as I got. "I haven't slept."

She raises her eyebrows. "I can tell. What's wrong?"

"Do you have a minute? My first patient's not for another twenty."

"Mine's in five," she says, checking her watch. "But it's okay. What's wrong?"

I take a deep breath. The tears start welling up before I can spit it out: "Owen cheated on me."

Her hand goes to her chest. *"What?"*

I put my head in my hands, and the next thing I know, her arms are around me. She smells like cinnamon and talcum powder, like the good mother of three that she is.

"Some woman he works with," I say, clutching her shoulders.

"Oh, Daphne," she says. "Oh my God!" I can hear it—the immediate fury in her voice—and I know that it's not just because I am one of her closest friends, and until thirty seconds ago, Owen was, too. A few months after Annie started working here, we were having a glass of wine together after work when she told me how her mother ran off with an old boyfriend when she was twelve. She has no tolerance for infidelity.

"I know." I swallow hard but the tears keep rolling down my cheeks.

She reaches and plucks a tissue out of the box on my desk. "I mean—" She shakes her head. *"Owen?"*

"Apparently so."

"I just can't..."

"I know." The tears keep coming. I swipe them away, quickly. "I can't believe I'm still crying. I cried all night. I can't stop."

"I don't understand this," Annie says, shaking her head. "Just three weeks ago..." She points a thumb over her shoulder, as if gesturing back to the Saturday last month when the four of us went to dinner—she and Jack, me and Owen—and then back to their house for drinks afterward when they needed to relieve their sitter. It was the kind of perfectly uneventful, wonderful night that you can only have with good friends, sipping our drinks in our socks in their family room, reaching into the bowl of chocolate-covered almonds on the coffee table that Annie had improvised to serve for dessert. "I had the longest talk with him that night about all of us renting a place at the beach together this summer," she says, shaking her head.

"He mentioned it on the way home, too," I say. *And then after we got home, we had sex in the hallway at the bottom of the stairs. This was not like us lately. It was not married sex. It was—was it because of her? Was he thinking of her?* My chest clenches, remembering how we both laughed the next morning when he came downstairs and caught me picking up the clothes we'd strewn across the floor. "I don't even know..." I feel my chin start to wobble.

"Oh, Daphne." She leans down to hug me again but I put my hands out to stop her.

"It's okay," I say, standing. "Well, it's not okay, not at all, but I need to pull myself together."

She reaches forward and hugs me anyway.

"Thank you," I manage. "You really need to get ready for your patient."

"Yes." She squeezes me one last time. "I do." She stands there, staring at me.

"Honestly, go," I say.

She starts to walk toward the door. "We'll talk later?"

I know it's not her intention but I can't stand the way she looks at me, the pitying, *poor thing* look in her eyes. I can hear Dr. Moyer, our practice's token idiot, talking to one of the nurses out in the hallway about Duke basketball. I hate his laugh, the throaty, heaving *huh-huh-huh*.

I look at Annie. Her hand is on the doorknob and she's about to open the door when my phone rings. We both freeze. I reach to pick it up.

"*Oh.*" I sigh, looking at the screen. "My mother." I send it to voicemail.

"Have you told her?"

I shake my head and put the phone back on my desk.

"Let's get dinner tomorrow," she says, coiling her long, curly hair into a bun at the nape of her neck. "I wish I could tonight but the kids have a school thing."

*The kids. The life. The warm house that smells like supper.* I nod as someone knocks on the door.

"You going to be okay?" Annie asks.

"Open it, it's Carol," I answer.

"Good morning, girls," Carol says when Annie lets her in. "What are we gossiping about today?"

Everyone in the office knows that Annie and I are close, but Carol, my nurse, is the only one bold enough—and old enough—to tease us about it.

"Here you go," she says, waving the paper printout of the day's appointments that she hands me each morning.

"Carol, you do realize that the office went electronic years ago?" Annie teases.

Carol swats Annie's arm with the paper before walking it over to me. "What can I say? Old habits die hard."

Annie's still in the doorway, still giving me that look.

"So Mary Elizabeth Foster is our first appointment of the day?" I say, skimming the printout.

"Theoretically," Carol says, already halfway out the door. "If she shows up."

"At least your morning won't be a dull one," Annie says. Aside from when I need to get a second opinion, Annie is the only person in my office whom I ever vent to about my patients, and vice versa.

"Dull actually sounds wonderful," I mutter, putting on my white coat and stuffing the folded printout into the front pocket.

As usual, Mary Elizabeth is late, but I manage to fit in another patient while I'm waiting for her. She arrives thirty minutes after her scheduled appointment time, and when I knock on the exam room door and she calls for me to come in, she's still not ready for me. I find her standing in the middle of the room, attempting to get an arm through her paper gown while she holds her phone between her ear and shoulder. She is wrapping up a call, speaking in one long run-on sentence, and she smiles at me, rolling her eyes and pointing to the phone as if the person on the other end is the thing that's holding us up. "I know, it was too late," she says to the caller. "*Way* too late for a Tuesday, but oh well. Listen, I have to go, I'm at an appointment and my boss is going to fire me for being gone again and so I doubt I can meet you before nine tonight. Okay, sorry, have to go. Okay, sorry. Bye."

She hangs up and turns to me. "Sorry!" she squeals. "One of my girlfriends…" She rolls her eyes again and shakes her head. "How are *you*?" I hear the *yew*—the toothy-smiled, cotillion-bred, over-enthusiastic homecoming queen influence. Mary Elizabeth has been my patient for three years now, ever since she finished law school at UNC, where her mother sits on the Board of Governors. She's twenty-seven, a Chapel Hill native, a junior attorney at a seersucker practice, and an utter mess. At our first visit, she told me that she'd been diagnosed with juvenile diabetes when she was three but that she's never been able to control it. In high school she was a competitive swimmer, destined for the Junior Olympics, but because of the huge calories she needed to consume to fuel her workouts, her blood sugar numbers careened all over the place. In college, she quit swimming—five a.m. workouts didn't complement her social life—but continued to eat like the champion freestyler she'd been, and when her weight ballooned, she turned to bulimia, which is probably not the best choice of disorder if you're a diabetic and have to control every bite of food that goes into your mouth.

But there's more: Once she dealt with the bingeing and purging—or her mother did, sending her to a top-of-the-line inpatient rehab center—she discovered alcohol, which, she says, joking but with a bit too much conviction, is her one true love. It is also poisonous for someone with her health history.

Our office is what some people call a *concierge practice*. For an annual fee, you receive comprehensive care from a variety of providers, so in addition to me, Mary Elizabeth sees Denise, one of our shrinks, and attends a weekly meditation class in the glass-walled atrium at the back of the facility, not that it's done anything obvious to even her out. Despite the fact that I'm not the staff member being paid to listen to her problems, I'm the lucky one to whom she often pays her penance, maybe because we're closest in age.

"So what'd you do last night?" I ask, looking over her chart. Her blood pressure's higher than normal.

"Well…" she says, sitting on the exam table now, swinging her legs like a girl. "It was my friend's birthday, so we went out for margaritas."

I take her slender wrist in my hand and press two fingers onto the underside to take her pulse.

"It was a late night, from what I gather?" I ask.

"Umm…" She wrinkles her nose in a cutesy way that is supposed to look apologetic. My sister does the same thing. "It's actually funny that I had this appointment this morning because, well…" Her breath is sour.

"Yes?" I know what she's about to say but I want to make her say it.

"I got hypoglycemic. I almost had a seizure."

"Mary Elizabeth." I put my hand to my temple, as if this surprises me. "What happened?"

"I just…one margarita turned into two and then three…" She shakes her head. *Margaritas.* I think of the Mexican takeout I bought last night for Owen's birthday and how, this morning, I realized it was still on the kitchen counter, untouched, and that I hadn't eaten a bite of anything since the bag of pretzels on the plane the day before.

"Did you have dinner?" I ask. "Or just drink?"

She presses her lips together and shrugs. Her eyes are watery. I wonder if she's still a little drunk.

"So what happened?" I could tell her, as I have before, about the risks that hypoglycemia poses for her, and how if she drinks too much, especially if she hasn't eaten, it can cause a seizure. She could lose consciousness, even die. But we've been over it a dozen times over the course of our partnership. No matter how many times I explain the mechanics to her, no matter how many times I talk to her therapist, even her mother, nothing ever changes.

"Well, fortunately," she says, twirling a lock of hair between her fingers, "when I started to get a little dazed, my girlfriend noticed. She's seen it happen before and, well, we've all seen *Steel Magnolias* a billion times and they remembered that scene with Julia Roberts and the orange juice." She starts to giggle and then straightens up when I don't follow suit. "I was fine within twenty minutes."

"Listen," I say. "This has to stop and you know it. You have to take better care of yourself. This is about you leading a long, healthy, and happy life, and you're not nineteen anymore, not that this would be okay even if you were younger." *Nineteen.* I think about Michael, my boyfriend when I was nineteen. Last I heard, he was living out West and working for a federal judge. I bet he's happily married. I bet he'd never cheat. We used to drive an hour south from our college campus to the beach, where we'd put his dorm room quilt on the sand and stay up all night to watch the sunrise. He was my only significant relationship before Owen. And Owen had only had one serious girlfriend before me, Ainsley from New Hampshire. They dated in college and during his first year of med school. She was nice and they stayed friends. She even came to our wedding. My husband's not—*was* not—the kind of guy who runs around.

"Are you okay, Dr. Mitchell?" Mary Elizabeth asks. I notice the cracks in the corners of her lips. "You seem like you drifted off somewhere for a minute."

I clear my throat before I speak. "Listen, I don't want to sound like your mother and if I could grasp your shoulders to shake you, I would, but you need to find a way to blow off steam that doesn't involve alcohol."

She sniffs hard. "I know."

"We can't keep having this conversation."

She smirks. I almost think she's about to laugh.

"What is it?" I ask.

"You do kind of sound like my mother." She smiles at me. A sorority girl smile. A *Bridget* kind of smile, I think.

I walk to the door, closing my laptop. "You can get dressed now," I say.

# CHAPTER FOUR

I almost always arrive home from work before Owen, and while I didn't really expect him to be here when I head up our long driveway at the end of the day, I'm bothered when I don't see his car, because where *could* he be? And shouldn't he be here, begging for forgiveness, fighting for the marriage that I thought we had?

I sit in the car for a moment after I turn off the ignition and lean back against the headrest, looking at the house. On the night that we moved in last October, we drank a bottle of champagne together on the porch swing that we'd installed just hours before. Our muscles ached from the strain of moving and we'd spend the next several weeks unpacking boxes, but in that moment, I felt so settled. People love to use that word to connote something negative—you *settled*, do you think you're *settling*—but I mean it in the best possible sense. Everything I had ever hoped for, had ever planned for, was working out how I'd envisioned it.

I was a kid who spent hours playing doctor's office, making patient beds for my Barbies out of shoeboxes that I stacked on their sides in my closet, and I am now an M.D. living in a town that the city limit signs declare is "The City of Medicine." My home is slowly becoming the exact replica of the magazine pages I've been tearing out of *House Beautiful* and *Country Living* for years. My husband—my *husband*—is a man I've known for most of my life. He is a lovely, funny, gentle, smart, good, and generous man. Or so I thought. We were on the cusp of the next phase of our life together. It was all happening.

That night on the swing with the champagne, Owen got up at one point to walk the invisible border where we thought we might put a flagstone patio. We talked about where the swing set would go, pointing at potential spots with our tilted champagne flutes. There would be Thanksgiving Day football games and maybe someday a swimming pool. The possibilities were endless.

He slept with Bridget three months later, which makes me think that when I was rattling on about paint chips and rearranging the furniture and making unsubtle comments about the spare bedroom that I wanted to use for a nursery, he had possibly, probably, already met her. Their friendship, if I can bring myself to call it that, was likely well under way.

I finally pull myself out of the car. After I greet Blue and take her outside, I find myself walking aimlessly around the living room. I fold the afghan that Owen's mother knitted for us after we moved into the house and lay it over the back of a chair. I go into the kitchen, opening the refrigerator and then closing it. Owen's birthday present is still on the table. I carry it into the mudroom and shove it into a cabinet next to the washing machine.

What should I do? When will I hear from him? Will he call? Do I want him to? I feed Blue, then go upstairs to unpack my suitcase from my trip. I take a shower, using the fancy lavender body wash labeled "stress relief" that I'd splurged on a few weeks ago, as if I'd even known what stress was then, as if I might be able to scrub this thing off of me, and then I pull on some old jeans and a T-shirt and go outside.


Right on schedule, we got married just a few months after I finished my residency. We were living in a small apartment just off Duke's campus, within walking distance of the medical center, which was convenient because Owen still had two years of training to complete and spent more time at the hospital than he did at home. I was settling into the five-day schedule I'd been daydreaming about for years, and with Owen always at work, the weekends rolled out before me, unrestrained acres of hours to be filled. One spring Saturday morning, I woke up when Owen went to work and couldn't fall back asleep. I eventually got in the car and started driving with no plan or destination. It was still early, and I could go anywhere—out for a long quiet breakfast to read the newspaper, for a walk in Duke Forest, or even the short two hours to the coast for the day. Instead, I ended up in the concrete expanse of the parking lot of the local Home Depot, deciding that I was going to learn how to garden. Our only outdoor space was a sad, rusted excuse of a balcony that was really a glorified fire escape. I bought a bougainvillea. Little did I know, bougainvilleas are like Hollywood starlets: Without relentless fawning, they wither away. Mine was dead by Thursday.

But I was hooked. Our balcony soon resembled a local garden center, and Owen joked that I was becoming the horticultural version of a crazy cat lady. It wasn't lost on me that my newfound hobby stemmed from the same place that led me to become a doctor. In both, there's a certain manipulation of life, a discovery of cause and effect, a doting and hopeful attempt to make things better. And most of the time, you can.

But then, sometimes things just happen. You till the soil, accounting for its composition and drainage, you consider sunlight and seasons, pests, disease. You plant carefully, choosing just the right thing for just the right place, thinking you've covered all of your bases, and then, despite everything, you fall flat. The dahlias wither days after they've bloomed, the tomato plant produces barely enough fruit for one salad. The same goes with patients. You prescribe the treatment that works for *almost* everyone. You give advice and provide referrals, knowing that you may or may not be heard. Usually, the formula works. Sometimes—as with Mary Elizabeth—it's not enough. I suppose now that the same could be said for relationships. Sometimes things just happen. *How the hell did this happen?*

I have filled a plastic cup halfway with wine and am kneeling, pulling up weeds, next to the family of tangerine-colored tulips that has poked up in the side yard like a gift. It was a lucky accident that the previous owners of the house had once been avid gardeners. There are dignified, hearty boxwoods bordering the house, roses climbing a trellis near the chimney. Blue settles in near me and gnaws on a stick. Gardening has always helped me feel better. Last month, on the day after another one of our go-nowhere baby talks, I spent three hours clearing two of the larger beds behind the house and tilling the soil to prepare it for spring planting, thinking that one of the beds would be a perfect spot for a vegetable garden. Early that evening, when I went into the house, Owen was finally home and taking a shower. I dampened a washcloth to wipe the specks of dirt from my face and after he'd wrapped a towel around his waist, he walked over and hugged me, a long, swaying, *we're going to get through this* kind of embrace. He kissed me and looked into my eyes and assured me that we'd figure this out. It only now occurs to me how odd it is that his first priority after coming home from a few hours at the office on a Saturday was to shower.

I wipe my nose with my sleeve and move to a spot toward the back of the house, where I've wanted to do some sort of pergola and train wisteria to grow around it. I stand there, trying to plan it out, but my mind starts wandering. *What am I doing? Really, what kind of future is going to happen here next week, much less months from now? Let's say I plant the goddamn wisteria. Will I even live here by the time it blooms? Will Owen? Is it even a possibility? Do I want it to be a possibility?*

We all know what people say about men who cheat—take them back and they'll do it again. But Owen's not a cheater. He's *Owen*. I can't connect the two, no matter how many times I replay the scene of him sitting in our family room—our *family* room, how ironic—last night breaking the news about his mistress.

*Mistress.* What a stupid word, meant for daytime television and romance novels, not real life. Not *my* life.

This is the problem: I don't have an answer for anything that's happened to me. I throw my pruning shears across the yard, as if that will help.

And then I'm walking over to get them, and I hear a car crunching up the driveway. I stare for a minute, looking at his familiar silhouette in the driver's seat of his Wagoneer and the white coat hung over the back of the passenger's side. The front of his car—the headlights, the wide grille—looks like a face, sneering at me.

Maybe I shouldn't just stand here. My heart thumps. My shoulders ache.

Part of me wants to run at him, claw at his clothes, and demand, with all of the anger that pulsates behind my eyes, that he explain to me how he could do this to me.

We lock eyes, and so I stand there, angled toward him—there's something about facing him head-on. Blue leaps up and jogs to-ward him, and it pinches at me. *He's done this to you, too, you know*, I think, watching the way that she licks his chin when he kneels down to scratch her. The back of my throat burns. The aftertaste of the wine I've been drinking is suddenly too strong and too sweet.

I'm not ready for this. I turn and go around back. Not a minute later, I hear him following behind me.

"Daph?"

I turn.

Blue lumbers up the steps to me, tail wagging. *Good girl.*

"We should talk."

I glare at him.

"Can we please sit down? Just for a minute?" He twirls his car keys in his hands and then walks toward the old iron scroll-work bench left by the previous owners. I rest against the door, if only to keep myself from falling to the floor. I feel light-headed and it's not from the wine. He sits and leans on his knees, still twirling his keys in his hands. I notice his simple gold wedding band that we picked out together at a jewelry store in Chapel Hill. He rocks back and forth on his heels. *Who are you?* I think.

"I can't imagine what this has done to you," he says.

"What *you* have done to me," I correct him.

He nods but doesn't look at me. His voice is even. I can't tell whether he's angry or contrite, calm or nervous. I want so badly to hate him.

"I know that it's not what you want to hear, and I know that it sounds canned, but, Daphne, you have to believe me when I say that I didn't want this to happen."

"I don't have to believe anything." My voice breaks. I can't get out *one sentence* before my voice breaks. I swallow hard, as if I can force it down. "I don't owe you anything."

"I know you don't," he says, under his breath. "Trust me—"

"Please!" I interrupt. "*Trust* you? I don't even know who you are."

"I'm sorry. That was a stupid thing to say," he says. "But I want to make this better."

"Do you understand the enormity of this, Owen? What you've done?"

Blue is lying on the ground with her paws on either side of her wide head. She looks just like a bear rug, like we always said.

"Of course I do," he says. "And that's why I told you, Daph. The guilt has been eating me up inside."

I feel like I've been kicked in the stomach. "Then why?" *Dammit.* The tears well up and I squeeze my eyes shut, trying to hold them back. Forget it. Let him see me cry. He should see how he's hurt me. "Then why, Owen? *Why?*" The sobs come quicker and harder, straight from my gut, from some deep horrible place inside of me. "Why would you do this to us? Do you know how crazy it is, Owen? How fucked up?"

His head falls deeper between his shoulders. "I know."

"I need to know why you did it." I'm shaking. I take a deep breath and try to collect myself. I need information. Information will make this better. If I can understand it, maybe it will fix it. When I put my hands to my face to wipe my tears, we both notice how I'm trembling. I see the way that he looks at my hands. The same thing happened—for entirely different reasons—on our wedding day. We were standing beneath the canopy of a massive oak tree in a grassy corner of Owen's grandparents' backyard in the Berkshires. The minister, a family friend, had just proclaimed it: *I now pronounce you husband and wife.* I started to shake, I was so happy. I was trembling, bursting with euphoria. We were laughing as he started to kiss me.

"Tell me how it happened." I can feel the acid churning in my stomach, corkscrewing through my center.

He takes a deep breath. "We've been friends for a while," he says.

"How nice," I say. I look up at the ceiling, where the planks are painted a color that people call *haint blue*, a Southern tradition thought to help keep out evil spirits. "Amazing that I never heard you mention her."

He rubs his hands over his face and then looks at me. "It's hard to explain. I can't even explain it to myself. I know that you don't want to hear that and I don't expect you to sympathize."

"I realize that there are a lot of people in my situation who probably wouldn't want to know the details, Owen, but unfortunately for both of us, I do. If I know the facts, then maybe my mind won't keep replaying everything I've imagined over the past twenty-four hours. Tell me," I continue. "How did it happen?"

He clears his throat and jingles his keys again. "When it first started, it wasn't... it wasn't anything involved," he finally says. Owen is never like this in an argument. He is direct, even, and steady. I was always the one who had trouble articulating what I needed to say.

"*Involved?* Come on, Owen. Be frank with me. So it was purely physical?" Once it's out of my mouth, I second-guess how much I really want to know.

"It started out as just flirting, harmless office flirting," he says.

"Harmless?"

He shakes his head and starts again. "We got to know each other better, started getting lunch every once in a while. And then, in January..."

"You slept together."

He nods. "Daph, I was so guilt-ridden, it fucked me up so much, I cut things off with her right away."

"And that's supposed to make me feel better?"

He sighs.

"Where did it happen?"

He looks up at me.

"I want to know, Owen."

"Her apartment."

"And I was where?"

"Here."

I nod. I feel sick thinking of myself at home reading, shopping online, folding laundry, oblivious to what was really going on.

"I thought about telling you right away. But it was just the one time and I told myself that that was it. I knew that if I told you, you'd never forgive me, and I couldn't face that."

My stomach is roiling. "But you can now."

He sucks in his lips and shakes his head. "Daph, the thing is, even though it was just the one time, I'm still confused."

I feel that leg-buckling feeling again. "*Confused?*" I say. "Confused about *what*? About your feelings for her? About us?" The tears start to come again. I blink them back.

He puts his hands behind his head and looks up at the ceiling. "It's not about her. To be honest, it's not even really about you. It's about me. I've started to worry that you and I want different things," he says, standing. "You know, we've been talking about having kids for so long and I know how badly you want that, and I know we can't keep talking about it forever. I keep waiting to feel the same way—I *should* feel the same way—but I don't. You know, I'm finally where I want to be career-wise, after all of the years of training, and we have the house, and it won't be much longer until our med school loans will be paid off. I should be ready but I'm not. And I don't know what to do with the fact that

I don't want the same things as my wife. I wish it were simpler but things have changed, and I can't keep ignoring the way that I feel."

I suppose that it should be a comfort to know that it's not her that he wants but it's not. "It's so like you to make this all about *you*," I say. "Do you realize how selfish you sound? So what, do you expect me to wait around while you figure out what you want, never mind our vows, never mind our marriage?"

"Daphne, I wouldn't blame you if you left, not after what I did."

I shake my head at him. "You should have talked to me," I say. "I don't care how confused you are, Owen, it never should have come to this. It's so cowardly, what you did."

He nods. "I realize how bad this is—the worst thing, really."

"That doesn't make me feel better."

"It kills me, knowing how much I've hurt you."

"That doesn't help, either."

He takes a step toward me. "Don't," I say, raising my hands. He stops.

"I don't know where we go from here," I say.

"I simply need time," he says. "I need a break, some time away from us to think."

"A break?" I say, wiping my cheeks. "We're not fifteen, Owen, we're married. You want a *break*?"

He nods and turns away from me. He could never stand to see me cry. "I'm so sorry."

"And how am I supposed to explain this to people? To my family?" We both come from long lines of together-forever Catholics. His parents have been married for forty years. Mine for thirty-nine. We are not the kind of people who *take breaks*.

"You should tell them whatever you think is best," he says. "I'll deal with my parents."

*And your mother will probably send you a big care package to nurse you through it*, I think. Joanne is a seventh-grade math teacher whose wardrobe consists largely of dorky "math humor" T-shirts that say things like "There is a fine line between numerator and denominator." I've never seen her angry or upset (which is saying something, given Owen's father), and she's an excellent mother-in-law—I'd like her even if I didn't have to—but she's always coddled Owen, who is an only child. It hasn't always made him the easiest person to live with—obviously, especially, now. *He wants a break?*

We stand there for a few minutes, neither of us sure what to do.

I want to ask him to change his mind. I want to plead with him, fall to his feet, prostrate myself, beg for my life. Because that's really what this is about, begging for the life that I thought I had. The image of myself on the ground, the dirty speckled porch, the thought of being eye to eye with the floor—I can't take myself there. It takes every bit of my will to keep my rubbery legs from collapsing, but I don't do it. I don't say another word. What am I supposed to do with this? *My husband cheated on me. He wants a break—from me.* It's like he's described a surgery and I'm the thing that needs to be removed.

Blue pulls herself off of the floor and ambles toward the door and then looks up at me, wanting me to open it. There is a scar over her right eye where the fur hasn't grown back. One night last November, I let her out before bed and a raccoon that'd found its way into our trash cans attacked her. The sounds that came out of her sent me screaming reflexively for Owen, who wasn't home. She wrenched herself free by the time I made it into the yard, and I raced her to the emergency animal hospital where Annie's husband, Jack, works as a vet. So there we were, me cooing in her ear while she got stitches and shots, a patch over her eye, and antiseptic applied to the gashes in her jaw.

The next evening, not even twenty-four hours later, I let her out like always, fully expecting her to be tentative and anxious. Her leash was in my hand in case she needed help. But when I pushed my weight into the door to open it, she slipped past, bounding forward, her legs scrambling down the back steps so fast that she cleared the last two. Her tail wagged as she trotted out into the yard and then she sped up and raced figure-eights into the grass in the dim, gauzy moonlight, because, well, why not? I thought about it for days afterward, how resilient she was. How could I not have, when what I see on a daily basis is the opposite, all of us licking our wounds and aching and griping, our big fucking case of *mired down*. I used to pride myself on being so tough. People have called me a lot of things over the course of my life—single-minded, tightly wound, ambitious—but never meek, never doormat, never victim. How on earth will I ever recover from this? How will *we*?

"I need to get a few things out of the house," Owen says as I'm going inside. I start to ask where he's staying but then I change my mind. I don't want to know. I go to the kitchen. He goes upstairs. And then, while I'm filling Blue's water dish, I hear his car, and he's gone.

# CHAPTER FIVE

Annie and I are watching a waitress at the end of the bar. On her tray is a bottle of wine and four stemmed glasses, two fat tumblers of something dark and alcoholic, and if she can squeeze it on, a pint with a local microbrewery's logo.

"Damn," Annie says, chuckling as she turns back to me. "Are Mary Elizabeth and her girlfriends here?"

"Oh, Annie," I gasp. "You're awful."

She shrugs and makes a face, and I can't help but laugh. It feels *so good* to laugh. "You are really a terrible person," I say. "I'm glad you're not her doctor."

"That goes for both of us," she says.

I shake my head at her and then I stab my fork into my plate and collect one last bite of pad thai. I was actually hungry for dinner, and I know that I can credit Annie with bringing back my appetite. We have spent our entire meal discussing my situation (*crisis? personal tragedy? How does one describe what's happened to me?*), but she hasn't forced me to pull the thing apart. I don't have a next step and she's not pushing me to come up with one. She doesn't want me to *cry it out* or *find something to take my mind off things*. She is simply being my best friend.

"Another?" she says, pointing at my empty wineglass with her fork.

"I don't think so," I say. "But are you up for ice cream? I feel entitled to be a stereotype and drown my sorrows in a sundae." There's a place at the other end of the shopping center.

"Works for me," Annie says. "And when you get to the part where you need to drink too much tequila and sing bad karaoke, I'm up for that, too."

I pick up my napkin and wipe my mouth. "Let's hope it doesn't come to that."

It's just starting to rain when we leave the restaurant, the kind of fat droplets that leave marks on your shirt. I check my bag to make sure I have my umbrella. Annie loops her arm into mine as we walk under the awning lining the shopping center. If any other friend of mine ever touched me in the way that she does, I might find it strange, even off-putting, but with Annie, it is innate and comforting, and I let myself lean into her.

"Oh, look at that!" she says, pulling me toward the storefront of a gift shop that I've been in only once, last year, when I was looking for a birthday gift for Owen's mom. There's a window display for Easter, with artfully cut paper flowers, tin buckets spilling over with candies, and sweet handmade bunny stuffed animals arranged in a vintage toy wheelbarrow. *I wonder whether he's told Joanne yet*, I think. *And if he has, why haven't I heard from her?* "I bet I could make something like that for the kids," Annie whispers, inspecting one of the Easter baskets through the glass.

I turn away and watch a middle-aged woman across the parking lot helping an older woman out of a car. They have the same hooked nose, weak chin. *I need to call my mother*, I think. I scan the cars and the people milling about. I can't go anywhere now without feeling like I have to look over my shoulder. What would I do if I ran into him? Or *her*, now that I know what she looks like? Into people I know from residency, from our old neighborhood—innocent bystanders who wouldn't know better than to ask the questions that should be innocuous: *How are you? What's Owen up to?*

When I turn back to Annie, she's staring at me in that same funny way that she did at the office. "Please don't pity me," I say. "You know I can't handle that."

"Listen," she says. She stops and licks her lips, considering me. "I'm probably going to regret saying this, and it's completely the wrong time. But you know, this reminds me of what happened with my mom."

"I know," I say, stepping toward the store window. *I really don't want to talk about this.*

"What I've never told you is that she left us lots of times before she went for good. Actually, the first time that I remember was when I was in kindergarten."

I turn to her. "I'm so sorry," I say, imagining five-year-old Annie in wool tights and a corduroy jumper. "You told me that you were twelve when your mom left."

"Nope, not the first time." She shakes her head again. "But it's fine." She sighs deeply, her shoulders rising and falling as she exhales. "Actually, it was awful. It was the second day of school and I'll never forget it. But the thing is, she came back."

"Oh."

"And then she left a couple of months later," she says. "And then she was back. And then she left the following June." She counts off each incident with her fingers. "And then she came back a few weeks before school started—like she'd been away on summer vacation or something!" She snorts. "She stayed for about a year, but when I was in second grade, she left again. And on and on."

"I didn't know about that back-and-forth," I say. "That must have been awful."

"It certainly was," she says pointedly, her tone deliberate.

"Have you heard from her lately?"

"Not since her Christmas card. She sent each of the kids ten bucks. Did I tell you that?"

"No. You mentioned the socks."

"Oh, yes. The socks she gave me. *Sorry for abandoning you, hope your feet stay warm.*" Her mother had come back into her life, wanting to reunite, when Annie was in college. She showed up at the restaurant where Annie was waitressing, sat in her section, and said she wanted to start over. Annie told her to go to hell. Her Christmas gifts are about the only contact they have.

"Anyway," she says, "I've been thinking about you a lot, as you can imagine, and I guess what I want to say is that it took years and years of therapy for my father and me to move past this, and revisiting the details just dredges up all of the resentment that I have for her, which is why I never talk about it. And while she had other issues—I think bipolar disorder, definitely alcoholism—she cheated on my father from the day that she met him and never stopped. I never actually knew about all of it until last year, when Dad and I got into Jack's bourbon on Christmas Eve after we finished stuffing the kids' stockings. Daphne, the way she jerked him around..." She stops herself and shakes her head, considering whether to say it. She doesn't need to, of course. I know what she's going to say. This is the *cheaters always cheat* speech. I suppose that I should be glad that we're getting it over with.

"Listen, I know that Owen's not like my mother," she hedges.

"He's not." I cross my arms over my chest. I don't know why my first instinct is to defend him, but strangely it is.

"I just don't want to see you get hurt."

I chuckle. "Too late."

She cuffs her hand around my arm, just above my wrist. "I'm sorry. I know that this is so new and I probably shouldn't have even brought it up. I just can't believe that Owen did this. It's like Jack said last night—he must be sick. Only someone who needs serious help could do this sort of thing."

I shake my head at her, not knowing what to say. I can't handle the thought of Annie and Jack sitting up in bed with their books opened on their laps, discussing the drama of my falling-apart marriage like it's something they watched on cable.

"It's unbelievable, absolutely abysmal," she spits, suddenly riled. "He really had us fooled, didn't he?" *I am not going to get angry with her*, I tell myself. *This is her personal stuff talking.* "Are you sure there weren't any signs? Nothing at all?"

I raise my eyebrows. "I'm quite sure, Annie."

She shakes her head, looking into the distance as if this is some baffling cosmic mystery. "My father never got over the way that my mother trampled on him," she says. "He's never remarried, as you know. Hardly even dated. It's taken him years to be able to trust people again. You deserve better, Daphne."

"I know, Annie," I say. My face is hot and my heart is pounding. I didn't need this—not from her, not tonight. *Am I going to be like her dad, destined for a lonely life of bitterness, unable to trust anyone? No. No, of course not.* "I know you mean well but I need you to stop, because what you don't understand is that I haven't even begun to consider the possibility of him *coming back* yet because I'm still getting used to the fact that he slept with someone else, first of all, and that he's left, at least temporarily." I don't add how that very phrase has been haunting me ever since this happened—the *leaving*. Break or not, temporary or not, I was *left*. He *left* me.

"You're right." She puts her hands up. "You're absolutely right."

I nod.

"It's just the Mama Bear in me, I guess," she says, smiling

sheepishly. She hooks her arm around my neck, pulling me in for a hug. I wish that I could say that I hug back, but I just stand there, arms at my sides, wisps of her hair tickling my cheeks, and I think, for at least the hundredth time today, that I can't believe that this is my life now.

I'm halfway into the house when my phone rings. I yank it out of my jacket pocket. I wonder how long it will take for me to stop reacting this way to a phone call.

It's my mother. I feel the dread roll over me. Telling her is going to be like reliving the whole thing all over again.

"Hello, stranger," she says by way of greeting.

"Hi, Mom." I collapse into the armchair in the family room. I have a feeling that I will need to settle in for this. My eyes land on a pile of oncology journals Owen left in a corner of the room. I remember him thumbing through them the night before I left for my conference.

"Daphne, where on earth have you been? I don't think we've spoken in a week." The thing about my mother's voice is that no matter whether she's happy or sad, furious or thrilled, she always sounds like she's talking over a crowd.

"I know, Mom, I'm sorry. Things have been really busy. I had that conference in Philadelphia." I thought I'd wait and come up with a right way to break my news—or if all else failed, I could tell my sister Lucy first and she could do it for me.

One of my many failings as a woman in my family is that I don't enjoy the telephone. I've been in the room with my mother when she's called my sister and vice-versa, and I've often felt a distinct envy listening to the long, lazy way that they can connect, chatting about the big salads that they had for lunch or the scarf that Mom picked up at TJ Maxx. Lucy says I'm "like a man" on the phone. "It's like you use it just to communicate information," she said once, as an insult.

"Busy," Mom moans. "You're always *busy*. I should've named you that." My mother actually named me after a character on *As the World Turns*. She often comments about my approach to work—*You're so busy, slow down, stop and smell the roses every once in a while, take a deep breath, relax.*

"So I had an idea and wondered what you two are up to this weekend," she says, changing the subject. "Oh, and by the way, I called Owen to say happy birthday but he never called back. Did he get my card?"

I suddenly realize that I haven't checked the mailbox since this all happened and that tiny departure, that simple misstep from my everyday routine, makes my stomach drop. Everything's upside down. Nothing feels normal.

"I'm sorry that he hasn't called you back," I say, anger washing over me as I say it. *Why should I apologize for him?*

"It's okay, honey. I figured he was just tied up at the hospital," she says. I hear clanking in the background. She's emptying the dishwasher.

For a second, I consider lying to her, but I can't.

"Mom, here's the thing," I start.

"Oh God, what is it?" she interrupts. She sucks in her breath so loudly that it makes a crackly sound through the receiver, and I can just picture her, plunking down at the kitchen table and bracing herself for whatever it is I'm going to say. This is the way I knew it would go with her. The second that you mention even the possibility of anything negative to my mother, she goes five-alarm fire on you.

"Mom, I need to tell you something, but promise me that you'll just listen to me explain before you say anything."

And because it's not the kind of thing that I've *ever* said to her before, she does. I tell her everything, from the moment that Owen told me about Bridget until last night, when I stayed up until three in the morning, twisted in my sheets, watching a self-inflicted picture show on the ceiling of Owen and Bridget. *Owen and Bridget.* It sounds insane, impossible, even grotesque. Owen and *Daphne.* That's the way it should be, the way that it's always been.

My mother doesn't say anything at first, which is the most obvious signal that this has, in fact, devastated her as much as I thought that it would. "Honey, do you want to come up here for a little while?" she finally says. "It must be so hard, being in your house all alone."

This is the thing about my mother, and about me. If I could only open up to her, she would give me enough tenderness to cushion a lifetime's worth of disappointments. Once, when I was home from college, I was in the kitchen by myself one afternoon when I came across a tax form of some sort on the counter. Under her occupation, she'd written in big, deliberate letters: MOTHER. It looked like a declaration, and it's an accurate one. She is a mother with a capital M. If she'd never had my sister and me, she would have found some other way to take care of people. I'll confess that I like to think that I inherited at least a little bit of that.

"Honey, I'm so sorry," she says.

I picture her fighting back her tears, holding the phone receiver away from her mouth so that I won't hear her cry. In a few minutes, she will hang up and tell my dad. I can see the two of them sitting side by side on the sofa in our family room, matching bewildered expressions on their faces.

"So this other person..." she starts.

"Yes," I say.

"She knew about you?"

"Apparently so."

She doesn't say anything. I wonder whether she's feeling the same swirl of emotions that I am—anger toward them, fear for me, confusion about the whole mess of it all.

"Have you called your sister?" she asks.

"Not yet."

"*Oh, honey,*" she moans. I know what she thinks—the fact that I haven't told Lucy, coupled with the fact that it took me this long to tell her, must mean that I'm in dire condition. *Because if I'm too weak to pick up the phone…* "I hate to think of you in that house all by yourself. Do you know where he's staying, during this…time apart?"

"I don't," I say. "I assume a hotel or something."

"And you don't think…" I know what she wants to ask.

"No, he said it was over between them. He said it's about *him,* and figuring out what he wants." As the words come out of my mouth, I realize how naïve it sounds, but I have no choice but to believe him, even if it's only to keep my sanity intact.

"Well." She huffs. "I just can't believe this, Daphne. It's just not *like* Owen."

"I know, Mom," I say, as Blue nudges her head under my arm. I hoist myself out of the chair to walk to the pantry and get her a biscuit. "I'm sorry to have to tell you."

"I'm so sorry," she says. "Oh, Daphne."

I'm worried she might go on and on like this, and if she starts to cry, I won't be able to handle it. "So what were you going to ask me about the weekend?"

"Oh! Well. Your sister and Bobby might be coming down."

*Ah.* She was calling because she wanted Owen and me to come up, too. I bet she'd already dog-eared a few recipes in her cookbooks for a Saturday night dinner for six.

"Honey, why don't you come home?" she says.

"You know, I'd like that," I say, looking around the room. "I think it's a good idea for me to get away."

"Good, honey. That will be good."

"I'll come up on Friday."

"Perfect," she says, her voice trilling. "That sounds great. I'm going to call you in the morning to check in."

"Okay," I say. I clear my throat. "I'm really fine, Mom. Really."

We both know I'm lying.

"Just promise you'll answer when I call this time, honey," she says.

"Don't worry about me," I say. "I promise, I'm fine. And I'll answer."

"Okay."

"You don't mind breaking the news to Dad?" I ask, praying she won't offer to put him on the phone. I don't have it in me to tell the story all over again, not now.

"I'll tell him."

"Thanks, Mom. I'll call him tomorrow."

"No need, we understand. But you can call us whenever you want. You go get some rest and we'll see you in a few days. I love you."

"I love you, too," I say, choking back tears. I hang up quickly, before I stumble over my good-bye.


When I get off the phone, I text Owen, telling him that I need him to watch Blue from Friday to Sunday. I'd take her with me but Lucy's allergic. It's an hour before I hear back from him. He writes that he can watch her, saying that he was planning to come by the house on Friday during lunch to pick up a few things anyway. I don't ask where he's staying. He doesn't ask where I'm going.

When I'm lying awake in bed later, I find myself thinking about the morning six years ago when he proposed at his grand-parents' farm in the Berkshires, the same place where we decided to marry. Over the four years we'd been together, we'd spent sev-eral sunny weekends there, sitting at his grandmother's Formica table playing cards late into the night, gorging on her famous ap-ple turnovers, climbing into his grandfather's ancient pickup truck for long country drives. At some point during these weekends, we always pulled their old wooden canoe into the water and glided on the lake, where we'd have the grown-up version of the long, lazy conversations we'd had as kids at camp.

On that morning, he woke me just after six o'clock and I groaned, turning over in the creaky iron bed as he nudged me to get dressed. He coaxed me out with a plaid Coleman Thermos filled with coffee, led me across the wide lawn and then down a narrow path through the woods. I started to catch on. He turned and smiled, laughing a little. The canoe was already edged into the water. A flannel blanket was folded carefully over my seat in the front of the boat. *What on earth are you up to?* I kept saying, and he continued to grin at me, barely saying a word until he'd paddled us out to the middle of the lake.

He knelt down in the center of the boat, looking like a boy with his bedhead, his bare feet, his fraying khaki shorts. He took my hand in his and started talking, saying all of the right things, none of which I can remember now because, in the moment, all I could think was to repeat to myself: *This is happening, this is happening, my God, he's proposing, it's happening.* The next thing I knew there was a ring on my finger and we were hugging and kissing and the sun was coming up over the trees and the air smelled grassy and sweet and it was perfect. I loved him. He loved me. It was perfect.

We were married a year later, and after the buzz of being new-lyweds wore off, we settled into the kind of married life I've always assumed is the universal experience. Our daily lives were like separate parallel tracks, each with our own individual responsibilities and to-do lists, but we were never more than a figurative arm's distance away from each other. No matter what I was doing, I was always aware of the third life we'd made together. We shared voicemail messages, an address, a laundry hamper. He was always *around* in some sense, even when he wasn't physically present.

So it's incredibly strange to imagine him just going about his life without me now—pumping gas, getting money from the ATM—as if our marriage doesn't exist, when, meanwhile, I'm here, unmoored, flailing, questioning how I'll make it through the next few hours, much less the next few days. I wonder whether he realizes what this has really done to me. I wonder whether he's even thinking of me at all.

I kick the sheets off the bed and sit up to check the time on the alarm clock across the room. It's past three. I lie back against my pillow, cursing the hour, the burning tension pulsing in my shoulders, everything. *Did he notice her first? What was their first conversation like? How did it happen, when they went back to her place? If I'd done something differently, would it have happened at all?*

# CHAPTER SIX

Mom opens the front door before I've even put the car in park. When I get to the front stoop, "Honey" is about all she can manage before she starts to cry.

"I'm so sorry," she stage-whispers into my ear, her nails digging into the back of my shoulder. "I just hate this for you."

"I'm fine, Mom." My mother has a distinct and wonderful scent—a mixture of Nivea cold cream, which she's famously used since her thirteenth birthday, when my grandmother presented her with her first jar, and Good & Plenty candy, which she eats by the handful from the crystal dish that she keeps on the kitchen counter.

I let go of her and step over the threshold into the house, then toss my bag into the same corner of the hallway where my backpack lived every day after high school.

"I'm going to go use the bathroom," I say, trying to sound cheery and light, like there's nothing more to my being here than a desire to visit.

"Was there a lot of traffic?" Mom follows me down the hall. I can almost smell the worry coming out of her pores.

"Just around Richmond. Nothing unusual." I keep walking, down the hall past the spot where my wedding photo sits on a table next to my parents'. I can feel it there. I don't look. "Where's Lucy?"

"She's upstairs napping. She got in late last night."

"Okay. I'll be out in a minute."

I close the bathroom door and push the lock and stand in front of the gold oval mirror that's been over the sink since the day we moved into this house. I examine the bags under my eyes, my chalky complexion, and note that I have the unmistakable look of *Someone Going Through Something*. My mother, being a woman who not only keeps a tube of lipstick in the front pocket of her pants at all times but actually thinks to reapply it throughout the day, has already noticed this, surely, and I'm certain it has only compounded her anxiety about me.

When Lucy and I were eleven and thirteen, Mom signed us up for an "Etiquette for Young Ladies" class at the Lord & Taylor at the mall. In a cheerless fluorescent-lit conference room, where an ancient "20 percent off" poster hung cockeyed on the wall, a middle-aged woman in a too-tight skirt spent three hours of an otherwise perfectly good Saturday morning instructing our gloomy table of awkward preteens on everything from how to set a table to how to properly wash our faces. But what I remember most from this *training*, antiquated even then, is the distinct realization, as I squirmed and sweated in my suntan-colored pantyhose, that this was another thing that separated me from my mother and my sister, who had not only applied her lipstick perfectly during that particular lesson but had raised her hand and taught the teacher a new trick about how to hold the tube.

Standing in front of the mirror in my parents' powder room, I am certain that the next forty-eight hours will mean defending myself against Mom and Lucy as they preen around me, poke the tender spots of my psyche, and make me face things that they, as a team, have surely already decided I need to deal with, regardless of whether I am ready.

An hour later, my sister, just up from her nap, flops down on the opposite end of the couch from me. She stabs a cracker into the log of goat cheese that Mom set on the coffee table along with a pile of Triscuits, the ritual cheese and cracker plate that she puts out every time people are in her house.

Twenty minutes after I broke the news to Mom the other night, Lucy called to check on me, and in a rare moment of sensitivity, she said that she'd meet me in Virginia. She would leave her boyfriend Bobby in the city. ("He's on my nerves anyway," she moaned, which irked me, of course, since I would kill to have Owen simply be on my nerves right now.) "We'll have a girls' weekend," she said. "We'll drink wine, eat junk food, watch old movies, paint our nails," proving once and for all that my sister still thinks that the cure for a grown-up heartache is the crap we used to read in *Seventeen* magazine and, more to the point, that we really are polar opposites.

"Daphne," she says now. "I can't believe this. It's just…" She throws her hands up in the air. "It's unbelievable."

"It sure is," I say. She and Owen have a normal brother–and–sister-in-law relationship—nothing more, nothing less. Their interactions are essentially polite cocktail party chatter. They pretend to be interested in each other's jobs. They talk about movies, current events, books.

When we were kids, Lucy was an obsessive reader. I yanked books from her hands to get her to come to dinner and knocked them out of her grip when it was time to get ready for school. I thought for sure that she'd be a great writer someday, or a book critic, an editor, an English professor. But then she surprised everyone when she decided to become a beauty editor at *Glow*, a woman's magazine. From what I can tell, this means that she spends her workday sifting through the crates of cosmetics sent to her by the manufacturers and zipping around to events at high-end Manhattan hotels to celebrate a new mascara's "lash technology" (these are the terms that she uses) like it's the cure for cancer. She is pretty and always has been, in a young Faye Dunaway sort of way, but now she's as well groomed as a contestant at the Westminster Dog Show, all polish and sheen. Bobby, her longtime boyfriend, is a hedge fund manager. They make piles of money, will likely get engaged within a year, and will live a glossy, superficial existence. It's not for me, but it seems to make her happy.

"So you took the train down last night?" I ask, changing the subject.

"Yes, after work. You're lucky to have a car. Bobby offered to let me take his but, God, I haven't driven in almost a year." I remember Bobby's car. He is one of those BMW owners whose license plate references being a BMW owner: BBYZBEEM.

"It worked out anyway," she says. "I actually like taking the train, and I had a ton of work to get done."

I'm tempted to ask what kind of urgent beauty editing would require such attention but I bite my tongue. I don't want to endure a twenty-minute monologue about moisturizer.

"So he did this a few months ago?" Lucy says, stretching her legs out on the couch and flipping her hair to one side. I once heard a story on the radio about a person's *definitive gesture*—a physical trademark like Bob Hope's imaginary golf swing, Bruce Lee's air-punch, Carol Burnett's tug on her ear. With my sister, it would be the hair flipping, the incessant, never-ending hair flipping.

"Sure did."

"Ridiculous," she says through a mouthful of food.

Our mother is in the laundry room, just off the den, not missing a word of this. She is many things, but not a housekeeper, and from the spot where I sit, I can see her folding my father's undershirts as methodically as if she were packing away my sister's and my baptismal gowns. I can feel her looking at me. I wish she'd give up the act and just come join us.

"And the girl?" Lucy says, her left hand swiping at her phone.

"What about her?"

"She's younger? Works with him?"

"Yup. A classic tale."

"What does she look like?"

My mind flashes to the pictures I found on the Internet. "Like the girls in your magazine."

This gets Lucy's attention. "Hmph," she says quietly, almost as if she's saying it to herself. She shakes her head. "So he's confused or something? That's what you said the other night on the phone."

"Apparently. I haven't really talked to him since the other day."

Mom can't help herself—she puts down the laundry and rushes over to where we're sitting.

"You haven't talked to him?" Mom asks. She sits on the arm of the sofa and clasps her hands tightly in her lap like she's cold.

"I really haven't, Mom. Why would I?"

"Umm?" Lucy says. They exchange a look.

"What?"

"If I were you, I would demand more of an explanation from him," says Lucy. "Not just about how he let this all go down but also about how he plans to fix it. You can't just let someone walk out of your life like he's walking out of a restaurant. Not without some repercussions. I mean, you guys have been together for how long?"

"Ten years."

She looks at me like I've just told her that it's been that long since I've been to the dentist.

"I see you're still wearing your wedding ring." She points at my hand.

"And?" I *knew* she would say something. "I'm still married, Lucy."

"Really, Lucy." Mom pats my hand. "It's not like they're getting divorced or something."

Lucy's eyes widen. "Of course they are!" she says to Mom, as if I'm not sitting right there. "She can't stay with him—not after this."

I pick up a cracker and jam it into the cheese. When I crunch down on it, I immediately wish that I hadn't. It tastes like glue.

"Nobody's getting divorced," Mom says.

Lucy looks at me, obviously wanting me to clear this up for them.

"Guys, this *just* happened," I say. "Do we have to analyze it right away? Can't we just *hang out*?"

"Of course," Mom says, squeezing my shoulder.

"Sure, let's just hang out," Lucy says unconvincingly, picking a piece of lint off her top. It is gray and thin and hangs off of one shoulder, reminding me of when we were kids and used to cut up Dad's old running T-shirts to make what we thought were fashionable late-eighties nightgowns for ourselves.

"Lucy, come on."

"I just…" She sits up, her spine snapping straight. "I know that I don't know him the way that you do but I just never would have pictured him doing this. Do you think he's always been this fucked up?"

"Lucy, this is your brother-in-law you're talking about," Mom says.

"My brother-in-law who slept with his coworker!" she says.

"Well, you could be more delicate with your choice of words," Mom says.

"Why are you defending him?" Lucy says.

"I'm not defending him!" she says.

"It sounds like you are," Lucy says. "I mean, something could legitimately be wrong with him. You've met his dad."

"Lucy, be nice," Mom says.

I clear my throat. "Don't mind me," I say, waving my hands in the air.

"Daphne," Lucy says, leaning forward. "I'm just saying, maybe this is for the best. Again, look at his father. Is that the kind of man you want to be married to?"

"You've only met Owen's dad once or twice, you don't know what you're talking about!"

The truth is, she's right about Owen, Sr. He's a total asshole. On several occasions, I have heard Owen describe his father as "200 pounds of tough-guy bullshit," and I agree. He is not even a teaspoon friendly, and the worst part is that he doesn't have good reason to back it up. I might be more inclined to let his lack of personality slide if he was a veteran with a war story, say, or had a scrappy, Scorsese-movie childhood. But the bottom line is that he's just a jerk. He owns a sporting goods store with a room in the back where they make trophies for local sports teams—bowling tournament championship cups, Little League plaques, swim team medals. It's obvious that he has a hang-up about Owen's choice of profession. I've heard the digs—about Owen thinking he's a big shot, about the amount of money he'll someday earn. I know that when Owen told him that he got into med school, his response contained more complaints about the cost than compliments about his son's high achievement. Owen took on the student loans himself, of course. We said we'd take a big trip to celebrate paying them off. We were thinking about Spain.

"Lucy, listen," I say. "I appreciate your concern but I'm really not in the mood to dissect Owen's character. To be honest, I'd like to spend the weekend keeping him *off* my mind as much as possible."

"Fine," she says, her voice softening a little. "I'm sorry, I'm just so pissed off at him."

Mom reaches over and hugs me. "We're here for you, honey."


Later that evening, I am collapsed on Lucy's unmade twin bed, watching her examine herself in front of the full-length mirror on the inside of her closet door. We assumed these exact positions at least 100,000 times during our teens.

"So what about your friends?" Lucy says. "Have any of them taken you out to get rip-roaring drunk yet?"

"I'm not twenty, Lucy."

She shrugs and fiddles with her hair, then starts pinching at her cheeks.

"So get this," she says.

I stretch my arms up toward the ceiling, making a diamond shape with my thumbs and index fingers. "What?" I manage through a wide yawn. I put my hand on my stomach, where the hefty portion of roasted vegetable lasagna that my mother served for dinner sits like a brick. When Lucy and I went away to college, Mom discovered a penchant for recipe competitions. She's always testing something—a pot pie for a Pillsbury contest, crab puffs for the Virginia state fair. The lasagna (a tomato sauce contest) was one of her first blue ribbons.

"My assistant, who's from somewhere in the South—Missis-sippi. No, wait," she says. "Texas." I drop my hands to my sides. *Texas. Land of the Glamazon Husband Stealers.* "One of those places where beauty pageants are a really big deal. Anyway, she told me that somebody from home swears by Monistat Chafing Relief for makeup primer." She laughs. "But it has to be the chafing relief stuff, not the regular, yeast infection kind of Monistat. I tried to find it in the city but they didn't have it at Duane Reade. Apparently, it's kind of hard to find. We should go to CVS and see if they have it."

"What the hell is makeup primer?" I ask.

Lucy's mouth drops and she glares at me through the mirror. "Makeup primer, my dear sister, is what you put on your face before you put on your makeup. It helps it last."

"Oh, oh, of course," I say. "That's very important." I roll over and examine the doodads on my sister's nightstand—an ancient ceramic Miss Piggy figurine that she painted years ago (we loved those craft kits), a mall photo booth photo of Lucy and her giggly girlfriends—lots of hairspray, big earrings. A couple of her books.

"Are you reading these?" I ask, reaching for the one on top— Wallace Stegner. And beneath that, a Princess Di biography.

"Yeah," she says.

"Any good?" I ask, turning the book over to read the back cover.

An uh-huh is all she offers. I flip the book down on to my chest. She's separating her eyelashes with a straight pin, a horrendous habit that she's had since some friend taught her in college.

"Jesus, Lucy, you still do that? Surely you've discovered a better way."

"Nope, still the best," she says, holding up the pin.

"As a medical professional, I have to advise you that it's probably not wise to put the sharp edge of a straight pin within millimeters of your pupil."

She continues with her other eye, wiggling her brows at me as she does. "Make you nervous?"

"That's disgusting."

"I'm so glad that we can revert right back to our teenaged selves after a few hours of being in each other's company," she says.

"Agreed." I cross my arms over my face. No matter how often I lance a boil or diagnose chlamydia, I draw the line at watching my sister hold a stickpin to her eye.

"Let's go out tonight," she says.

"Go out?" I say through my folded arms. "Go out where?"

Lucy shrugs. "Doesn't matter. Anywhere."

"I'm pretty sure that the only real bar in town is still that disgusting sports bar where the waitresses have to wear those ridiculous uniforms." I was dragged there with high school friends once, during our first winter break in college, because somebody we graduated with waitressed there and was willing to serve us nineteen-year-olds.

"You mean Fourth Quarter?" Lucy says. "The imitation Hooters?"

"That's the one."

I pull into the parking lot of the bar, where a plastic sign next to the front entrance is advertising a St. Patrick's Day special. Corned beef and cabbage and Guinness for two, $12.99. *And a side of gastroenteritis*, I think to myself, crossing under the sign and into the bar.

Inside, it smells like onions and beer, with a faint back note of whatever watery antiseptic cleanser they use to hose down the place. A morose twenty-something is at the hostess stand, dressed in a tight referee's jersey and black shiny short-shorts. "Hi, welcome to Fourth Quarter," she says, not even trying to smile.

"Do you ever have to use those things?" Lucy asks her, pointing to the referee's whistle on a lanyard around the girl's neck.

She shrugs. "No. Sometimes I want to, just to see what would happen." She tugs at the hem of her shorts. Poor thing.

"You should," Lucy says.

*You* would, I think.

"We're just going to the bar," Lucy tells her.

"Okay. It's buy-one, get-one shots tonight," she says, hopping up on the stool behind her podium.

Lucy looks at me, raising her eyebrows.

"You've got to be kidding me," I say.

The light in the bar is too bright, casting a harsh topaz glow over the room. There are television screens everywhere, and the cacophony of sounds—blowing whistles, sportscasters screaming, motors roaring, music—doesn't appear to faze anyone else, but I feel instantly overwhelmed. I slide on to a stool and manage to politely grin at the bartender as he sets a cardboard Bud Light coaster in front of me. Lucy takes the liberty of ordering both of us a vodka soda.

I feel blindsided. How on earth did I land here? Last week, I had a husband, a home, and the shared (I thought) dream of starting our family, and now I'm drinking away my sorrows in a shitty sports bar behind a Best Buy? I pull out my phone and put it on the bar, if for no other reason than because Lucy is already typing away at hers.

I notice on one of the televisions that the Boston Bruins are playing tonight. Owen is surely watching. I wonder where. He preferred to watch games at home, where he could yell at the television in private.

"So here we are," Lucy says, turning to me. "A Friday night in Manassas. And I wonder why I ever moved away."

"Do you think you'll stay in the city forever?" I ask.

"I don't know," Lucy says, spinning her phone on the top of the bar with one hand. "Probably."

She reaches over my arm to grab my phone. "Do you have any pictures of him here?"

I nod. We determined on the drive over that the last time that

Lucy saw Owen was last summer at Mom's birthday party. She and Bobby had missed Christmas, opting instead for four days in Turks and Caicos. I remember one of the photos that she emailed afterward—the two of them holding up margarita glasses with a couple they met at their resort's pool bar. The couple had a boat. They went snorkeling.

"He is good-looking, that's for sure," she says, studying the picture of Owen. He's in profile, laughing at something, I can't remember what. He was driving when I took the picture. We were running errands for the house. Or grocery shopping. Maybe taking Blue to the Eno River for a hike? It was something regular and easy and dull, which is a shame. Our time off together was rare, and when we had it, we filled it with the to-dos of our home life—renovation-related errands, shopping. I should have worked harder to make that time count. Did he know her yet, when I took that picture? His smile in the photo is real. You can't question it: He looks happy.

I take a sip of my drink. I'm a firm believer in a glass of wine at the end of the day, but I don't think I've had a vodka drink in ten years.

"And a pediatric oncologist." She shakes her head, sneering, as if it's him in the flesh and not his picture that she's looking at.

The bartender, who's short and barrel-chested and has a face like a French bulldog, walks over to check on us.

"We're fine," I say, before he has a chance to ask.

"Okay," he says. "No problem." He sticks his hand under the bar and then it emerges holding a sad wooden bowl of wasabi peas. It's like I've time-traveled back to the late nineties. I was two years into med school at UVA and too focused on classes to give any serious thought to relationships, but I'd briefly dated a guy named Derek, a former college hockey player, who was planning to do orthopedics. We watched the Stanley Cup finals in a bar like this one. I wonder what happened with him. Why things never went further with us. When we first met, I was wary. The orthopedics guys, especially the former athletes, weren't exactly viewed as boyfriend material, and while Derek was a little wild—far more like the kind of guy that Lucy dated than I ever had—he was cordial and sweet, a gentle giant.

I wonder, had Owen and I never had that childhood history, whether we ever would have noticed each other in that sandwich shop that day. I always thought we were fated. I loved when people asked how we met. "Well, we kind of met twice," I'd start, smiling at Owen as I said it.

"So do you guys live here?" the bartender says. "Haven't seen you before, I don't think."

I clear my throat and look to Lucy, who clearly doesn't look like she lives in suburban Virginia or frequents this bar. I don't want to be a jerk, but I'm not interested in making an effort. Plus, chatting people up is much more my sister's game.

"We grew up here," Lucy says. "Just back in town for a visit."

"Ah," he says. "Well, welcome home."

"Thanks," we say in unison.

"Sisters?" he says.

"Yes," she says.

"So what's the occasion? Anything special or just visiting to visit?"

"Just visiting to visit," I say, before Lucy can offer my sad story. I pick up the stirrer off the cocktail napkin that I plucked from the stack on the edge of the bar and stab it into my drink to break up the ice.

"Can I get you another one of those?" the bartender asks.

I tilt my glass to get a better look at its contents. It's nearly empty.

"Yes, she'll have another, please," Lucy says.

"No, really, I don't need it," I protest.

"I'll drive," Lucy interrupts. "Or we can take a cab. Please get her another."

The bartender grins, baring the wide gap in his teeth. "You sure?" he says, pointing at me.

I shrug and shake my head at Lucy. "I guess."

An hour later, the bartender has taken a shine to Lucy, as have the two gentlemen on the other side of her. They are dressed in enough Nascar gear to be mistaken for members of a pit crew, burly, unshaven, maybe in their mid-fifties, and they're stopping in town on a drive down the coast to a race in Darlington, South Carolina.

Hank, the one next to Lucy, has been married for thirty-five years and has two daughters and four grandchildren. Joe, his buddy, has been married for thirty-four and has six children ("Old-school Catholic!" he shouts at me, by way of explanation).

Lucy is telling them the story about how our parents took us on an introductory trip to D.C. right before we moved to Virginia. *Our mother said she was taking us for a walk on the National Mall, and we get there, and I'm all, Where are the stores? Where is the mall?*

*Ha, ha, ha.* I think. Hank and Joe snicker. The story's always funnier to Lucy than it is to anyone else. My concentration keeps swerving in and out of the conversation, catching a phrase here and there. Lucy took the liberty of telling our new friends my story. I didn't have to add a word as she rattled off the details, and I was fine with that—*I* didn't want to. Hank and Joe gave me the standard, chin-in-their-chests condolences that you'd expect from men of their generation: "Sorry to hear that." "That's really too bad." Lucy was on a roll, her indictments of Owen flying from her mouth like parade streamers. *Such an asshole. Deceived her. Cheated right after Christmas and they'd just moved into their new house.* The two men just shook their heads and stared into their bottles. "Just awful." "Terrible." "So sorry."

Alcohol is a depressant, for the record. It blunts the functioning of your central nervous system, which impairs you physically and psychologically. There is an initial high after a few drinks, a stimulating effect, but alcohol ultimately blocks your nerve receptors' abilities to send messages to your brain, so you start to slur, your motor skills loosen, your emotional state destabilizes.

Inhibitions are lost. Men punch each other. Women profess their love to each other. My sister laughs louder. The women across the bar—two of them, both a little puffy around the edges in the way that suggests a lot of nights like this one—sing along unoriginally, embarrassingly, to Prince's "Kiss."

I feel myself sinking, emotionally bottoming out. I remind myself of the way that three vodka drinks have affected me physiologically, because somehow, going through the biology takes away the blame for feeling what I'm starting to feel. Tears just behind my eyes. The suspicion that nights like tonight could become more regular now. Owen, on the prickly edges of my mind, beckoning me to think back, what it was like, what we had planned, the memories. The years and years *and years* of memories.

My phone rings. Owen's face pops up.

Lucy huffs when she sees it. The two men peer, heads bent over the bar, watching me. I want to answer it.

"Let me," Lucy says, her hand poised to take the phone.

"Lucy, please," I say, putting my palm over it. I'm about to answer it, I really am, but then it hits me that I'll have to tell Owen what I'm doing, which is fine, except that I really think that I might cry. I might sob. It will be a slurry, mucousy mess of a thing. The ringing stops and Lucy smiles at me in a satisfied way. *I wonder if everything's okay with the dog*, I think, watching and waiting for the voicemail alert to chime. It doesn't. *He'd leave a message if something was wrong*, I tell myself.

"You know, I did that once," Hank says, pointing at the phone with his chubby finger.

"What?" My heart is pounding. *Why did he call?*

Hank looks over at his buddy, who's nodding in a way that suggests that he knows what Hank's about to say.

"I cheated on my wife."

"Hank, no!" Lucy says and slaps her hands on the bar, as if they're old friends and she knows him well enough for this to be shocking.

"It's true," he says, shaking his head at the memory. "Worst thing I ever did."

"Hmph." Joe sort of laughs, agreeing with him.

"Why?" I ask. "Tell me."

"Our kids were little—babies, really. Things had changed, they always do once you get married and start a family. Nobody was sleeping—well, my wife wasn't sleeping. It's just around the clock, the stress about money and the worry about the kids, and it's hard as hell." He shakes his head.

"I was weak," he says, raising a finger to make the point. "I could tell you that I was tired, or that things had changed between Ramona and me, and all of that's true, but I was weak to do what I did. That's the bottom line. It was a nightmare."

"But she found out eventually? Or you told her?"

"It was a woman I worked with, just like your, uh..." He puts his palm in the air and wiggles his fingers for a reminder.

"Owen."

"Right," he says. "Anyways, she caught me. The woman from work, it had lasted a while, she went a little...she got a little attached. She came by the house one time. Ramona was at her mother's with the kids, just for an afternoon visit, and she came home as I was standing there in the doorway, telling this other woman that she had to go. She couldn't be at my house. Well, she just lost it then. And Ramona was walking up and saw the whole thing. It was awful, a big confrontation. Fortunately, the kids were too young to really remember."

"So what happened?"

"I moved out for a while, but every day, I begged for her forgiveness. I came by the house every night to tuck in the kids. Brought flowers and candies for Ramona. Wrote love letters—I'd never done *that* before. I knew what I'd done. I knew what a mistake it was. The worst thing you can ever do to somebody."

I remember how Owen said the same thing on the back porch the other night.

"Eventually, she took me back. It took a long time to win her trust. Years, really. I don't think she said more than a few words to me for the first six months that I was home again, but I deserved the punishment. I *didn't* deserve her forgiveness. Thank God, she took me back." He stares into his beer. "Thank God. I don't know what I'd do without her."

The words reverberate in my ears. Lucy puts her hand to her chest and purses her lips. "That's so sweet, Hank."

"Well, I don't know if I'd put it that way, but..." He shrugs. "I got lucky."

He gives me a lingering look and I manage to smile at him. I feel the teensiest glimmer of hope, like finally somebody understands what I'm going through. What Owen did doesn't have to end our marriage. A U-turn is always possible. But does he want that? Do I?

# CHAPTER SEVEN

I'm standing in the kitchen early the next morning, watching the sun come up over the trees, when my dad walks in.

"You're up early," he says, patting my shoulder.

"I am." I had a lot of trouble falling asleep, despite the three vodkas. I spent the night trying to decide whether to call Owen back. Was he getting in touch for a logistical reason—something to do with the house or the dog? Or was the call something more? *I'm reconsidering, Daph. I made a huge mistake.*

Dad puts his arm around me. "Jesus Christ, gal," he whispers. "What happened?" My father's favorite phrase is *Jesus Christ*. Not in the holy sense but in the *Jesus Christ, are you kidding me?* way that he yells at the television when he watches the Patriots or the *Jesus Christ, what are we going to do with this kid?* that was frequently employed during Lucy's teen years.

"I don't know, Dad. But it's obviously bad."

"Yeah."

"It's real bad."

We stare out at the backyard together. A bluebird is hopping along the back of one of the patio chairs. One summer night several years ago, Owen and I, acting like kids, stood out there and tossed pebbles up into the air to make the bats circling above us swoop down, silhouette black against the navy sky. We were probably out there for forty-five minutes, just doing that, having the time of our lives. That kind of relationship doesn't come out of nowhere. It happens slowly, over time. I don't know if you get more than one.

"What do you think you're going to do, Daphne?" Dad asks.

"I don't know. Any advice?"

He makes a *pffft* sound like a dud firework that's really perfect, like the deepening bleakness that's wedging its way into my chest. "I don't know, gal. I really don't." He's quiet for a beat. "I could kill him, you know."

"I know."

"Did you have any idea?"

"None, honestly."

"I guess you just keep doing what you've always been so good at doing. You figure out the next step." He reaches for the bloated sponge in the bottom of the sink, squeezes the water from it, and deposits it back in the soap dish. We've always been alike that way, my dad and me, tidying up around the tornado that is Lucy and my mom.

It's unintentional, of course, but what he says stings. I *have* always been the kind of person who figures things out, haven't I? I have always been able to so seamlessly move from point A to point B, as easily as if my life were a simple equation. So what now? How do I solve this one?

"I don't know how to figure it out, though, Dad."

"You will," he says, patting my shoulder again.

"Will what?" my mother says, coming into the kitchen.

"Figure out what I'm going to do," I say, going to the cupboard for a coffee mug. "It's not even really under my control, or remotely straightforward. I can't just, you know, write a prescription and make it better."

"Oh, but you'll find your way, honey!" Mom exclaims, her

voice exploding into the room. I think of Lucy upstairs sleeping. "*Of course* you will! You're going to get through this! These difficult things only build character! What doesn't kill us makes us stronger!" She reminds me of those generic motivational posters, like the one my idiot colleague Dr. Moyer has in his office, the word "courage" in all caps over a photo of a mountain range.

"Honey, you simply need to take some time and get some perspective," she says, now rifling around in a mound of baked goods on the counter—a couple of tins of shortbread, Lucy's favorite bagels brought from New York, the cinnamon scones that I occasionally request before a visit.

Her cheery encouragement is starting to get to me. Can't I just wallow a bit more? Does she really not understand that the last thing I want to hear right now is how this will "make me stronger"?

She starts to hand me a scone.

"That's okay, Mom," I say. "I'm not hungry."

Her shoulders drop—just barely, but I notice it.

"On second thought." I take the scone from her and manage a nibble, and then as I'm walking to the refrigerator for the half-and-half, my phone starts to ring. I whip around to where I'd laid it on the kitchen table and there's Owen's name at the top of the screen, the simple familiar four letters, and that picture of him, laughing. My parents look at me in an alarmed way, like the phone is a bomb that only I can disarm. I snatch it and hurry upstairs to my room, where no one else has to see this.

"It's me," he says. There's a hollow whirring sound in the background that makes me think that he's outside somewhere. "Something happened, Daph."

I feel my skin start to prickle. "Is it Blue?"

"No, she's fine."

I sigh. "Then what is it, Owen? The house?"

"No." He pauses. "I need your help."

"You've got to be kidding me." This isn't what I was expecting. This isn't what I was *hoping*. "I'm away at my parents' house— *retreating, because of what you did*—and you need my *help*? This better be good."

I'm sitting on the floor of my bedroom, where nothing has changed, down to the mint green wall-to-wall carpet that Mom put in when we moved here. I pull my shirt over my knees and wait for one of us to say something.

"It's Bridget," he finally says. My stomach clenches. I feel an instant dead weight in my gut that makes me breathless. "I'm sorry, Daph. I'm sorry to ask…" He pauses a beat. "She was in an accident last night. It's really bad. We're in the ICU." *We.* I can't help how it announces itself, even now, in this context. "I know how awkward this is. I don't know why I called. I'm sorry. I just needed to talk to you. I need you." Something in his voice hitches and cracks. I think he's crying.

I can only think of two times when Owen's cried in front of me and one of those times, it was happy tears—our wedding day. The other was the first time he lost a patient—I think her name was Miriam. She was thirteen, from Tennessee.

"Do you want me to come home?" I say, breaking our long silence.

"Will you?"

I quickly throw my things into my duffel bag and go down to the kitchen, where Lucy's sitting in a chair with her bare feet up on the kitchen table, telling Mom about a new anti-aging cream she's testing at work.

"Where are you going?" she says when she turns and sees me standing there with my keys and my bag.

"She was in a car accident," I say.

"Who?" Mom yelps, her hands going to her cheeks.

Dad rushes in from the family room, holding the crossword page in one hand. "Is everything okay?"

"Is it Annie?" Lucy says, taking her feet off of the table and sitting up.

"No, Bridget," I say, and it strikes me how odd it feels to say her name in this way—like I know her, like we're friends.

Mom and Lucy exchange a glance.

Dad narrows his eyes at me, perplexed.

"The girl that Owen—" I start to explain, but Lucy cuts me off.

"What are you doing, Daphne?"

"Owen asked for my help. They're in the ICU. I have to—"

"You don't have to do anything," Dad says, taking a step toward me.

"He's still my husband," I say. I see Mom behind him, her eyes full of fear. She nods ever so slightly.


They walk me out to my car, and as I'm reversing down the driveway, Lucy walks alongside me, like she's about to throw herself on the hood to get me to stay. "Call me!" she says, holding her thumb and pinky to her ear.

I nod, glancing one last time at my parents, who stand side by side on the front stoop, the worry in their expressions revealing everything that they can't bring themselves to say.

# CHAPTER EIGHT

I pull into the parking lot next to Duke Hospital and turn off the ignition. It's the very same parking lot where Owen and I used to meet between shifts during residency. Most residents took their breaks in what's called "the bunker," a computer room in the hospital's basement, but Owen and I always met outside, eager to pull oxygen into our lungs after countless hours of breathing stale hospital air. We would rest against my car, neither of us saying much because we were exhausted, and lean into each other, sipping the good coffee I'd bring in a Thermos from home. We would watch the cars and city buses rumble past, watch the smokers (a surprising number of whom were doctors and nurses) get their fix on the corner, and comfort each other by cracking jokes about all of the stupid mistakes we were sure we'd made over the course of our shifts.

A statistic that people used to talk about during residency was the high divorce rate among members of the program, particularly the surgery program. But I always felt like the exception to prove the rule: During those years, I felt I was falling more deeply in love with Owen each day. It was so many things—the initial spark of our childhood history and our shared passion for medicine, of course, but so much more, too. A lot of it, perhaps, comes down to the fact that we really *talked* to each other back then. We were constantly telling each other stories—big things, like his issues with his father, my obsessive desire to succeed—and all of the little things, too.

One day early on, outside in this very parking lot, Owen told me why he'd chosen pediatric oncology for his specialty. When he was six, his mother noticed that her normally rambunctious boy, who'd been scaling trees in the backyard since he could walk, was suddenly only interested in lolling about on the living room sofa in front of *Tom and Jerry*. Two visits to Mass General confirmed that Owen had acute lymphoblastic leukemia, the most common form of childhood cancer. His little life suddenly became about chemotherapy, spinal injections, and daily handfuls of candy-coated pills that were nothing like candy. By the time he reached his ninth birthday and was formally declared cancer-free, he knew that he was going to be a doctor exactly like the ones who'd saved him. His career is about so much more than work to him. His heart is involved. I know that he sees himself in each and every one of the kids he treats. I was proud to be married to such a man.


I take a deep breath and get out of the car. During the four-hour drive back to Durham, I made a conscious decision to not analyze what I'm doing, but walking through the parking lot, I can't help but start. I am so angry and yet…I love him. I want to help him. I feel out of place and like this is the only place where I can be. The voice on the phone—the only man I've ever really loved, my *husband*—needs me. I need to be needed. It makes my stomach flip, even just admitting it to myself. *Maybe it's selfish? Am I here because it's good for him or good for me?* I think that I'm allowed to not care about her. *Bridget is a stranger*, I tell myself. I am a doctor and it's acceptable and understandable, even a good thing—even a *helpful* thing—for me to disassociate myself from any emotion regarding her condition. *Think of her like a patient*, I say to myself as I walk under the awning and into the building. *Think of this like any other case.* Because my practice is affiliated with the hospital, I'm able to use my ID to get into the intensive care unit, and as soon as I'm there, it hits me that it's been a very long time since I've been in an ICU. There is a veiled, hushed sort of decorum like that of a library or a museum. And almost because of the quiet, you can't help but notice the faint droning and beeping of the machines in the background, all running for the sole purpose of keeping hearts beating, lungs expanding and constricting, blood pumping. I scan the room of pinched, austere faces and am about to approach the thin-lipped woman standing behind the nurses' station when I spot him.

He is speaking to a doctor, the person I assume is in charge of Bridget's care, and I am instantly struck by the look on Owen's face. He's in the hospital where he spends more time each week than he does anywhere else, including his home, but he does not have the steady expression of someone who's comfortable here. Rather he has the anxious, worn face of a visitor. Beyond him is a curtained enclosure and I wonder if Bridget is lying behind it with a breathing tube and bandages, looking nothing like the photos I've fumed over.

I catch his eye and he waves, one palm up. I don't go to him. I stand there and watch the way that he nods at the doctor, his arms crossed, listening expectantly, wanting answers. A couple of minutes later he comes to me, and as he approaches, it's obvious that he's trying to gauge whether he should hug me or...what? I shove my hands into the pockets of the down vest that he picked out for me at the L.L. Bean outlet a couple of years ago when we took a trip up the Maine coast with his parents.

"So what happened?" I say, my heart pounding. *Just a patient*, I remind myself. It's immediate and obvious: Being here feels like a mistake.

"She just got out of emergency surgery," he says. "She was driving home from work. Some asshole tore out of that shopping center on University, where Thai Café is?"

I nod. He's unshaven, and looks like he's been here all night. He's wearing the old jeans and long-sleeved T-shirt that he always wore when we worked on house projects, which makes me think that he must have gotten the call about her accident when he was picking up the dog. I wonder who broke the news to him. *Why was he the one who was called? Where is her family?* I'm suddenly aware of the bright buzzing overhead lights and the stale, choking airlessness of the room.

"What's the prognosis?" I ask, trying to ignore the anxious way his eyes are flitting around.

"It's bad," he says, running his hand over his chin. "Blunt abdominal trauma. Splenic rupture. Orthopedic injuries." He starts to sound like the doctor that he is, and it's a comfort. We can pretend that there's nothing between us, that we're just two doctors discussing a case.

"She had emergency surgery for the abdominal, I assume?"

He nods. "Also a chest tube. There's blood in her lung cavity."

*For some reason, I didn't imagine it could be this bad.* "And the orthopedic?"

"Hip fracture, her head." He looks away and takes a deep breath. "I'm sorry for bringing you into this. I didn't know who else to call."

I don't know what to say. If the accident had happened to anyone else—his best buddy from residency whom he occasionally cycles with, a parent, his boss—I would have run to him as soon as I saw him here. But though I *want* to comfort him, to put my hand on the back of his neck and whisper into his ear that everything is going to be okay, I can't.

*I should have stayed in Virginia like they begged me to*, I think, my head pounding. I could lie to myself and say that it's empathy and that I came here purely out of concern. I could tell myself that I am a bigger person and that I am the kind of woman who simply acts when called on for help, no matter whom the asker is or what he's done. But deep down I know that the only reason why I'm not back in Virginia, eating egg salad at my mother's kitchen table, is because hearing Owen's voice—*I need you*—sent a tidal wave of hope crashing over me. Now, my *other* status is suddenly so blatant and I'm wondering what on earth I was thinking by even coming here. I'm such a fool.

"You've been here all night?" I ask.

He nods.

"Is this why you called last night?"

Our eyes meet and it all comes together. He's been here since the accident. He's an emotional wreck. She's not just some one-night stand.

"It's not over between you two, is it?" I ask.

He doesn't need to say anything for me to know the answer. We stare at each other for an awkward, gut-wrenching moment.

"Daphne," he starts.

I put my hands out, stopping him. I believed that I knew everything there was to know about my husband. I probably thought that I could pick his fingerprint out of a lineup if I needed to, but I know now, looking at the pained expression on his face that I've never seen before, not once, that he's done something I never could have predicted.

I feel my skin start to prickle, heat on the back of my neck. I shake my head at him, unable to find words strong enough to express what's bubbling up inside of me.

"I can't be here," I manage.

He closes his eyes and nods. "I'm sorry."

I turn and leave, hurrying down the hall, away from him. I push through the double doors with two hands, into the bright, blazing day.

# CHAPTER NINE

What I discover when I arrive home crystallizes, in the most painful way, just how much he's deceived me. When I go upstairs, Blue trailing behind me, I find Owen's suitcase open on our bedroom floor. He was not packing for just a few days—pairs of his socks are jammed into the spaces on the sides and shirts and sweaters are piled so high that he might need to sit on it to close it.

I thought that he was going to swing by to get the dog and pick up a few things—a couple of shirts for the weekend, maybe his cycling gear in case he wanted to go for a ride. It's obvious now—though he didn't bother to make it clear to me—that he was actually going to move out. This "break" was about much more than needing time to figure out *what* he wanted—it seems that it was about deciding *whom* he wanted, too.

I feel dizzy, like my legs might give out at any moment. I sit down next to the suitcase. I know all of his things as if they were my own: the gray sweatshirt that he liked to wear on the weekends, the cache of blue checked button-downs that I teased were his work uniform, the jeans with the holes that have been in his life longer than I have. I start to push the suitcase into the closet, where I won't have to see it, but stop halfway and pull out a shirt. It is green and plain and soft and I hold it to my face and breathe in the sweet-spicy smell of him, one last time, before I make myself get up to see what else he was planning to take.

I walk down the hall to the office, where I discover a box on the floor, half filled with his books. This might be worse than the suitcase. It's one thing to see his clothes piled up, when I can pretend that he is just packing for a trip. Our office, a place that we worked hard to make comfortable for the two of us, is home to an L-shaped desk made by a woodworker in Hillsborough, all of our diplomas, and a needlepoint of his grandparents' farm. There's no denying it, I think, running my fingers over the stitches: He is leaving. I shove my books together on the bookcase, closing the gaps where his books were. This should make me feel better, I think, but it doesn't. Extricating him is not my choice. This is *our* house.

*How did it work, exactly?* I wonder. Was this all planned? Did they decide together that he was going to move out and that they'd move forward together, or is what he told me on our back porch true—that he's honestly confused and remorseful about what he's done, and needs time to sort it out? Either way, he's lied to me about the nature of their relationship. It almost doesn't matter whether it's past or present—it happened.

I go downstairs. He left a half-full glass of water on the kitchen counter. I dump it and put the glass in the dishwasher, shoving the door closed with my foot. His pile of journals remains in the corner of the living room, and I scoop them up and deposit them in the recycling bin. I pull a garbage bag from the box under the sink and shake it open. There are pictures everywhere. The vacation photos—at a blues club in Memphis with Annie and Jack, wine tasting with my med school friends in California, skiing in Vermont, it all goes in. I hardly let myself look. And then in the hallway by the stairs—the photo of me with his mother, standing beside the first Thanksgiving turkey we ever attempted together, another of Owen walking with Blue down a leaf-strewn path just after we got her. *Don't cry*, I say to myself, shoving them in.

The house is quiet, which feels appropriate. This awful extermination (that's what this is, isn't it?) deserves a reverent silence. I know that he is still littered everywhere, in the boxes of childhood memorabilia in the attic, in the formal clothes that still hang in the back of our closet, but this is a start. *This is for the best*, I tell myself, not believing a word.

My phone rings. I rush into the family room, digging it out of my purse, which I'd thrown on the sofa on my way in.

"Hi, Mom," I say after glancing at the caller ID.

"Daphne, honey, I've been so worried."

I'd forgotten to call her when I arrived, as I always do when I leave my parents' house, to let her know that I've made it home safely. "Mom, I'm sorry, I got wrapped up with everything here. I'm home now." I pull out one of the chairs at the kitchen table and sit down.

"How is Owen? How is the girl?"

"Oh," I say, pausing to decide whether I should flood her with the entire story. "The accident was pretty serious."

"Oh, no!" she says. "That's horrible."

"Yes, Owen was pretty distraught. More than I realized he would be."

"So it's really bad."

"Yes, but I was still surprised by how he reacted, given that he had given me the impression that their relationship wasn't serious."

"What do you mean? Is it serious?"

"Seems that way." I sniff.

"Oh, honey," she moans. "Is she still in the ICU?"

"She is," I say, forcing myself to answer her questions. I'm ashamed to admit it but I'm suddenly angry—perhaps it's irrational on my part, but why is her first instinct to worry over Bridget? I need to get off of the phone. I can't do this right now.

"So what will you do? Are you going to go back there? What do you mean about their relationship being serious?"

"Mom, to be honest, the whole day has been a bit of a shock. It's just—at the hospital, it was very obvious that their relationship is much more than I thought it was."

"Sweetie, no."

"I'm sorry, Mom, but can I call you later? It's been a long day."

"Are you okay?"

"I'll be fine, really. Just let me call you back in a bit."

Reluctantly, she lets me go. I put the phone on the table and pull my legs up to rest my chin on my knees. I'm realizing something: The very worst thing about Bridget's accident, for me—and only for me—is that I no longer feel entitled to be angry about what's happened to me. And I am *so* angry. I know that I should compartmentalize the two things—my tragedy, hers—but when I'm really honest with myself? My situation feels every bit as tragic. There, I've said it. I *mean* it.

Every time I think about what's happened, the image that comes to mind is of a million tiny pieces of paper fluttering in the sky, blown to bits by some unexpected pop. My life, over in a snap, bombed away. And it's their entire fault.

There isn't a piece of me that wants to feel sorry for them. I don't care how much he's hurting. I didn't deserve this. None of it. And had Owen been brave enough to come to me when he decided that our marriage was no longer fulfilling him, then none of this would be an issue. I would've fixed it. I would have done anything.

Later that night, after I've locked up and brushed my teeth, I stand in front of the bathroom mirror for a long, long time. I look normal. Utterly, inarguably normal. A little on the short side. Pretty, but not sexy. Owen liked this about me—my T-shirts, my ponytails. I think of Bridget. I know that I shouldn't compare us in this way, especially not now, but I can't help it when the woman who's replaced me looks the way she does. My eyes scan my reflection—the freckles from teenaged summers by the pool, the scar near my collarbone from a bug bite I couldn't stop scratching, my hands. I turn my engagement ring and my wedding ring around my finger. And then, swiftly, I yank them both off, pulling hard, willing myself not to remember that day when we stood in front of everyone we loved and made our vows, reciting the words as we looked into each other's eyes and placed the rings on each other's fingers. *For better or for worse. Till death do us part.* I hold the rings tightly in my hand, biting my lip to try to stop the tears rolling down my cheeks, and remember another vow we both made, at our respective medical school graduations, a doctor's ethical promise: *Primum Non Nocere*—"first, do no harm." He's lied to me—about our marriage, about the man I thought he was, about everything.

I take a deep breath to try to collect myself as I walk to the bedroom, and as I'm opening the lid on my jewelry box, I stop myself. Instead, I pull open the top drawer of my dresser, and I reach to the back, past my old running socks and snagged tights, and I bury my rings down deep in the corner, where I won't come across them, as if I might be able to forget they ever existed at all.

# CHAPTER TEN

Last summer, a local magazine ran a story about our practice. There were photos of the spa-like waiting area with its pillow-soft chaises and the buffet of teas and healthy snacks. There were descriptions of the New Age music that's pumped into each exam room and the state-of-the-art LED lighting system meant to simulate natural light and, therefore, lower blood pressure. The writer talked at length about the atrium where the daily yoga and meditation classes take place, the menu of services offering everything from biofeedback to acupuncture, the wide windows overlooking walking paths maintained by an army of volunteer master gardeners. But what the writer didn't mention were the caregivers themselves and how despite all of the bells and whistles and the truly talented team, our practice is like most other workplaces in that it has its black sheep. Just today, as I was standing at the nurses' station waiting to talk to Carol about our next patient, I overheard Dr. Moyer and Dr. Anderson giggle like fourteen-year-old boys over the digestive distress that Dr. Anderson's last patient had come in complaining about. They were going on and on, and I eventually cleared my throat loudly and gave Dr. Moyer a look—I'm never in the mood to deal with him, but I'm especially not these days. He was licking the foil top that he'd just pulled off of a yogurt container (completely unaware, of course, that that's something no one should ever do in public) and whined, "Oh, please, Mitchell, like you've never bitched about a patient."

And he's right. Guilty as charged. When a patient cops to a steady diet of fast food and then gets pissed off because you won't diagnose her "irritable bowel syndrome," you can't help but vent about it. Same goes for the ones who log five hours of sleep a night but are convinced they have chronic fatigue syndrome and the ones who haven't exercised in years but are sure there's a thyroid problem to blame for their steady weight gain.

So I may occasionally air my frustrations about my patients, but it's only ever to Annie, and I have *never* breached the patient/doctor code of confidentiality in any serious way. Until now.

When I go into my personal office at the end of the day, ostensibly to record notes about the day's appointments and answer emails, I lock the door and then jiggle the doorknob to double-check it. I open my laptop and log onto the Duke Hospital system website. I almost consider using Owen's ID and password, which I'm sure I could figure out because the password he uses for everything is his mother's maiden name plus 45 and 9, the jersey numbers of Pedro Martinez and Ted Williams, his two favorite baseball players.

My hands shake as I type in my personal access code and then Bridget's name and birth date, which I unburied in an unusually detailed triathlon results listing from 2009.

I remind myself that people do this all of the time. I remember how I teased Annie last year about looking up a potential nanny's health record before she hired her, as if discovering that the woman had had a precancerous mole removed might reveal how she'd treat her kids. Still, this confidentiality breach is something that our electronic system probably can track—with malpractice risks these days, everything's tracked—and I would have some serious explaining to do if Bridget's doctors caught me digging through their files.

*Oh, well*, I think, taking a deep breath while I wait for the system to locate her record. Like so many things lately, doing this feels like something beyond my control. I feel *awake*, hyperalert, and I know that it's because there is enough adrenaline pumping through my body for me to run to the California coast and back.

I'm concerned about her, I tell myself. More than I would be if she was an anonymous stranger. I want Bridget to be okay. Mostly. It's horrible that this has happened to her.

Though, earlier today, as I was doing an annual checkup for a regular patient and half listening to her tell me about her new grandson, it occurred to me that maybe this experience will make Bridget and Owen see the grave error they've made and set them straight. And, okay, if she has to endure a painful bit of rehab, or if the head injury leads to the kind of facial scarring that leaves Duke's best plastic surgeon flummoxed, well...I guess it's my first revenge fantasy. I shouldn't be judged for it. It's sort of all I have.

Finally, the record appears. *Shit.* I lean toward the laptop's screen and press my fingers to my lips. It's bad. Much, much worse than I'd realized. I read down the list:

*Blunt abdominal trauma*
*Splenic rupture with left hemothorax*
*Pancreatic trauma*

A variety of orthopedic issues—her hip is fractured, her left knee is basically obliterated, there's a hairline crack across her forehead.

The positives: Her emergency abdominal surgery was a success. She's had a chest tube inserted to reinflate her left lung. But her spleen has ruptured, and there's the blood in her left lung cavity that Owen mentioned. She'll be in the surgical ICU for some time. I scan her physicians' names but don't recognize any of them. I make a mental note to look them up later.

I feel a headache coming on. I log out of the system, and then, because I've gone this far, I click over to Gmail and log in to Owen's account, knowing that the password, Sullivan459, will work. There's nothing, just a few forwarded jokes from his mother, a subscription renewal request from *Sports Illustrated*, automated bill pay messages from our bank, and, farther down, messages from me. I start clicking through them.

> Hey. Any ideas yet about what you want to do for your birthday? I have that thing in Philly but I'll be back early enough for dinner. Could make a reservation somewhere?

> Hey—B's vet appointment is next week. Could you do it? I have a practice meeting. If not, I'll reskedge.

As was often typical, he hadn't replied to either. I remember how I nagged him about the vet appointment and then finally just dealt with it myself because it was easier than trying to pin him down. I keep scrolling and find another—a back-and-forth between us from several weeks ago. He's forwarded an article he read in the local paper about a new restaurant downtown. Want to go this weekend? he'd asked.

And my reply: Actually, I don't know—it's been such a long week. I would rather stay in, I think. Rain check? I click over to the sent folder to look at his response:

> No problem. I should probably spend some extra time
> at the hospital anyway—if you don't mind, I'll plan on
> working late on Friday. XO.

I log out and slam the laptop shut. I hardly remember reading his email. I thought everything was fine. *Wasn't everything fine?*

I pick up my phone. I want to call him, but what would I say? *How is your girlfriend doing? If I'd gone to that restaurant with you, would everything be okay? Were you really at the hospital late that Friday night, or were you with her?* No amount of explaining will make any of this better.

I dial Lucy. "I need to talk to you," I say.

"Is everything all right?" I can hear the honking horns of the city in the background. I apologize for speeding out of Mom and Dad's house and tell her about the accident, the encounter with Owen at the hospital, how I came home to discover that he was packing up his things, the computer sleuthing, the way that I turned down Owen's dinner date requests, all of it.

She's uncharacteristically quiet, muttering "uh-huhs" and "yups" as I talk, and I start to wonder whether she's actually paying attention to a thing I'm saying.

"Lucy, are you listening to me?" I finally ask.

She sighs. "Of course I am." She sounds rushed and weary.

"You know what?" I bark, as tears come to my eyes. "Never mind. I'm sorry to have bothered you with the inconvenience of my crumbling marriage."

"Daphne, stop."

"What? Stop *what*, Lucy?" I wipe my cheeks. I know I'm being sulky and petulant but I think I'm entitled.

"Daphne, I'm sorry," she says. I hear her take a deep breath. "Listen, let me be honest with you."

"I wouldn't expect anything less," I say.

She ignores my sarcasm and continues. "I think you're spending entirely too much time dwelling on the reasons *why* Owen cheated when you should really be focused on how you're going to move on."

"Move on?" I wail. "Lucy, this is my marriage!"

"Your marriage may very well be over," she says. "I'm sorry to be so blunt, but no amount of *should haves* is going to change things. He made that call when he slept with his coworker. I assume he's with her now? At her bedside?"

"*Lucy.*" My head is pounding. I massage small circles into my forehead with my fingertips.

"Am I wrong?"

I sigh. "But…"

"Daphne, I'm sorry," she says. "I really don't mean to sound insensitive, but if what you're telling me is true—if it wasn't just one night of straying but that he actually had a relationship with her, well, that's much worse, and you have to move on. You realize that, right? There's a big difference between physical and emotional infidelity."

"Oh, is that so?" I say curtly. "That's great input, Lucy. Thank you for pointing that out."

"Well, it's true!" she says. "It's one thing to stray sexually but to have an *entire relationship* with another person, to become emotionally attached. *Much, much worse.* I mean, hello, did you not sit in the same family room with me after school and see this over and over again on *Oprah*?"

I can feel my heart rate speeding up, like a ghastly little motor revving up against my will. "Okay, Lucy."

"Daph—"

"No, never mind. Go back to whatever it is that I interrupted. I need to go."

"I really didn't mean to upset—"

I hang up on her—I don't need to hear any more. I turn in my chair and look out my office window, where I see a longtime patient walking down a pebbled path with Dr. Billings, my boss. I wonder where Owen is, whether he is, in fact, holding her hand while she lies in her hospital bed, or whether he's at his office, like I am, burying himself in his work. I turn and check the time. It won't be long before I'm the only one left in the office. My stomach rumbles and I reach for the Tupperware of chocolate chip cookies that Annie brought this morning. She keeps leaving little gifts in my office—a slice of carrot cake from my favorite bakery, candy. I can't bring myself to tell her that her gestures actually make me feel worse. They force me to acknowledge the fact that I am mourning my marriage as I knew it.

I know I should grab dinner, or at least get home to let the dog out, but home is the last place where I want to be. The last Saturday that we spent in the house together was three weeks ago. We stained the deck. Owen went to Lowe's to buy grass seed for the lawn. In the afternoon, we both took naps—he in our bed, the newspaper splayed open next to him, and me on the couch, HGTV in the background. I woke up later and made salmon. We ate it in front of the television, where we watched a basketball game. Or Owen did. I sat next to him, browsing a stack of back issues of home and garden magazines, ripping out pages to add to the "someday files" that I kept in the office, each carefully labeled for the area of the house: *yard, bedroom, bathrooms, paint colors…*

There were so many things that we talked about doing and we made a lot of good excuses—*after* residency, *after* the wedding, *after* the house is done, *after* kids. Would she have driven out to the Outer Banks to see the wild horses in Corolla, or watched the various Ken Burns documentaries—*Jazz, The Civil War, Baseball* (of course, baseball)—that I rolled my eyes at when we channel-surfed and Owen suggested them? Did he daydream about their life together, the fun they would have? We never took a blanket and a bottle of wine to the movie series on the lawn of the state art museum, we never dressed up to see the North Carolina state symphony, we never so much as drove the fifteen miles to Raleigh to go out to dinner. Hell, we rarely even had dinner together, and when we did, it was usually takeout, often in front of the television. *Had we stopped being interested in things together?* I wonder. *Is this why? Worst of all, had we stopped being interested in each other?*

The bulk of our shared life was so logistical:

*Have you fed the dog?*

*Did you pay that bill?*

*What time will you be home?*

*Did you call your mother back?*

*When is that thing again?*

We'd settled in without an ounce of fanfare. I thought we had a normal marriage, but maybe I'd set my expectations too low. Should I have seen this coming? I reach across my desk, where a pile of medical journals, newsletters, and conference invitations has been piling up for weeks. I pull the stack toward me, telling myself I'll stay just a bit longer. I'll get a few things done, I think, and then go.

# CHAPTER ELEVEN

A week after Bridget's accident, I am sitting at the kitchen table on a Friday night, sipping a glass of white wine and nibbling on a takeout panini, when I break down and text Owen, asking simply, "How are you?" I'd checked Bridget's progress earlier, in my office during my lunch break. She is doing better. Her breathing has improved and she's been extubated, so she can probably even talk a little bit now. I bet her voice is hoarse. I picture him helping her, holding a cup of water to her chapped lips.

He calls almost immediately after I've hit the send button. I sit there, stunned, watching the phone buzzing on my table like a belly-up beetle. I can't answer it. I know, now that he's reaching out, that there isn't anything he can say to take the pain away. Speaking with him, at least for the time being, might even make it worse. The phone stops after just a few rings—he hasn't bothered to let it go long enough to leave a voicemail.

When I go to sleep later that night, I dream about our baby. It isn't the first dream I've had about our child, but it's the first since everything happened. I want to blame the vividness of this particular episode on one of the over-the-counter sleeping pills that I finally broke down and bought, but I know that's not it.

When I wake up on Saturday morning—I never knew, by the way, that a person can wake up sobbing—I stay under the covers for a long time, my arms crossed over my waist, thinking about the squishy, delicious, sweater-suited infant that I'd dreamed was crawling across our kitchen floor. I was unable to see its face, or tell whether it was a boy or a girl, as it was crawling away from me (a detail that must be significant) toward one of those old-fashioned wooden pull-trains on wheels. It was a dream baby like in a diaper commercial: big, round bottom, chirpy gurgly mumbles, biscuit-dough thighs.

I turn over in bed, thinking about the child that may now never be. Our mothers had rhapsodized about their future grandchildren for years. I remember the two of them joking together at the brunch on the morning after our wedding, about how they'd be battling it out for babysitting shifts. It made them both crazy that we'd decided to wait to try until Owen's training was behind us and then, once that happened, that we wanted to pay down the med school loans just a bit more before we started. That was more him than me—I can admit that now. I would have started three years ago when he finished training and got his job, but he was worried about money, which is a trait of his that I both valued (better to have a thrifty husband than the type who spends your life savings on a sports car) and blamed on his father, who can't go five minutes without complaining about someone ripping him off. I told myself that kids were a foregone conclusion—it would happen, that was the important thing.

A year after Owen started working, we got Blue. I called Mom afterward, saying "Mom, guess what?" and she squealed, "*You're pregnant!*" the words finally unleashing themselves. They'd been on the tip of her tongue for years.

"A *dog?*" she gasped, a sort of whinny escaping from her mouth. "A *dog?*" She kept repeating it, as if she needed to talk herself down from the disappointment. Now she sends Blue birthday gifts and fills her stocking at Christmas—bones, rawhide chews, canisters of tennis balls, a canine backpack for hiking.

I somehow let myself believe that the dog and, later, the house meant that we were on track, that each benchmark for our family would lead to the next logical step. I had no reason to believe otherwise. Until the more recent fights, whenever I talked about a baby, daydreaming about what would it feel like to be big and pregnant, whether it would be a boy or a girl, Owen indulged me, even chiming in with his own fantasies about coaching Little League and teaching our child to ride a bike. Our timetables might have been off, but I never doubted that he wanted a child. I remember a rare lazy Sunday morning a couple of years ago, when we were sipping coffee and passing the real estate section of the paper back and forth. He put down his mug and said, out of nowhere, "You know what will be fun? When our kids are old enough for us to send them to camp." He wanted it. I know he did.

Over the past year, and especially since we moved, I grew more impatient. It became the thing I talked about. I brought it up over dinner, during the morning rush before work, on the weekends, in emails. *I'm almost thirty-seven, Owen. We can't wait much longer, Owen. If you're so worried about money, just imagine what IVF will cost us.* I can hardly bring myself to think about the fact that this coincided with the beginning of his relationship with Bridget. While I was cruising pregnancy websites and walking around in an anxious haze each month, talking, *talking*, he was . . . *I can't even think about it.* The images of her that have played in my head, in something lacy, beribboned, seducing my husband, the two of them discovering each other—it makes me sick. And it shames me. Sex for us had become so rudimentary; I knew the *series of things that we did* so well that I could do it in my sleep and, sometimes, pretty much did. Had I become a nagging wife (is that something I even believe in?) when he had decided that what he really wanted was a girlfriend?

After I get out of bed, I have a cup of coffee and go outside to throw a tennis ball to Blue in the backyard. I'm halfway out the door when the house phone rings. I consider letting it go to voicemail—Owen and I used to joke that the only reason we have a landline is so that telemarketers and our mothers can reach us— but then I picture Mom at home, calling from the kitchen phone, her anxiety growing with each unanswered ring, and I race across the kitchen to pick up the cordless phone off the counter.

"Hello?" I answer.

"Daphne!" A lump instantly forms in my throat. It's Joanne, Owen's mother. I've been wondering when I'd finally hear from her. "Daphne, how are you?"

"O-oh!" I stammer, startled by the direct route she's chosen to take the conversation. I'm frankly hurt that it's taken her this long to call—and to tell me that she's on my side, if I'm being honest about it. I'm tempted to say as much. "Well, I've been better," I say.

"Oh, no, Daphne, what's wrong?" she asks, and then it hits me: *She doesn't know.* I can't believe he hasn't told her. I wonder if I should.

"Honey, are you there? What's wrong? You're worrying me."

Owen and his mother's close relationship was something that the three of us sometimes joked about, with Joanne's standard line being that until I came along, Owen would call her to let her know when he sneezed. I can't believe she doesn't know, and it occurs to me, given their relationship, that maybe the fact that he hasn't told her means he actually hasn't worked out what he wants to do. If he hasn't told his mother, maybe his intentions regarding Bridget aren't what I thought. Is it possible that I misread what I saw that day in the ICU?

I clear my throat. "Oh, Joanne, it's nothing—just a really long week at work. Did you call for anything in particular?"

"Oh, no, dear. Just thought I might catch you two before you run off to whatever it is you have planned this weekend. Is Owen there or is he working?"

*Should I?* A part of me wants to tell her. I can see her calling Owen, screaming at him, horrified by what he's done to me, but then I think of how devastated she'll be and I don't want to be the one responsible for revealing the news. She's not the person I want to suffer for this.

"He's at work, Joanne."

"Oh, okay. I'll try him there. You have a good Saturday, dear."

We hang up and I take the dog outside. I toss the ball across the yard and feel, with each passing minute, that I need to find something to do that doesn't involve being at the house, which has become such a minefield for me, with every corner revealing another painful memory.

After I shower and dress, I drive downtown, taking the long way through Duke's campus, and feel the gloom lift, just a bit, as I notice what a beautiful spring morning it is. The azaleas are already beginning to bloom, and the sky, as they like to say a few miles down the road in Chapel Hill, is a perfect, cloudless Carolina blue. I decide to drive to Stone Brothers, my favorite garden shop, to seek out inspiration for the yard, but first I pass over the railroad tracks toward the old tobacco and textile warehouses that now house restaurants, bars, and boutiques, and pull in at my favorite breakfast spot, Parker and Otis. I choose a table that's partially hidden behind a counter piled high with cookbooks and cast-iron bakeware, on the off chance that Owen might stop in for breakfast. The hospital isn't very far and Durham isn't a very big place—we're destined to run into each other eventually.

Minutes later, I am savoring the cheddar biscuit that came with my bacon and eggs when I feel a tap on my shoulder.

"Jack!" I say, greeting Annie's husband as I wipe the crumbs from my lips and stand to hug him.

He laughs. "Sorry to interrupt." He points at my plate.

I narrow my eyes at him. "Very funny. Is Annie with you?"

"Nope," he says. "Just meeting a friend for breakfast." Jack grew up in Durham, and like most of the people I've met who were raised here, he appears to know everyone in town. Rarely have I been out with him when he hasn't run into his old babysitter, or his first boss, or the neighborhood kid whose house he toilet-papered.

"How about you?" he says. He takes a deep sip from his coffee mug. "Just enjoying a leisurely Saturday morning breakfast?"

"Yup." I shrug. "You know. I'm surprised that you found me. I was trying to hide out."

"Sorry," he says with a smile. "I guess I sensed your presence."

"Listen, Daphne—" Jack starts, shuffling his feet.

I put my hand on his arm and shake my head. "It's okay, Jack. You don't have to say anything."

He clears his throat. "Well, I'm really sorry." He shakes his head again.

"I know."

He squeezes my arm. "I don't want to disturb your quality time with your biscuit," he jokes, winking. "But would you like to join me and my friend?"

"Oh, that's okay," I say. I gesture toward the local indie news-paper that I grabbed on the way in. "I'm good here. Reading."

"Come on," he says. "It's just my friend Andrew. He just moved back to Durham six months ago. We played soccer together in high school."

"Of course you did."

"What is that supposed to mean?" He laughs, knowing the answer.

Before I can respond, the person who is presumably Andrew appears from around a rack of hand-stamped tea towels.

"Hey!" he says, pointing at me. "Bean Traders!"

"Yes!" I say.

"You guys know each other?" Jack says.

"On the same coffee schedule," I explain.

I often stop at a local coffee shop before work, and at least once a week, I see the man whom I now know as Andrew in line. He is impossible to miss—tall, with skin the color of caramel (*Spanish?* I've wondered. *South American?*), but his most distinguished characteristic is that he is always impeccably dressed, especially for someone in a strip mall coffee shop in Durham, North Carolina, at seven on a weekday morning. It's not the kind of thing that I normally go for (not that I've ever been the kind of woman who "goes for" a specific physical something in the opposite sex), but compared to the T-shirts and regular-guy oxfords and khakis I'm used to, it's hard not to notice someone like him.

We've been at Bean Traders at the same time on enough occasions to have started smiling politely at each other, and we've had a handful of short, cordial, early morning exchanges as we've doctored up our drinks at the crowded table that holds the sugars and half-and-half. Nothing particularly memorable, just your typical earth-shattering small talk about the weather, the early hour, and our shared gratitude for caffeine.

"I'm Andrew Scott," he says, putting out his hand.

I can't help but laugh a little. One of my dad's idiosyncratic rules, this one always delivered with a wink, is to *never trust a man with two first names.*

"I'm Daphne Mitchell."

"Daphne is Annie's best friend," Jack says.

"Ohhhh," Andrew says, nodding.

"Now you *have* to join us," Jack implores, grabbing my plate. "No excuses."

"So you just moved back here?" I ask as I settle into a seat.

"Sort of," Andrew says, taking a careful sip of his coffee. "I live in San Francisco, but my father's having some health problems—he's had a series of strokes—so I'm helping my mother out for a while."

"Oh, I'm so sorry," I say.

"Thanks," he says, unfolding his napkin. "He's actually doing great, so I'm not sure I'll be here too much longer. It's been kind of nice, though, being back. It had been a few years since I'd spent any significant time here."

"Durham's changed a lot for you, I imagine."

He laughs. "I'll say. When I was growing up, nobody went downtown. Now, I swear, the restaurants could give the ones in the Bay Area a run for their money."

"It does seem like every local restaurant gets written up in national media within months of opening," Jack says. "Annie always says that the *New York Times* must be getting kickbacks from the Durham mayor's office."

"It's changed so much since *I* moved here, I can only imagine what it's like for the two of you," I say.

Andrew turns to me. "What brought you to Durham?"

"Residency," I say, purposely keeping it short and sweet. "I'm an internist. How about you?"

"I work in the hotel industry."

"He's being modest," Jack interrupts. "Andrew is a partner in a boutique hotel group. You've probably read about them—they rehab old buildings and turn them into luxury hotels that are way too hip for the likes of me. I'd be turned away at the door."

"Not true." Andrew smiles.

"Totally true!" Jack says. "What's the one that just opened?"

"It's in Chicago, in an old bank."

"You walk through the vault to get to the bar," Jack says.

"That sounds fun," I say.

"Well, don't get the impression that they're, like, theme hotels," Andrew says. "It's a bit more sophisticated than that."

"So you're not putting chocolate coins on the guests' pillows in the former bank?" I say.

"Not quite," he says. "Though that's not a bad idea." He smiles at me and I notice the way that the outer corners of his eyes crinkle.

"You should look into some of the old warehouses in Durham," I say.

"That's what I keep telling him!" Jack says.

"I don't know that there are many left up for grabs," Andrew says to me. I'm starting to feel like he's *only* speaking to me—he hasn't looked in Jack's direction since we sat down. I glimpse at Jack, who raises an eyebrow at me. I give him what I hope is a subtle smirk. "So where do you live in Durham?" Andrew asks.

My heart leaps. *How do I answer this?* "I live a bit south of here, toward Chapel Hill, in an old farmhouse." I immediately kick myself—*why invite questions about the house?*

"A big old farmhouse just for you? That seems like a lot."

"You should see Daphne's house," Jack interjects, saving me. "She's amazing. If the doctor thing doesn't work out, she could easily flip houses for a living. She'd be a star on HGTV. Hell, you could hire her to work on your hotels."

Andrew nods and takes a sip of his coffee. "I used to go running out that way a lot. It's so pretty." My mind jumps to Owen, who loved riding his bike through the country roads surrounding our house.

"It's very peaceful," I say, laughing to myself over my choice of words. *That's exactly what it's been lately, as peaceful as an* E. coli *outbreak on a cruise ship.* "So are you living with your family?"

He shakes his head, making an *eek* sort of face, stretching one corner of his bottom lip toward his chin. "No. Absolutely not. I'm over forty. I couldn't possibly—not even under the circumstances. As much for my mother's sake as for my own!" he jokes. I'm impressed by how light he seems, how unaffected despite the awful circumstances that have brought him home. *Over forty.* I wonder why he's single. I wonder if he's gay. Not that I'm remotely ready to entertain the idea of another man. I'm not even...*separated.* I wince to myself, turning the word over in my head.

I listen as Andrew and Jack recount a story from high school about a soccer tournament trip to Nashville. What if he wanted to ask me out? What if *I* wanted to ask *him* out? I could, after all. *But it's not me*, I decide, watching Andrew and Jack banter back and forth about which one of them thought it was a good idea to try to buy beer at the convenience store across from the hotel during the soccer tournament. *I'm not one of those people who jumps headfirst into the next thing. I'm not the type of person who, say, if my dog died, would go right out and replace it with a new one, transferring over the water dish and the leash to the new model.* I drag my last bite of biscuit through a puddle of rich, golden egg yolk on my plate and look up to see Andrew watching me, amused. I was never a delicate eater, not even on my first dates with Owen, who told me soon after we got together that he loved to watch me eat, for the hilarity of it. I smile back at Andrew and then Jack, who's watched this whole exchange.

"Excuse me," I say, putting my napkin to my mouth. "I'm hopeless when it comes to these biscuits."

Andrew laughs. "It's adorable."

*Adorable?* Is he *flirting* with me? He's most definitely flirting with me. Grown men don't just throw out the word "adorable."

I think of Lucy and her admonition on the phone the other night that I "for the love of God, treat myself to some fun." So okay then, handsome Andrew, friend of Jack's. Maybe a drink would be fun. I can feel that my cheeks are flushed.

"Well." I crumple my napkin between my hands under the table. "Now that I've cleaned my plate, I should probably get going and let you two catch up." They both stand after I do, good Southerners that they are. "Thanks for letting me crash your meal," I say.

Jack and I do that sideways hug thing that men do with their female friends, and Andrew shakes my hand. Firm handshake, I notice. Another one of Dad's rules.


Before I reach my car, I have my phone out, ready to call Annie, who will love to hear about my breakfast and frankly deserves a light-hearted story from me after what I've put her through over the past few weeks. I slip into the driver's seat and check my voicemail first—there's a message from a phone number I don't recognize.

At first, it doesn't register. The voice is small, like a child's. "I know that this is awkward." I hear a faint lazy drawl. "But I'd really like to chat with you. I'd love for you to call me back. I understand if you don't. But I'd really love to. Thanks *so* much."

That last part—the girly enthusiasm, the *so much*, is what burns most, like too much salt on your tongue. What on earth could she want? Why on earth would she want to talk to me?

I call her back, turning the dial for the air conditioner all the way up as the phone rings. It's not even sixty-five degrees outside, according to the display on my dashboard, but I'm sweating.

"Hello?" Her voice is light, sweet.

"This is Daphne Mitchell calling you back."

"Thank you so much for returning my call," she says. She speaks slowly, taking little baby breaths. I know she's still in the hospital. *Why would she call me?* "I'm sorry, Daphne. Would you mind holding one minute?"

"Would I mind?" I laugh, I can't help it. "No, Bridget, I don't mind one bit."

Her voice becomes muffled. She's put her hand over the phone. *It's okay. I'll be fine. Maybe ten minutes or so. Okay, hon. Thanks, hon.*

Do you call your mother *hon*? A friend? A nurse? A sister? Who could be *hon* besides...? My pulse starts to race.

"I'm sorry about that," she says.

"Was that Owen?"

There's a pause, revealing everything.

"Yes."

"Bridget, what is it, exactly, that you want from me?" I adjust the vents so that the air blows on my neck and chest.

"I wanted to call and speak to you directly. To apologize."

*Apologize? I swear, has there ever in the history of the world been a more conscientious piece of trash?* "You want to *what*?" I gasp.

"As you know, I've been in an accident," she says, speaking over me like she's trying to calm me down.

I don't say anything. What does she expect? *Condolences?* Not from me. I know that she's been though a lot, but she'll be fine enough to ride off into the sunset with my husband, to steal *my* life. I wipe the sweat that I can feel beading along my hairline.

"I've had a lot of time to think," she continues. "We both have, and I wanted to let you know that I feel horrible about the way that things—"

Before she has a chance to continue, I hang up and throw the phone into the passenger seat.


I shake the whole way home. Here I was, having my first "up" morning since this happened, my first kind-of-good day—and then this, like a glass of something cold and wet tossed one-handed, deliberate and reckless, to wake me up and startle me back into reality.

When I get home, I slam the front door behind me so hard that Blue jumps, and fling my bag to the floor.

I have my phone in my hand and pull up *my husband's* number. "Owen," I say after he picks up. I spit his name out, practically kick it at him. "I need to explain something to you."

He tries to tell me it's a bad time. I barrel past. I don't care. I am screaming and I never scream, and it feels good, so right that I wonder why I haven't done it every day of my life so far.

"I don't know what the fuck she was thinking, calling me. Doesn't she have enough to worry about right now? What was it, exactly, that she thought she would gain from that? Did you tell her to do it? Did you think it would *help* somehow? What the hell is wrong with you, Owen?"

"Daphne, I didn't—"

I grit my teeth. "You can go to hell, Owen," I say, my throat burning. "And you can tell that *whore* to never call me again. And I don't want to hear from you, either, ever again, not after what you've done." Tears roll down my face, hot, expunging. It feels exactly right. I'm not sure that I mean it—*I don't want to hear from you*—but it feels good so I keep going.

"You do *not* get to call me anymore. Do you understand? You lost the right to be in my life the second you started to deceive me. You made your choice and that choice was her, so you don't get a single piece of me. Not anymore. We are finished. Do you understand?

"Our marriage is over!" I wail.

"We're done. It's finished."

"Daphne, please listen to me," he says. "I had no idea she was going to call. She's in a very fragile emotional state. I know she just really needs you to understand. I really need you to understand—"

"You *what?*" I scream. "You must be kidding me. Listen—" I take a deep breath. "Don't miss a single syllable of this, Owen. This is *over*. We are *over*. *You* chose this, and you are getting exactly what *you* wanted. So you need to get your things out of this house and we need to call a lawyer and we need to end this, like *you* wanted. I am setting a firm line in the sand, Owen. You are no longer a part of my life. Do you understand?"

I hang up, not needing to hear his answer, the reasoning, the excuses. I hang up before I change my own mind. I throw the phone across the room, hearing it skid across the hardwood floor, and then I fall to the ground, put my head in my hands, and sob. I know that this is it, finally. This is rock bottom, the end, and not a thing about it feels good.

# CHAPTER TWELVE

When I see Mary Elizabeth's name on the day's schedule on Monday morning, I'm puzzled. She isn't due in to see me for another week. I read Carol's printout three times, making sure that I'm seeing her name correctly, not so much because it's a massive surprise to have an unexpected patient visit but because despite two cups of coffee this morning, I feel foggy and out of it. My mind keeps hitching back to the phone call with Owen on Saturday, replaying the words I said to him.

"Which room?" I say to Carol as I approach the long hallway where the exam rooms are located.

"Number three," she says.

"Okay."

"Hey," she says, stopping me as I'm heading past her toward the room. "Everything okay with you?"

"I'm fine," I say, forcing what I'm sure is an unconvincing grin.

She's nods, one swift dip of her chin. I know she's noticed my bare ring finger—she's the type to notice—but she hasn't asked anything outright and I haven't offered.

I've waffled on whether to tell her. While we have a great relationship, there isn't much that Carol loves more than good office gossip, and once she's heard my news, the rest of the practice will, too. I'd like to hold off on that until I know where my marriage has headed.

I continue toward the exam room, telling myself to focus. *Mary Elizabeth*. Maybe something has finally clicked and she's here to declare that she's ready to get her life in order. After our last appointment, when she confessed her margarita binge and the near seizure, I talked to Denise, her therapist, in the office, and we agreed that it's time to talk to her about rehab again. I have my fingers crossed that we'll be able to chat about it today.

My hopes are dashed the minute I walk into the exam room. She is lying on the exam table, facing the wall, and as I shut the door behind me, I wonder if she's even awake. "Mary Elizabeth?"

She flinches like I've startled her.

I walk across the room, ostensibly to place my laptop on my desk but really to give her a moment to collect herself. It's Monday morning—she should be dressed in office clothes, here on a break from her workday. Instead, she's wearing a pair of jeans that look like they haven't been washed in months and a stretchy black top that exposes most of her back, the sharp bumps of her spine running down the middle like a zipper.

When she finally sits up and brushes the hair from her face, I notice the black smudges under her eyes, what is clearly yesterday's makeup. She coughs and smiles.

"What up, Doc?" She laughs, a girlish giggle, and that's when I'm sure she's drunk. My heart sinks. I've seen plenty of addicts over the course of my five years at the practice, but I've never had one come to see me while blatantly wasted. I consider calling Carol into the room right away. *Why didn't she say anything?* Surely she noticed this when she brought her back.

"I'd like to do a blood panel today," I say, deciding in the moment that the best approach is to be businesslike and firm. "But I don't know that you're in any shape for that."

She rubs her hands over her eyes. "It's no problem," she says, a dopey smile on her face. Her eyes are bloodshot and swollen. I start to wonder whether only alcohol is to blame.

"What's going on, Mary Elizabeth?" I ask.

"What's going on, Mary Elizabeth?" she mimics through clenched teeth. *What's your problem, Mary Elizabeth?*

She's always animated, a hyperkinetic mess, but also charming and smart and agreeable. It suddenly strikes me that this specific combination might also be at the root of what gets her into so much trouble.

"You're drunk," I say.

She furrows her brow at me. "Are you kidding?"

I shake my head.

"It's like eleven o'clock on a Monday," she says. "No, I'm not drunk."

I put my stethoscope in my ears, though it isn't her heart rate I'm interested in, it's her breath. I place the silver disk on her chest, through her shirt, and lean in, pretending to take a closer listen. Her heart is beating a little fast. Finally, she exhales, and it's putrid, a humid stink.

"Did you come from work today?" I ask.

"Have the day off," she says, struggling to enunciate.

"Did you drive yourself here?"

"Because?" she says, drawing out the *zzzzzz.*

"Have you eaten anything?"

She rolls her eyes.

"Do we need to go over this again?" I say, perhaps a bit too sharply. I told myself on my way into the office this morning that I would leave my personal concerns at home—I cannot bring it into the office, not only because it's what my patients deserve but because I need a mental break from it, too. I take a breath and start again. "You know that being Type 1 means that you have specific guidelines you need to follow. You need to eat at regular intervals every day, no exception." I've said this to her so many times now that I ought to just record it and play it for her when she comes into the office. *This is how parents must feel when their kids don't listen to them*, I think. Everything I say to her seems to just bounce off and disappear into the ether.

She smirks. "I was diagnosed when I was in preschool," she slurs, the preschool coming out like *priss-coo*. "I'm a grown woman, I can feed myself."

"You sure about that?" I say, taking a different tack. Maybe if I get a rise out of her, she'll start talking.

"I'm under a lot of stress, Dr. Mitchell."

*Try having your marriage implode*, I think.

"I actually wondered if you might be able to give me an anti-anxiety prescription, like a Xanax or something."

"You're kidding." I want to shake her for even considering that there's a chance I'd prescribe something.

"I'm working on this really tough case. I just need enough of a prescription to get me through the next month or so."

It's obvious that she's rehearsed it, and I'm alarmed. If she's added pills to the mix, I can only imagine what else she's doing. I stand in front of her, our faces barely a foot apart. "Mary Elizabeth, listen," I say. "I think it's time you start thinking about a program."

Her mouth drops and then her eyes narrow. In a split second I've gone from friend (or potential drug supplier) to foe.

"Mary Elizabeth, we've been over this so many times. You are killing yourself. You need more help than what we can offer you here."

She doesn't say anything. She just wobbles on the table, staring vacantly, and then the next thing I know, her head starts to dip. She braces herself on one arm and I sprint across the room to press the call button and bring Carol into the room.

Pro that she is, Carol doesn't react at all when she walks in seconds later and sees Mary Elizabeth.

"Could you get a breathalyzer kit please?" I ask.

"*What?*" Mary Elizabeth screams. "A *breathalyzer?*"

"It's for your own good," I say to her. *And for the practice's, too. God forbid your mother brings a lawsuit.*

"But I'm not drunk!" she screeches. She pushes herself down off of the table and stumbles. I leap forward to catch her before she falls.

She pushes me away and starts to collect her things. I can't let her leave, not like this. I reach out and grab her arm. I've never touched a patient like this before but I'm desperate. I just can't let her leave and get herself killed.

"Jesus, get off me!" she screams. "I'm fine!"

I take my hands away. "Mary Elizabeth, please," I plead. "Let me at least get someone to give you a ride somewhere. We can call a taxi." Carol comes back into the room and raises her eyebrows at me. I could kill her for not warning me about this.

Mary Elizabeth turns and scowls. "I have a friend with me, in the waiting room. I'll be fine." She bumps past Carol and starts down the hall. I follow after her.

"Listen," I say, my voice low as I walk alongside her. "This could be a turning point for you. Let's just go back to the exam room, do the test, and we can talk. We can change everything for you right now."

She shakes her head, stumbling faster, trying to lose me.

"If you'll just work with me," I beg. I've never pleaded with a patient before.

She swerves into the waiting room and while I'm relieved to see that there is, in fact, someone waiting for her, it alarms me that he doesn't seem the least bit fazed by the way she's acting. He looks unremarkable, like any standard young former frat guy—polo shirt, Carolina baseball cap. He stands, tossing aside the magazine he was reading.

"Let's go," Mary Elizabeth says.

There isn't much I can do. She's my patient and I can't reveal information about her to some stranger in a waiting room. "Will you get her home okay?" I say.

He smiles. "Oh, yeah, sure," he says, his hand waving back at me as he's halfway out the door.


I rush back into the office, ignoring the woman in the waiting room who's been pretending this whole time that she was engrossed in the *Southern Living* she was holding in front of her face.

"What the hell was that?" I say to Carol when I find her putting the breathalyzer kit back in the storage area near the nurses' station.

She flinches. I've never lost my temper at work before.

"Why didn't you tell me what to expect before I went into the exam room?"

"Dr. Mitchell," she says, looking at me in the gently scolding way that my grandmother once did when she caught me with my finger in the cake she'd just frosted. "Of course I would have alerted you. Diana, that new young nurse, took her back because I was finishing up the blood panel for Mr. Dawson."

I feel my cheeks instantly flush. *Of course.* I knew she was busy with Mr. Dawson, the patient before Mary Elizabeth, because I asked her to do the panel. What the hell is wrong with me? "Carol, I'm so sorry."

"It's okay," she says, squeezing my arm. She looks into my eyes, letting her arm stay put for an extra few seconds. "You've done everything you could do for that girl," she says.

I nod.

"It's sad to see that happen to a girl like her. So much potential."

"Awful," I say. "She's determined to self-destruct."

"She's been damn lucky so far."

"Sure has," I say, pulling out the printout with the schedule. "We have until one, yes? I'm going to grab a quick bite to eat."

"Okay," she says. "Go take a break."

"Again, Carol, I'm sorry. I'll see you in a bit."


I walk down the hall to Annie's office. "You will not believe what just happened," I say, standing in the threshold of her open door.

"What?" she says, through a mouthful of the noodles that she's eating out of the container in her other hand.

I close the door behind me and sit down and take a deep breath, in through my nose and out through my mouth, and then another.

"Did Orlando teach you that?" Annie jokes, watching me.

I roll my eyes at her. Orlando is the patchouli-drenched stress management expert who works in our office. "Actually, I have Mary Elizabeth to thank."

"What?"

"She just walked out on our appointment. She was drunk."

"Are you sure?" She puts down her food.

"You can't smell the liquor from here? Honestly, I'm surprised you didn't hear anything. I asked to do a breathalyzer and she flipped out."

"Wow. Do you think she'll be okay?"

"Nope." I look up at the ceiling and groan.

"I'm sorry," Annie says.

I rub my hands over my face. "You know what I need right now? Some good, basic, boring cases. Spring allergies, that kind of BS."

"I did three of those this morning," Annie says. "And I suspect my next patient will be the same. If it makes you feel any better, I had to leave early yesterday because Samantha's school called to tell me that she has head lice."

I make a face. "And you're sure you don't have it?"

"I'm sure," she says. "Though every time I think about it, I start itching." She picks up a pencil off of her desk that obviously found its way to her through her daughters—instead of the standard orangey yellow, it's pink and ladybug patterned. She uses the eraser end to scratch the back of her head. I make a face at her.

"I'm really fine," she says.

I nod. "I hope so."

"Difficult patients aside, how are you holding up?"

I shrug one shoulder. "Haven't talked to him. I'm not really sure what the next move is. I can't bring myself to think about anything logistical—his stuff, the house." I take a deep breath. "I'm running a lot. Six miles last night. And the yard's never looked better."

"I'm so sorry."

"I can't stand being in that house." I lean forward and pluck a piece of butterscotch hard candy out of the jar she keeps on her desk. "The girl…Bridget…she's doing better," I say. "I've checked the records a few more times. She's stable. Will be hospitalized for a while still."

Annie nods. "Feels weird, I bet."

"What?"

She points over the desk at my left hand, where I'm caressing the inside of my ring finger with my thumb. "Oh," I say, shaking my head when I realize what she's talking about. "Yes, I keep touching the place where it was. Some sort of phantom limb phenomenon."

"I hate this for you."

I shrug. "Yeah, well."

"You know what I'm thinking?" she says. "We need to do something fun, something to look forward to. Do you want to go away for the weekend? I can get Jack to watch the kids."

"Nah." I think of Lucy and the awful sports bar in Virginia. A change of scenery won't do any good.

"How about a party?" she asks, raising her eyebrows.

"Really?" I say, chuckling. "I know you're only trying to help but no thank you." I take another butterscotch from the jar and start unwrapping it. "To be honest, I prefer binge drinking by myself and singing along to Linda Ronstadt."

"That's really pathetic," she says, cracking a smile. "I hope you're kidding."

I shrug. "The dog doesn't mind."

"Well, I wasn't thinking so much about a 'get-over-Owen' party, I was thinking about a birthday party."

"I don't know, Annie." My birthday's in just a few weeks.

"Well, we don't need to have a party *for you*, but we have been wanting to do a cookout now that the weather's getting nicer, something low key. We could invite Andrew, Jack's cute friend."

"You could," I say, smirking. I stand and go around to her side of her desk and lean down to give her a quick hug. "I love you," I say. "Thank you."

"I love you, too."


I go back to my office and plunk down at my desk and massage my temples with my fingers. I decide to check my email quickly before I walk down the hall to see Denise, Mary Elizabeth's therapist, and fill her in on what happened this morning. I feel a sharp, stabbing pain in my chest as soon as I click on my inbox and scan the new messages. There's Owen's name. The subject: *Please read.*

# CHAPTER THIRTEEN

I try to concentrate on the words on the screen but they jump around like they're alive. I read it five, ten times, but I can't seem to ground myself in what it says. I feel like I've been handed a loaded gun. I take a deep breath and start again.

I hope that you'll read this without deleting it. I know that you don't want to speak to me, and I fear that if I call, you won't talk to me, or if I stop by, you'll slam the door in my face. So, a letter. I think that the last one I wrote to you was that summer after camp, which is far too long. It's just another example of the many things I should have been doing over the past ten years to show you how much I love you.

You probably, rightfully, despise me. I would. And on many levels, I do—hate myself, that is. For what I did to us.

Here's the thing, Daphne. I did develop feelings for Bridget. We did develop a relationship. But when I told you that I wanted to take a break to give myself some time to think, I was being honest. I didn't intend to continue on with her. I wasn't in love with her. I've never been in love with her. Like I told you that day at the house, I have been sincerely confused about what I want and whether we want the same things, but that has never had anything to do with her. It's about me.

Starting a relationship with another woman was an inexcusable way for me to deal with what I was feeling, but what's more important for you to know is why I think that it happened. I wasn't being honest with myself about what I needed from our relationship. We had fallen into a rut, and the daily grind of the house and our lives and even everything related to talking about a baby felt arduous, like another job. We weren't exactly a couple any more, were we? We were more like roommates. Siblings. Coexisting in a shared space but not really sharing anything beyond the stuff in the house and the bills. I guess that Bridget provided that "something new" that I must've craved on some deep-down level. I know that isn't something you need to hear. I guess I'm trying to explain what was going on inside my head when I did what I did. It's not original—I understand that—and it's not an excuse. But it's why.

Maybe you don't need explanations. Or want them.

Everything that has taken place over the past few weeks—confessing to you, Bridget's accident—has forced me to think hard, in the mature way that I should have been doing all along, about what the future holds. I suppose that, in some ways, you and I were always doing so much of that—planning for the life that we would have together. But what were we doing in the meantime?

I guess that what I'm trying to get at is that I am drowning in regret over the decision I made. I know how pathetic that must sound to you but I can't shake the fact that I can't stop thinking about you. I constantly reminisce about the past: Sunday mornings spent running together on Duke Trail, the Saturday afternoons at the Federal, and how we would talk about nothing and everything (the brilliance of their garlic fries, my bad impressions of the car dealership commercials that came on the TV in the corner). That was the most fun I could have ever imagined. It was everything, you were everything. The emotions I felt were so strong they were practically unfathomable. For the first time in my life, I felt complete.

Remember the day that we drove to Asheville to get Blue, and how during the whole drive home, she insisted on lying cradled in your lap like a newborn? Or that horrible dinner with my dad at that awful Italian restaurant in Springfield, where he threw his plate on the floor and my mother cried and then we went home and got smashed in my old treehouse in the backyard? Camp—canoeing together, singing those silly songs while we sat in inner tubes on the lake, that first dance, our first kiss. All of it, all of us. It's all I think about, Daph.

Everything that's happened is my fault. I ruined it all. I miss you in a way that hurts so deeply and completely and I don't know what to do to make it better but I want to. You are, after all, everything. I miss my best friend. And I know that this comes too late, but I'll never tire of saying it: I'm so, so sorry.

I don't know what to think. *He can't stop thinking about me? He constantly reminisces about the past? He wants to make it better?* Impossibly, my heart seems to race faster every time I read it. I don't know if I believe him—more than that, I don't know if I should.

The more I consider the words he's chosen, the more bewildered I am about the reasons he's outlined for why he cheated. So he was essentially bored. A "rut" is the thing that made him decide to pull my heart from my chest and wring it like a dishrag. That day at the house right after he confessed to me—a day that I know will leave a permanent scar—he said that we had changed. Things felt different to him. I didn't totally believe him about this being the sole reason why he did what he did. I thought there had to be something more to it. And after seeing him at the ICU that day, I knew that I was right. It was beyond whatever was happening with us. He wasn't just bored.

Dammit, though, it's not that I don't agree with him, I think, chewing on my thumbnail as I go over and over the lines. We *were* absolutely in a rut. We were definitely sometimes like roommates. But the solution, to me, *never* would have been to look elsewhere. I thought this dip was normal. Doesn't everyone go through it? Wouldn't any married person who took the time out of their day to scrutinize their relationship see the same dents and dings? Isn't that why most people *don't* scrutinize? Did he expect too much? And if so, can I ever be enough? I didn't give the state of our marriage too much thought because it honestly didn't worry me. Maybe that's the biggest problem of all.

*And then*, I think, my hands shaking as I bring them to my face to wipe my eyes, *what does it say about him that he decides to send this when the woman whom he cheated with is lying in a hospital bed? How can he be so callous?* The Owen I married doesn't hurt people like this. The only thing I can think is that he must feel such a sense of urgency to confess these things to me that he can't help himself. It's not like him to do the things he's done, I rationalize, but it *is* like him to try to right his wrongs.

I remember that drive back from Asheville with our new puppy curled in my lap, too. I remember sharing the six-pack in the tree house tucked into the oaks in his backyard. I remember the feel of the cool water as I dragged my fingers through the water in the lake at camp, laughing together at the bar as the sun set, all of it. And what makes me angriest of all, the thing that is most infuriating, is that they're still good memories. I can close my eyes and take myself back and still feel the way that we loved each other. Despite all of the ways he's hurt me, there is a pearl of truth lodged deep in my chest that I can't ignore. I still love him. I still want him. Despite everything, I don't know if I can let him go.

When I get home at the end of the day, I go for a run to try to clear my head. It's an ugly thirty minutes, huffing and wheezing as I try to convince myself that this is, in fact, a better option than taking a plastic cup of wine into the backyard to allegedly pull weeds but mostly to think about the email and stare into space.

By the time I turn the corner back toward the house and slow to a walk, I don't have any new insights. I'm tired and frustrated and mentally spent. I tear my earbuds out of my ears, collect the mail from the mailbox, and sift through it on the long walk up the gravel driveway—electric bill in his name, calendar for the Durham Performing Arts Center in mine, the latest issue of *Glow*, a subscription to which was this year's unsubtle Christmas gift from Lucy. *Could things be normal again?* I think. *Could we put it back together? Could I come home from a run, get the mail, go inside, and kiss Owen hello? Could this be our home still?*

I sit on the porch and stretch my legs and watch Blue sniff around the flower beds. It feels like it's about to rain. Normally, I find the sound of the wind through the trees on our property soothing, but today it is sharp and grating, like an impatient rustling of paper. I'm so confused, and I don't do indecision well. When I was growing up and got nervous about something—a test, a swim meet—my dad would always tell me, in his matter-of-fact, don't-sweat-it way, that the anxiety you feel leading up to something is always worse than the actual thing itself. I'm not so sure anymore.

I shift in my spot on the front porch and watch as the petals from four newly bloomed Bradford pear trees whirl through the sky without any discernible pattern. It reminds me of an undergraduate physics class and learning about chaos theory: how, from a scientific point of view, so many things that seem random actually have a sequence, an order that happens for a reason. It should bring me comfort, I think, but it doesn't.

# CHAPTER FOURTEEN

I stand behind Annie in my office as her eyes scan my computer screen, and when she finally finishes reading Owen's email—I know because her head starts to shake slowly back and forth—I swear that steam's about to come out of her ears. This is exactly why I decided not to show it to her when I received it yesterday.

"The nerve that he has to do this to you—it's *unreal.* Who does he think he is?" She spins around. "It shows such an absolute and utter lack of compassion," she says, her hands punctuating each syllable. "He's a total narcissist, Daphne, just like my mother. The similarities are actually kind of unbelievable."

I knew she'd be unhappy about Owen's sudden declaration— she's been my biggest cheerleader over the past few weeks, the head majorette in the *Let's Get Daphne a New Lease on Life* parade. In some ways, her reaction is validating. And somehow, it also makes me feel worse.

She shakes her head at me, her eyebrows stretched up toward her hairline. *What do I say?* I'm still angry—of course I am—but I don't believe he's a monster. Not one bit. And maybe it's just the shock wearing off, but the more I read the letter last night, the better I felt about it. This, in particular: *I am drowning in regret over the decision I made.* How many times have I read that particular line? The words have burned themselves into my brain tissue.

*I am drowning in regret over the decision I made.*

I can't think of anything else.

"Annie, come on. Read it again," I say, gesturing toward my computer. "Read it again and try to remember that this is Owen, the same person who has sat at your dinner table dozens of times over the years." I turn the chair back toward the screen.

She makes a sound that's half grunt, half laugh. Whatever it is, it reeks of disdain. "You've got to be kidding me. I mean, he says it right here," she says, pointing to the screen. "'It's about me,'" she reads. "Damn right it is, Owen. *All about you.* Do you believe this? What he's written?"

"Well, yeah, I do," I say, defensive. "I do know a thing or two about him. He *is* my husband."

She moans. It's a *disappointed* sound, a lamenting *you should know better.* "I'm sorry," she says. She turns to me and grabs my hands. Her eyes are the exact shade of blue gray as the cedar-shingled houses that my family used to rent on Cape Cod, and there's probably a deep-down subconscious part of me that finds some comforting affinity in her because of that. "I don't mean to upset you," she says. Her voice is like melted butter, like a mother's. "It just frustrates me so much that he's hurt you like this and now..." She motions to the computer. "It seems like he's stringing you along, Daphne. It's like he thinks he gets both of you."

"But I honestly think he's really confused," I say. "That's what I want to explain to you. I truly think he's remorseful."

"And?" She raises her chin toward me, waiting for me to give her the answer she wants to hear.

"I mean, yes, Annie, I hate this," I point to the computer like a TV trial lawyer pointing at a piece of evidence. "I actually do. I was starting to feel better—or, well, at least get used to my new reality. But I've also loved him for a long, long time and I can tell when he's being sincere. He was my best friend. For many years.

Imagine if something happened between you and me. And imagine that I wrote a letter like this to you. An apology."

She stares back at me, biting her lip, and I know that she's not buying it. *Some friend,* she's thinking. She fiddles with the tiny charms on her necklace—L, S, M, Luke, Samantha, and Molly's first initials—stamped in sterling silver.

"That said," I continue, "I can't gloss over what's happened. I know better. The past few weeks have left me bitter and angry and raw. I don't know whether it's right to trust him the way that my instincts are telling me to, and I don't know how to defuse the incredible amount of resentment I feel toward him. I'm furious, I really am, but this apology..." I stop and close my eyes. "I don't know how to deal with it. I feel like I'm being pulled in two directions."

"Well, you know what I'm going to say," she says, looking into my eyes.

I pick up my coffee mug from my desk and take a sip. "Yeah," I say. "I can't respond to him—not yet. This letter obviously clouds things, but no matter what happens between Owen and me, I have to put this—him—aside for a while. I need to think this through."

She nods at me.

"He did an awful, awful thing," I say. "I can't excuse it because of the things he's written in this letter." I look at her. "Right?"

"Exactly," she says.

I nod back at her, hoping that I look more certain than I feel.

Later that afternoon, I am in an exam room, entering notes into my laptop after a patient visit, when Carol pops her head in. "Dr. Billings wants to see you."

"Now?" I say, slamming the laptop shut. "Don't we have another patient waiting?"

She checks her watch. "You have ten minutes."

I hurry down to my boss's office. His door's open but he is on the phone, most likely with his wife, Valerie, because I hear him mentioning Dover, the King Charles spaniel that she drives around town in the front seat of her Jaguar sedan like it's the queen. I wait in the hallway, ignoring Carol when she walks by and gives me a look like I'm standing outside of the principal's office.

"Dr. Mitchell?" he finally says. In the five years I've worked for him, Dr. Billings has never called me Daphne and never asked me anything about my personal life, not even a simple "How was your weekend?" It's not so much that he's cold but that he is formal and brilliant and old-money wealthy, and the combination, along with his wire-rimmed glasses and ubiquitous bow ties, denotes the sort of eccentricity that makes it acceptable for him to forgo the usual social graces. Outside of work, at the annual summer barbecue that he and Valerie hold at their house overlooking the golf course at Hope Valley, or on the handful of occasions when I've run into him around town—at Witherspoon Rose once, both of us browsing the delicate hybrid tea roses—he is more relaxed but still plenty intense.

"How was the AMA?"

"Excuse me?"

"The American Medical Association conference. Philadelphia?"

"Oh!" I put my palm to my head. That conference seems like a lifetime ago. It *was* a lifetime ago. "It was good. I was on a panel. 'Is Concierge Care the Future of Medicine?'" I say, reciting the name of the talk.

He shakes his head and sighs. "Concierge Care" is a label we all despise. It sounds so pretentious, as if we're doling out diamond necklaces along with our diagnoses.

I rest my hands on the chair in front of me. He hasn't invited me to sit. The office is dark save for the small brass table lamp on the corner of his hulking mahogany desk. If I didn't know him, I would assume that he is playing up the gloomy intensity for effect. There are piles of papers strewn everywhere, crooked fading photos that suggest they were hung on the walls decades ago, a tower of files threatening to topple in the corner.

"So," he says, looking over his glasses at the computer screen as he does it.

His middle finger caresses his computer mouse as he scrolls. "I wanted to talk to you about one of your patients." He turns ninety degrees to face me and his small, sharp eyes land on me, like a mosquito ready to bite. I suddenly feel my skin start to prickle, goose bumps forming on my arms.

"Which patient?" I ask.

"Mary Elizabeth Foster." He laces his elegant fingers together and rests his chin on his hands. He is thin and fine featured, as my mother would say. *Like a hawk*, I think.

"Mary Elizabeth?" We've spoken about her before, nearly a year ago, in a meeting with the other providers in the office who treat her.

He nods. "She was in the office last...?"

"A week or so ago," I finish for him.

"I'm friendly with her parents," he says.

"Oh."

"They are worried about her care."

I frown. *This is puzzling.* "About *her* or about *her care*?"

"About her *care*, Dr. Mitchell." His eyes bore into mine and I force myself to hold his gaze. "When she was here last, did you give her a breathalyzer?"

"No." I shake my head. I can't imagine the impetus for this—I picture Dr. Billings and Valerie with Mary Elizabeth's parents, shaking the ice in their highball glasses at the country club bar while they discuss her in between conversations about their golf handicaps and their designer dogs.

"Are you sure?" He points his forehead at me.

"I'm positive," I say. "Because she wouldn't let me." He might be my boss and I'm aware that I'm capable of making mistakes, but I know that Mary Elizabeth has received nothing but the best treatment from me. She is my special case. Of all of the spinning tops I treat, she is the one who worries me most, the one most likely to fall first. "I could smell the alcohol on her the minute I walked into the exam room. She was behaving erratically and I wanted to test her. I called Carol into the room with me, and I thought about getting additional assistance."

"What was the reason for her visit?"

"Well, that's a good question," I say, trying not to sound defensive. I've never doubted his respect for me. While he's not a man who's generous with compliments, he frequently asks me to consult on other doctors' cases and often, in our practice meetings, asks me to comment when we're discussing a tricky situation. He values me. I know that.

"She had another appointment scheduled for a few weeks later—a standard blood panel. She asked for an anti-anxiety prescription—I'm sure it's why she came to see me." Internists are solicited for meds all the time—anti-anxiety, antipsychotics, painkillers of every variety—even in a practice like ours, where the patients are paying us to pay close attention to their behavior.

"Okay," he says, rapping his fingers on his desk.

"I skipped the blood panel. She was in no shape for it," I say. "And I offered to arrange a ride for her but she had a friend waiting for her in the lobby."

"Did you walk her out? Did you see the friend?"

"I did. He was about her age. Did something happen to her?" I think of how I pleaded with her to stay.

"Fortunately not," he says. "But she went missing for several days. Disappeared from work, didn't call anyone."

"Denise doesn't know anything?"

He shakes his head.

"You were the last person who saw her before she..." He makes a *poof* motion with his hands.

*And so I'm somehow to blame?* I think. "Where is she now?"

"She turned up yesterday morning. She's been in Asheville with a *friend*." He says the word like it's rancid.

"And she's okay?" I can feel the dampness on my hairline and on my upper lip, behind my neck. I can't believe that he'd question me like this.

"She may lose her job. I hear that this isn't the first incident."

"Dr. Billings, I have talked to her on many occasions about entering a program and about how dangerous her behavior is, given her particular circumstances. As you know, the decision ultimately has to come from her unless there's some sort of intervention. Is her family thinking about that? Because I talked to her mother about that once. We spoke on the phone less than a year ago. I can look it up in my records." I leave out the part about how her assistant kept me on hold for nearly ten minutes, and how, when she finally came to the phone, she seemed highly burdened by my desire to talk about her daughter's health, despite the fact that I was returning her call. Our conversation probably clocked in at less than 120 seconds, and she talked *at* me the entire time.

"I don't know what her family's intentions are, but I wanted to get your opinion. They are not..." He squirms in his seat. "They are not the type to mention these sorts of things socially, not that anyone is. I was curious about your assessment."

"My assessment is—" I feel a buzz in my front coat pocket. *Ugh!* I'm getting a call. We both hear it. He grimaces at me. *Dammit.*

"My assessment is that she needs a program," I continue. "Denise and I have discussed it. She's had several seizures related to her alcohol use. I prescribed—" *Buzz. I wonder who it is? I wonder if it's Owen.* "I prescribed Klonopin to her once," I start again. "Under Denise's advisement, but that was a couple of years ago and I've refused to since."

"Okay. That's helpful," he says.

"As I mentioned, she's due in for the routine tests," I say. My heart is beating faster. I can practically feel it in my fingertips. *First Owen and his email, now I'm questioned about my ability to do my job...* The phone buzzes again.

"If she shows," he says.

"True, but she's never actually missed an appointment before. She's always late, but she shows up. To be honest, I think we have a good connection."

He squints at me like this is the strangest thing he's ever heard. The phone buzzes again.

"Why don't you go answer that?" he finally says.

I hurry out, yank my phone out of my pocket, and answer without bothering to see who's calling. "Hello?" I bark.

"Hey, Daphne. This is Andrew, Jack's friend?" In contrast to my own, his voice is buoyant and upbeat, like it's following one of those animated bouncing balls that marks the words during the sing-along cartoons that Lucy and I used to watch on Saturday mornings.

"Andrew." I swallow, using the pause to settle myself. *Jesus, this day.* "Hi! Hello." *Jack must have given him my number.*

"Listen," he says. "I know it's last minute and you probably have plans, but I have a couple of tickets to a concert tonight, and my friend who was joining me just bailed. I wondered if you might like to come. Grab dinner first?"

"Tonight?" I say. *Tonight.* My plan was to see what's new on

Netflix, make some progress on the book I'm reading for Annie's book club, and maybe paint my toes if I could handle that much activity. "Um, well, I'm the doctor on call this weekend for our after-hours hotline," I say, remembering.

"Oh, I see," he says. "Like I said, it's totally last minute."

"No, it's...it's fine." I backtrack. *Can I go on a date? This isn't a date, though—just dinner, some music.* "I probably won't even get any calls, and if I do, they usually don't require more than a few minutes." *I wonder if he knows that I'm married?* I inhale sharply, taking a big breath of air into my lungs. "You know what?" I say. "Sure! That sounds fun." I force myself to smile as I speak and hope that it injects at least a little enthusiasm into my voice.

"Okay, good," he says. "How about we meet at Geer Street. Seven o'clock?"

"Seven o'clock!" I repeat. *It will be good for me*, I tell myself. *He is nice. He is handsome. And he's not Owen.* "Seven o'clock sounds great."

# CHAPTER FIFTEEN

This may not be a date but it's the perfect night for one. The sun is just setting, the sky is turning a velvety deep blue, and the trellis above the restaurant's patio is strewn with glittering string lights. We sit at a quiet table in the corner, away from the crowds crammed into the long, communal tables in the center of the room, and the candle set between us flickers from the gentle, early spring breeze. At the coffee shop across the street, a jazz trio is playing, the music just loud enough for us to hear it over the laughter and easy conversation coming from the tables around us.

The last time that Owen and I came here was last fall, right before it got too cold to sit outside. It was a Sunday night and we sat on the other side of the patio and I had a Reuben. That's about all I remember. I was blissfully oblivious to the way that my life was about to break open. *Blissfully.*

Andrew sits with his forearm on the table, comfortably slumped to one side. He drinks the same beer that Owen often ordered. His hair is still damp from his shower, but as expected, he is dressed better than Durham requires him to be. He wears a starched shirt, the sort of jeans that do not look like they came from the Gap, and loafers without socks, a Southern boy trademark that Owen rolled his eyes at in the same way that he rolled his eyes at grown men in superhero T-shirts.

We order—he lets me go first—and then I watch the waitress as she hurries off, her walk a sort of bounce-bounce like she's on a tether.

"So remind me, how long have you been back in Durham?" I ask. I take a big swig of my wine. I should slow down. When I was getting ready earlier, I guzzled a glass in record time, trying to quell my nerves. *This isn't a date,* I remind myself. *You have nothing to prove.*

"I've been here for about three months."

"And how has it been?" I wince as soon as the words are out of my mouth. *How has it been since you came home to tend to your ailing father? Idiot!*

"It's been pretty great, actually," he says fortunately. "You know, I come back fairly often. With all of my travel for work, it's easy to hop down for a few days if I'm already on the East Coast, but I haven't been able to spend any extended time here since before I left for college. Do you like it here?" he asks.

"I do," I say, leaving it at that. Earlier, when I was driving home, I noticed a For Sale sign in front of another farmhouse down the road from ours. I thought about how I always assumed I'd stay here forever. Now I could choose to go anywhere, do anything. I wonder when (if?) the concept won't seem so terrifying. "So you must travel constantly for work?" I ask.

"I've definitely logged some airline miles." He starts to tell me about his company, which started off with two small hotels—one in the Bay Area, the other in Oregon—and is now comprised of half a dozen properties in North America. Each is a restoration of some sort: an old zipper factory, a former post office, a dilapidated Woolworth's. He starts telling me about his latest prospect—the first outside of the U.S., a renovated seamstresses' workshop in Vancouver—and how he dreams about expanding outside of North America, with locations in Spain, South Africa,

Ireland. It's hard not to feel his enthusiasm, and before long, I am swept up in his wanderlust and thinking that Durham is indeed a very small place and that there are thousands upon thousands of people in the world and thousands and thousands of them get their hearts broken every day. The thought, distressing as it is, gives me comfort.

After we finish dinner—I resort to eating my fish tacos with a fork so as not to humiliate myself—he excuses himself to use the restroom. I sip my wine and gaze around the patio. My eyes land on a large group that I noticed while we were eating. There's a young couple sitting at the end of the table—he's bearded, wearing a plaid shirt, and she's wearing the kind of sweetly patterned sundress that I know from pictures that my mother wore when she and my dad were first dating. But what really draws me to them is the chubby toddler she's bouncing on her lap. His chin is shiny from drool and she holds a piece of her fried chicken out for him to try. He yanks the drumstick from her hand, wields it like a pint-sized caveman, and they all laugh, watching him.

I turn away, twisting in my seat for a moment to see if Andrew's on his way back to the table. There's a couple just behind us. I try not to stare. She has dark, wavy hair that tumbles down her back, and he is clearly mesmerized by her, leaning almost into his plate to get closer. They are deep in conversation, obviously in love, or lust, or some combination of the two. I feel the telltale ache in my chest that is with me so often lately. *Were Owen and Bridget ever bold enough to go out in public together—maybe driving to some out-of-the-way place where they wouldn't be discovered—and did he look at her like that? Did he reach across the table and take her hand, the way that I'm witnessing the man next to me do it now, and slowly caress it with his thumb, staring at her with that sort of adoration?*

Andrew returns and sits. "This is a fun place," he says.

"Yes," I say, plastering a smile on my face. "Yes, it is."

Andrew pays, insisting on it, and then we walk up the street to Motorco, the music hall where we're seeing a band that he described over dinner as nuevo-bluegrass, whatever that means. He doesn't know the dirty little secret about me and concerts, of course. Precisely, that I can't stand them. I know how it makes me sound. Dull, unfun, like someone who would wrinkle her nose at an ice cream cone. Who doesn't like a concert?

It's not that I don't like music. I do—a lot, actually. My hang-up with concerts are the stumbling, sweaty crowds, the fact that I can never see the stage because I'm not tall enough, and how I always get restless after a few songs and wish that there was something to look at besides the armpits of the people around me.

The show has already started. Andrew points me toward a wall of gymnasium-style bleachers on the side of the stage, and I squeeze my way through the crowd of T-shirts and denim and climb to where there is half an empty row. I watch the people below us in front of the stage; they are singing along, moving their bodies to the beat of the music in ways that suggest they can anticipate every boom and pop of the drums, every riff, every bass line. The band is clearly popular.

Andrew offers to go to the bar and I watch the band, a quartet of young guys I think are related in some way. Before long, I am bobbing my head along to the music. And when the song ends and the crowd erupts into applause, the woman next to me hopping up to stand and shout, I clap along, raising my arms up almost over my head. *Maybe this whole night is a lesson,* I think. *I shouldn't be so quick to assume that it's impossible for me to have a good time now. There is still plenty for me to look forward to.*

Before the next song begins, I dig into my purse to quickly check my phone for any work-related hotline calls. My stomach drops. I have six missed calls, all from within the past half hour, but they're not from the office—they're from Owen. No voice-mails. I search the crowd to see if Andrew's on his way back and find him making his way up the side of the bleachers, taking care not to spill the pints he's carrying. I could say that I got a message from a patient. It would be so easy to step outside for a moment and find out what Owen wants.

Andrew is squeezing himself down our row. *Excuse me! Sorry! Excuse me!* We lock eyes and he smiles at me. He passes a woman who might be young enough to be a student, wearing a short top and an armful of bracelets, and I notice how she looks him over in an approving way. I wonder again why he's single. I wonder why Owen called. *Just ignore it,* I think. *Just let yourself have the good time you deserve.*

He goes to hand me my drink, but to take it, I have to shove my phone clumsily into my bag.

"That was an effort." He laughs.

"What? Oh," I say, realizing that he was talking about going to the bar. "Yes. Thank you very much."

I take a sip of the drink and angle myself just the tiniest bit toward Andrew. *Forget Owen. Forget him,* I think. *Remember what he did to you.* I think of Bridget, the two of them in bed—I can't help it, but my mind so often goes to the physical first, some reptilian impulse kicking in. I think of their bodies, sweaty and twisting, I think of them holding hands, sweet, tender, the most evident physical expression of emotional love. I think of that couple at the restaurant and how Owen must have looked at Bridget like that. I think of how he lied to me, about working late or needing to go into the office when he was possibly with her. The deception wasn't random or impulsive. He planned it and let his actions follow the outline, forgetting me a little bit more with each passing day. *He said in the email that they had a relationship*, I remind myself. I force myself to think through the details, one after the other, building a case for why I ought to sit right here and enjoy myself. *Don't think about him.*

I glance at Andrew, who's watching the band. His eyes meet mine and he grins. "They're good, right?" he says, nodding toward the stage.

"Yes," I say. *They* are *good*, I tell myself. *Stop thinking.*

"This is fun," he says, nudging me with his elbow.

"It is," I say, nudging him back. I nibble at the inside of my lip and then lean into him. "I'm having a really great time."

I turn back to the stage. I watch the bass player, humble and earnest, the jerky, hyperjauntiness of the fiddle player, the rhythmic hopping and flapping of the crowd in front of them. And then I start tapping my foot. I make it move, and it feels silly, like it's on a mechanical lever, but I don't stop. *Let it go*, I tell myself. *Let him go.*

After the show, Andrew walks me to my car. I'm nervous, cringing at the thought of an awkward good-bye. We both say the things you say—*had a great time, let's do it again*—and then he leans in for a hug and I don't know whether he's going to kiss me but I turn my head away, just in case, and it's obvious, what I'm doing, which makes it worse, because how bad would it be for him to kiss me on the cheek? And so, maybe inspired by the comfort of his arms around me, the faintly damp masculine warmth of him, I turn my head back and I kiss him on the cheek quickly, appropriately—not a lingering, passionate embrace, just a gracious, grown-up thanks-for-a-nice-night peck.

I step back.

"It was a really fun night," he says, grabbing my hand for a moment and then letting it go.

"It was," I say, running my hand over my hair.

"Let's do it again," he says. He means it. I can tell. Is it possible that Jack hasn't told him anything about me? He didn't ask me a thing about my personal life during dinner—but then again, I didn't ask him, either, not wanting to open that avenue of conversation. Bad first-date etiquette—*not that this is a date.*

"I'd love to do it again," I say. I open the door to my car and he holds it for me as I slip inside.

"Get home safe," he says, closing the door after I'm in.

I nod, waving, and once he's turned, I watch him walk away. I pull out my phone. No more calls. *Could Owen have sensed that I was out?* I muse. *Could he have seen me?* It's funny to feel vengeful, but even better, I realize, to feel good about it. I look back out my window but Andrew's already gone. There is a food truck parked on the corner outside of the music club, and people are milling about, eating pizza and clutching the band T-shirts they've just bought.

Let Owen think that I'm moving on. *It's fine,* I think. Because whether I'm ready to or not, I'm starting to have something to show for it.

# CHAPTER SIXTEEN

I am halfway up the driveway when I see Owen's car parked in his old spot. I park and fly inside. *What is he doing here?* I realize that he still owns half of this house, but he *cannot* just show up here like this. He lost that privilege when he did what he did with Bridget.

"Owen!" I scream, letting the door slam behind me. "Owen!"

I cross the threshold into the kitchen and he's sitting there in the dark, the only light the pendant over the sink that I turned on before I left for the evening. Blue is lying at his feet.

He has his elbows on the table, his open mouth resting against his interlaced fingers. His eyes are red and puffy. His cheeks are streaked from tears. I notice that he's not wearing his ring.

"Owen, what the hell is going on?" I drop my bag. He looks me over—I'm dressed up for once, in the silk shirt that I bought for a New Year's party that we went to two years ago, heels, and even makeup. "What are you doing here?"

"I'm sorry," he says. His voice is thick with mucous. He clears his throat. "I called first."

"I saw. You called a lot of times. What is it, Owen?" *Dammit, can't I have one good night?*

He closes his eyes, squinting them shut. He looks physically pained.

"She died," he says.

I put my hand to my mouth. I'm not sure I've heard— *"What are you talking about?"*

"Bridget. Bridget's dead."

It started three days ago. First they noticed her breathing—she was having more trouble than would be reasonable despite what she's endured. But Owen thought that something was wrong even before that. He didn't think that she was progressing as quickly as she should be, regardless of the long inventory of injuries. He talked to her doctors, and after some back-and-forth about the best course of action, they discovered that they needed to do another abdominal surgery and, in the course of doing so, determined that she had more internal bleeding. They addressed it, and she started to progress again. Her breathing tube came out and she started to talk a little bit. She was getting better. *"You could tell, her color,"* Owen says, his voice drifting off. But then she reversed— an unexpected snap. The complications started piling on—they discovered posttraumatic pancreatitis, due to the initial accident. And because of the pancreatitis, the lag time from the accident three weeks ago, and the extent of the damage, she developed ARDS, acute respiratory distress syndrome. Her lungs were compromised, she was shutting down, her body wasn't getting enough oxygen. It all started moving faster and faster, in the way that it happens, one thing after another and then another. They reintubated her. She held on for another day. And then, this afternoon, she let go.

"I'm sorry to come here," he says. "I didn't know what else to do."

I pull out the chair next to his and sit down.

"I know I shouldn't be here." He sniffs hard, sucking in air.

"It's okay," I say. The refrigerator hums in the background. It's like a soundtrack, defining the moment.

"What about her family?" I ask. My heart is pounding. I feel like I can't take a full breath.

"They're here," he says. "They've all been here, the whole time, since the accident."

"I don't know what to say, Owen." I say it to the top of his head, which is hanging between his shoulders, which are curled over the table.

He shifts in his seat. "Daphne, can I stay here tonight? I know that it's asking a lot. I just don't know where else to go. I don't want to be alone."

I feel a jolt, a nervy electric current running through my veins. "Of course you can," I say.

He runs his fingers through his hair and looks down at his lap. "Thank you."

There is a difference in the way that you think about death once you become a physician. Pre-M.D., I thought about it as the end of a long road—what happens, mostly, at the end of a life, the concluding final chapter. Of course I was aware that people die much earlier from causes that have nothing to do with age—car crashes, wars, disease, freak injuries, swimming pool drownings, the stuff on the evening news. But mostly it was older people. Once I entered medical school and words like "longevity" and "vitals" became part of my daily lexicon, death became a sort of undercurrent. Not in a morbid way but in a realistic one. Death really does happen every day, hundreds of thousands of times, to every sort of person. A long battle with a chronic condition finally, mercifully ends. SIDS. An operating-room mistake. A suicide. Heart attacks, strokes. Murder. A kid passes out on a football field. A woman looks the wrong way before she crosses the street.

I don't deal with it in an immediate way with my work. Owen does. I am a preventer, a monitor, but he is an *undoer*. The damage, the cancer, is already there. He is a wonderful doctor, working in one of the best hospitals in the world, and some of the patients who come through his office die despite the best efforts known to mankind. He loses people in spite of everything.

But that's his job.

All four of his grandparents are living. There have been no horrifying stories about childhood friends who died young. He was diagnosed with cancer as a boy and it marked him, it changed who he would become, but it didn't kill him. The theme that has driven his life is *survival against all odds*. I watch him, so brittle, from across the table. Grinding his teeth, the anxious pulsating pop in the side of his cheek. His eyes are closed, like he can't bear it. I reach my arm out and grab his hand.

I can't believe that she's dead.

I know that this moment—sitting here and noticing the way that my feet hurt, the back-of-my-throat aftertaste of the dark beer that I drank at the concert, the cloying perfume that nags at me because I'm not used to wearing it—I can already tell that this will feel like the threshold, the line between *before* and *after*. Months from now, this will be the moment that sticks.

I let go of his hand and stand up and the chair sliding across the floor behind me, the deep skitter, sounds like a groan. My feet *click-click* a few scant steps across the hardwoods, sounding ridiculous. I slump over him, put my arms around him, and whisper in his ear. "I'm so sorry." My throat burns.

He cups his hands over my forearm, like he needs to hold on.

"I can't believe it," he says. "I just don't—"

"Shhhh." I press my cheek to the top of his head. "It's going to be okay," I say, sensing the hollowness of the words before they're even out of my mouth.

I fall asleep sometime after two, and when I wake the next morning, the first thing I do is text Annie. Call me.

She does, about thirty seconds later, and I lunge to pick up the phone so that the ring doesn't wake Owen, who's asleep in the guest room. At least I hope he's finally sleeping. He sat in the same spot at the kitchen table for hours, eyes closed, head on the table, or slumped back in the chair with his palms pressed together against the bridge of his nose, like he was begging for something. There are so many questions I wanted to ask. What does her family know about him? What's his role, exactly? Has he been staying at her place, driving her parents to the hospital each day? I couldn't ask, of course—it's not the time. I eventually went upstairs to the bathroom, found the sleeping pills that I've been using, and left the bottle on the vanity in the guest bathroom.

"*Soooo?*" Annie says, her voice bright, the *soooo* curling over itself.

Of course. She's wondering about my night out with Andrew. I'd already forgotten.

"Hey," I say. I hop up from the bed and close the door, which I'd left cracked just in case…I'm not sure. In case he needed me, I suppose.

"How was it?" Her voice is tinny, clanging. She can hardly contain herself.

I clear my throat. "It was good."

"That's it?" she says. "Oh, no. What is it?"

"Nothing, I had a nice time. It's what happened after."

"After? *Oh.*" I can hear the foreboding in her voice.

"No, not like that. Andrew is a lovely person. Really. But when I got home, Owen was here."

"Are you kidding me?" she wails. "I can't believe the gall—"

"Annie, stop," I interrupt. "It's Bridget. She's dead."

As I describe what's happened, I have to keep stopping to collect myself. We both keep saying the only thing you can say in this situation: It's unbelievable. We both agree that Owen needs some-one right now, and I can tell that Annie doesn't want it to be me but it's going to have to be. She keeps insisting, her voice consol-ing, soft, that I *take care of myself, don't let this overrun me, be very, very careful.* I know that what she wants to do is pluck me right out of this chaos, because she's right, it's not mine, but how can I not feel some of what he feels? It's so awful. After I hang up with her, I tiptoe down the bright hallway, the sun coming in slats through the windows that line one side of the wall. The guest room door is cracked and I peek in, pressing it open ever so slightly with my fingertips. He's not there. I continue downstairs to the kitchen, but he's not there, either, and when I look out the window to the driveway, I see that the space on the left that his car always occu-pied, the one that he parked in last night, is empty. He's gone.

I'm not sure what to do. I pace the kitchen floor for a minute and then, because I don't have any other answers, I call my mother.

"Hi, honey!" She is chewing something.

"Hey, Mom. Listen, I need to talk to you. Something hap-pened."

"What? *Oh!* What happened? What is it?"

I can hear NPR in the background, through the dusty, beaten-up AM/FM radio that my parents have kept on the kitchen counter for decades. My mother, I am certain, is sitting at the table in her floral-printed robe, picking pieces off one of the expensive French pastries that she buys every Friday afternoon for her and Dad to enjoy over the weekend.

She gasps throughout my story. "I can't imagine what her family must be going through," she says. "How old was she?"

"Twenty-six."

"Twenty-six! My God. A life is just beginning at twenty-six. It's tragic."

"It is," I say. Owen and I met for the second time when I was twenty-six.

"Her whole life was ahead of her."

"I know."

And then I begin to bawl. I can't hold it in any longer. It is all so sad, such a mess.

"Oh, honey," my mother coos. "It's going to be okay."

"I feel so confused," I say. "I can't imagine what her family is going through. And I'm worried about Owen. I really am. What am I supposed to do now?"

"I know, honey, I know," she says. "It's a terrible situation to be in. I think," she starts, collecting herself. "I think that the best thing that you can do—the only thing, really—is to take it one day at a time. Follow your instincts. Be there for him but don't forget to take care of yourself. Put yourself first. You won't be of any help to him or anyone else if you don't."

"You're right," I say. I rip a paper towel off the holder next to the sink and wipe my nose. "It's all too much."

"I know, honey," she says. "But do what feels best. Lead with your heart."

"Okay," I say, turning her words over in my head. "But what do I *do*?"

"Why don't you call him and find out where he is?" she says. "So that you won't worry."

"I'll do that," I say. "I'll call him right after we get off the phone."

"The thing is, you need to be there for him," she says. "As uncomfortable as it is between you two right now, he needs you. You're all that he has down there."

"You're right, Mom. Thank you."

When I hang up, I feel redeemed. For better or for worse, the validation—maybe permission—is exactly what I hoped to hear from her.

*Doing what feels right should be a simple solution*, I think, staring out the kitchen window.

Owen is grieving. I should help him.

But Owen started a relationship outside of our marriage with the person he grieves.

But she is dead *(how is this possible?)* and I should respect her.

And they both deceived me, so I should respect myself.

I open the window. It's a beautiful day. They all are in April. The breeze is gauzy and sweet. I start to cry again. Nothing is normal anymore. Everything feels fragile and out of balance. *Where is he?*

*I want him here,* I think, turning and gazing into our family room with its cozy sofa, the soft rug—this house we built, this *home*. And it's not because I want to take care of him, though I do. It's not *(admit it!)* because I'm worried about him, though I am. I simply want him home. With me. I pick up the phone and dial his number, but he doesn't answer. It just rings and rings.

# CHAPTER SEVENTEEN

Even though I've just called, I try Owen once more, and when he doesn't pick up, I head outside. I'm pulling the hose into the backyard when I notice a flash of pink—one of our rosebushes is blooming. I kneel to inspect the plant, gently running my fingertip over the new petals. My wedding bouquet had pink roses like these. Lucy teased me about them—flower freak or not, I'm not normally much for pink. The buds have barely opened but I pull my pruning shears from my back pocket and cut a few, then take them into the house and put them in a bud vase and set them on the kitchen counter. I know what I'm doing—puttering, wasting time. I check my phone. No missed calls.

It is warmer than it should be at this time of year, and while all I really want to do is wait so that I'm here when Owen gets back from wherever he is, I know that I will feel better if I get out, so I grab my keys and an old canvas bag and drive downtown to the farmers' market.

As usual, it's packed, and it takes me three turns around the parking lot before I'm able to find a space. I walk through the lot, hitch my bag over my shoulder, and am just about to walk into the L-shaped pavilion when I see Edward, Owen's boss, up ahead.

*Shit.* I stop at a stand, letting the crowd weave around me, hoping I won't be spotted. Edward looks like Clark Kent ("Super Doctor!" Owen and I always joked) and he looks even more so right now, with the sun behind him, all hazy, fuzzy edges framing his imposing stance. He's holding a bag open in front of his wife, Gloria, who's inspecting a bundle of asparagus. Edward and Owen are close—the nature of the work they do, I always thought—and occasionally grab lunch or a beer in the evening. I wonder how much he knows. I wonder if he's heard the news about Bridget. I surely don't want to be the one breaking it, so I hang back, waiting until they wander off.

It's nearly eleven o'clock, but the Saturday morning crowd is still half asleep, their bodies moving like they're wading in mud. Making my way toward my favorite vendors, I collide with two jogging strollers, a hippie-granola family of four, and a pair of head-in-the-clouds undergrads walking so close that you can practically smell the sex wafting off of them. I'm standing in line to pay for a bag of spinach, scanning the crowd for Edward and Gloria, when I notice an older couple at the Chapel Hill Creamery table next to me. The woman has that academic look about her, choppy gray haircut, long shapeless tank dress, delicate silver jewelry. She squeezes her beloved's arm when he points toward a soft, oozy round of cheese. "No, honey, you don't like that," she says gently, and I notice how he simply turns his attention to the next thing, trusting that she is right. Though they look nothing like my parents, it reminds me of how at restaurants my mother will poke her finger at some description on the wine list and say to my dad, *Do I like that?* I shudder, thinking of Bridget again, realizing how she will never know that sort of long, lifetime love. I wonder whether I will—with Owen, with someone. I brush the thought away, pay for my vegetables, and weave back into the crowd.

I am trying not to let the atmosphere get to me, but it becomes harder with each passing minute. I stop to let someone by, swerve to avoid getting trampled by a toddler, almost get whacked in the face by a massive bouquet on a young woman's shoulder. Before long, my inner monologue takes a nosedive—*Can't anyone in Durham walk in a straight line? Why did I think it was a good idea to come here in the first place? Where is Owen? What should I do?* Everyone around me seems so happy and carefree and...happy. *Dammit!* I sneak a finger under my sunglasses to wipe away a tear. I think of her mother. I wonder if she had a sister, too. *I can't believe she's dead.*

I squeeze through a mass of people to get to one of my favorite stands, where a woman with long gray hair in a calico print smock sells fresh bread and baked goods. I select a pillow-soft, golden loaf of sourdough from the wire-shelving unit she uses to display her items, and then my eyes fall to the bottom shelf. They're there—the seven-layer cookies packed with butterscotch, chocolate chips, and coconut that I used to buy for Owen when we were first married. I would hear him come in early on Sunday mornings after spending all night at the hospital and I'd stay snug under my warm blankets waiting, smiling to myself as I heard him fumbling around the kitchen. When he finally crawled into bed and curled himself around me, I could smell the butterscotch on his breath. I pay for a bag and tuck it into my tote. *No harm*, I tell myself. *Don't overthink it.*

I pick up a few more items—a bouquet of ranunculus, a pint of jewel-like strawberries—and walk toward the food trucks that park around the perimeter of the market. I'm stopped in front of them, trying to decide what to buy for lunch on my way out, when I feel someone tap my shoulder. I turn around.

"Andrew!" I say.

"Long time no see!" he says, pulling off his sunglasses and tucking them into the collar of his shirt.

"Yes!" I say, putting my hand to my chest. "How's it going?"

"Great," he says, taking a sip from his plastic cup of iced coffee. "Last night was a lot of fun."

"It was," I say. *He'd never believe what's happened since.*

"What are you up to today?" he asks, rattling the ice in his drink.

"Oh, today? Well—" I start, grasping for an answer. I don't want to tell him. And then I see a woman walk up behind Andrew. Her eyes rake over me.

"Hello," she says when she reaches us. She stands a good foot taller than me, and maybe that's all it is—well, that and the smug expression on her face—but I suddenly feel intimidated.

"This is Daphne," Andrew says. "The friend of Jack and Annie's?"

"Oh, yes," she says, not offering her name. "You're the one who took poor Andy out last night. I was sorry to miss that show." She puts her hand on Andrew's shoulder. "He said it was great."

*Andy?* I glance at him but he seems unfazed.

"We had fun," I say, standing up a little taller. *Why is it that certain women have the capability to make me instantly feel like a child?*

"So you live here in Durham?" she says.

"I do. You, too, I assume?" I glance at Andrew and he smiles at me. *Who is she?*

"Just recently moved back," she says. "From San Francisco."

"Oh!" *So she was supposed to be his date last night and they both came here from the same city.* "Of course."

She playfully elbows him. "Yes, though I hardly ever saw him. I swear, I've seen more of him since we got to North Carolina than I ever did in California. Anyhow, I grew up here, like Andy. And now I'm back."

"So you know Jack then?" I ask.

She nods like it's a stupid question. "I do."

"I work with Annie—they're very good friends of mine." *Mine, not ours.*

"Oh," she says. She apparently doesn't care enough to ask more because she turns to Andrew, crossing her arms over her chest, and that's when I notice her wedding ring. "So what do you think, babe. Lunch?" she says. *Babe?*

"Yeah," Andrew says, and then he turns to me. "Daphne, do you want to join us? We could just grab something here and sit outside?"

"Oh, I don't want food truck food," she says, wrinkling her nose. "Let's go have a proper brunch somewhere. I feel like a Bloody Mary." She curls her hand around his bicep and though he's still looking at me, I notice how he doesn't flinch. Whoever she is—whoever her husband is—she and *Andy* are obviously very close.

"What do you think?" he says to me, oblivious to the fact that the woman wrapping herself around him definitely does not want me to join them. "Come on and eat with us. It will be fun." Suddenly it occurs to me that maybe Jack *did* tell him about everything that's going on with me. Does he feel sorry for me? Am I his charity case? His good deed? She looks down at me, her eyebrows ticked up, almost like she's daring me to come. *If only she knew what I've been through over the past twelve hours.*

"You know, thank you, but I can't," I say. "I have plans this afternoon, and think I'll just grab something here before I head out."

"Well, okay," he says. "Another time." His eyes linger on me for a moment and then he smiles. Last night, during dinner, I noticed his smile. I thought he seemed so genuine, but now, I wonder. In fact, I'm starting to question my entire ability to read people. I always thought that I had good instincts, but the past few weeks have proven otherwise.

"It was nice to see you," I say. *I can't stand here any longer.* "And to meet you," I say to the nameless woman. She smiles at me. It's not genuine.

"Let's get together again soon," Andrew says, stepping toward me. I readjust my bag on my shoulder. I don't want a hug.

"Sure," I say, waving as I walk off. "Have a great lunch."

When I get home, Owen's still not there. I feel that ache in my chest. I get a bottle of sparkling water from the refrigerator and go out back to the deck, where I carefully unwrap the grilled pimento cheese sandwich I bought from one of the gourmet vendors on my way out of the market. It's a decadent, gooey delicious mess that I've often treated myself to after a long week, but today it just tastes bland and gummy. I push it aside and turn my face toward the sun, hoping the warmth will help me feel better.

*Where is he?*

I bet he's at his office, drowning himself in a massive pile of paperwork. I always accused him of hiding behind his work to avoid dealing with things and he always accused me of the same. We were both right. We would fight and then retreat. A couple of wimps, really, both of us too stubborn and too averse to confrontation to be mature and say, *Hey, listen, we need to talk about this.* He normally backed down first. He could be the bigger person. He could let things go. I would make up obligations to avoid him when I was upset. I had work to do, a patient to see, a meeting to prepare for. *If we had just talked...* I hear the crunch of a car coming up the gravel driveway. Blue breaks into a trot when she sees him. I follow behind.

He steps out, so rattled that I can see it in his eyes: that look that is both frantic and exhausted all at once. I want to run to him but I can't. I shouldn't.

He walks toward me.

"How are you doing?" I ask.

His eyes dart around the backyard. He can't look at me. He shakes his head and starts to say something but then he stops. I've never seen him like this before.

"Owen." I take a tentative step toward him and put my arms around his waist, and the smell of him, so familiar, soothes me.

He locks his arms around me and shivers, just barely, and that's when I know that he's crying. We stand together for a long time, just like that. I don't want to be the one to let go first.

"Were you at the hospital?" I say after a while, my arms still clasped around him.

"Yes," he says.

I don't know whether it was for work or for her. And now that he's home, I don't care.


He sleeps in the guest room for the rest of the afternoon. I feel like I'm tending a patient, and even though there's a part of me, deep down, that's questioning if this is the right thing to do, I ignore it. For the first time in weeks, I feel a sure sense of purpose. I make a quick shopping list and when I get home from the store, I make chicken pot pie, his mother's recipe. Before long, the house smells wonderful, like butter and garlic and thyme. It smells like home.

The sun is just setting when we sit at the table together—me, in my seat, and him, in his.

"Thank you," he says as we begin quietly eating. The fading sun casts fuzzy shadows around the room. *How many meals have we shared like this?* I think, picking at the salad that I made with the spinach from the market. I still don't have an appetite.

"How are you?" I ask after a while.

He puts his fork down and looks at me, sheepishly biting his lip. "I don't know what to think," he says quietly, looking away. "Everything feels upside down. I don't know how...how this is happening."

"*Owen.*" I shake my head. The thing is, in some small way, a different way, I know exactly how he feels.

"Daph," he says, his eyes filling with tears. "I'm sorry to have brought you into this."

"It's okay," I say, reaching across the table to grab his hand.


Annie's sitting on the bumper of her minivan when I pull up the next morning to meet her for a walk on a popular trail. When she sees me, she stands and hurries toward me to give me a hug.

"Oh, Daphne," she says, holding me out at arm's length. "I can't imagine what this is like for you."

"I honestly don't even know how to explain it." I take a step toward the wooded trail and motion for her to join me. "Come on, let's walk."

"So how are you doing?" she asks as we enter Duke Forest, the shelter of the tall pines shading the trail.

I don't say anything at first. I listen to the *crunch-crunch* of our sneakers against the wooded path. "I feel sort of like I lost a patient. It's not quite like knowing someone, but it's not like an absolute stranger."

"That makes sense."

"It's, I don't know, it's terrible."

She nods. "How's Owen?"

"Owen." I suck in my lips. "He's not doing well. Not at all."

She doesn't say anything. She's made it clear how much she hates him for what he did to me and I wonder if she can let it go for now, the way that I'm trying to.

"Last night, after I went up to bed, I heard him crying. He had the eleven o'clock news on, but I could hear him crying over it. He has never watched the local news once in all of our years together. He was weeping, Annie."

She shakes her head. "Awful."

"I don't know what to do," I say. "He's going to the funeral. It's on Wednesday, in Texas."

"So he knows her family?"

"They've been here since the accident," I say. "I wanted to ask about them last night when he told me about the funeral, but he didn't seem like he wanted to talk and I didn't want to push. I wonder how much they know."

"There's no telling," Annie says. A couple of women jog past. They are students, quite obviously—young, beautiful, long dark hair in high ponytails, gazelles—the kind of women that, had I seen them just days ago, would have made me seethe, thinking of Bridget. Now it just makes my heart ache. I feel like I have a boulder lodged in my chest.

"I wonder, I don't know…" I say. "Did they think he was just this great guy from work? Did they know about me? Did they just meet him? I don't know. I don't know anything." *Did they think she hit the proverbial jackpot? A doctor! A good-looking, funny doctor!* I feel tears spring from my eyes. I stop and moan up at the sky.

Annie stops walking. She cocks her head, her eyebrows knitted together, her lips pushed out in a pitying pout.

"Ugh." I turn away. "Stop looking at me like that! *Please!*"

"I'm sorry," she says, glancing at a couple of walkers as they pass. They're older women, wearing loose T-shirts and comfortable sneakers. One is telling the other about a recipe—*You don't have to make the crust from scratch, I used store-bought,* I hear her say. On a normal day, Annie and I would joke after they passed about how that will be us someday.

"It's all so bizarre, Annie," I say. "I mean, this morning, when he got up, he stared into the pantry and asked whether he could have a bowl of 'my' cereal, everything in the house being mine now, or whatever. Yesterday, I watched him bring his suitcase into the house, like he'd been away on a trip." I shake my head. "I don't know." I start walking again. "What would you do?"

"Probably the same as you," she says. There is no ire in her voice, none of the bitterness I've heard so much of lately.

"Really?" I take a deep breath. "Okay."

"It's a crazy situation," she says.

"I'm worried about him," I say. "I feel like I need to take care of him, like he's sick."

She nods. "I think I understand."

"I think I do, too," I say, and then I stop and throw my hands up. "Actually, I have no idea. I don't have *any* idea. It's all a nightmare. A fucking mess." I close my eyes and press my fingers to the bridge of my nose. "It's all just very, very sad."

"I'm so sorry," she says.

"Yeah." I run my hands through my hair. People whiz past us. Two dogs bark, straining at each other as their owners pull them along.

# CHAPTER EIGHTEEN

Lucy thinks that I've lost my mind. She's been on a photo shoot in L.A. all week, and because I didn't want to catch her up over email, I wait and call her one night after work, while I'm grocery shopping.

"Why on earth would you let him stay with you?" she yells through the receiver, her voice as piercing as the noise that I can hear in the background. "I'm sorry, Daph, it's awful what happened to her. But this is dangerous. For both of you."

"But what else am I going to do?" I say. "Imagine if it were Bobby."

"Please, *Bobby*..." I've noticed how there's always sarcasm in my sister's voice when her boyfriend's name comes up. "The very fact that you say that you think it's okay proves how *not okay* it is. You can't live together and pretend like nothing happened. He's not going to get over his mistress dying like he's getting over the flu, Daphne."

"Thanks for that heartfelt insight, Luce."

"Daphne, I know that you still love him—you can't just turn that off in an instant. And I know that what's happened to him is a terrible, tragic thing that I wouldn't wish on anyone. But the bottom line is that this is a really bad idea."

"Okay," I mutter. I am walking down the cereal aisle. A part of me knows that my sister is right. Here's evidence: When I arrived here tonight, I stood for several minutes next to the automatic door trying to decide whether to get a basket or a cart. Am I buying groceries for two again? And now, here I am, in the cereal aisle, my hand on a box of Owen's favorite brand. *Don't overthink it*, I hear my mother say. I throw the box in the cart, where there are tuna steaks, the chicken sausages we grill and eat with couscous and sautéed peppers and onions, tortilla chips, Owen's favorite salsa.

"It has to be agonizing, Daphne, the two of you in that house together, after everything. It's not good for you."

"I'm fine," I say. "And where else is he going to go?"

"A hotel?" she says. "They have those down there, I assume?"

"Lucy, it's still his house, too, legally. And it's honestly not a big deal. It's fine," I say again.

"Really?" she says. "It's fine? So, what, you have dinner together and sort the mail and wash each other's breakfast dishes and do his laundry like nothing happened? Like everything's 'fine'? Is that how it is?"

I feel my cheeks redden. The truth is that the past several days have been a strange sort of flashback, though I don't dare admit that. On Sunday night, I was sitting in the living room, watching *The Big Chill* on cable. I was trying to relax—pretty unsuccessfully, given that I was mostly straining to listen for any clues as to what Owen might be doing upstairs. He eventually came down, and when he went to the kitchen to get himself something to drink, I went to the liquor cabinet and found the bottle of scotch and poured us each a glass. He watched me do this and didn't stop me. He sat on the couch and waited for me to sit next to him, and then we sat there silently for a long time, drinking. Owen is the one who taught me to like scotch. We had "tutorials," starting out first with just a splash in a glass of ice, then a glass with water, and then a half-inch neat. I got out the good bottle, the special-occasion stuff.

It occurred to me, sitting there, that if an objective observer had somehow taken an aerial shot of our living room on Sunday and one six months ago, he or she would have seen the exact same picture—my laptop beside me, Blue nestled in the space between the coffee table and the sofa, Owen on the other end of the couch. This recent one is slightly more somber but honestly, not all that different.

Lucy's voice jolts me from my thoughts. "You need to sleep with that other guy."

"Lucy, please." I've actually hardly thought about Andrew since I saw him that day at the farmers' market with the clingy nameless blonde. I don't exactly crave more drama in my life.

"I'm serious, Daphne."

"Your job has really infiltrated every part of your brain, hasn't it?" I snap.

"Screw you," she says. "And I'm serious. You need to do something to take your mind off Owen because I can see you falling right back into it and completely forgetting the fact that he had an affair, which, let me remind you, led him to question whether he still wanted to be married to you. Just a few weeks ago, he was moving out. I'm sorry that that girl's dead but he's a psychopath, Daphne, or at least selfish to the point of disease—a textbook narcissist. It is not your job to take care of him."

I lean against the shopping cart and put my head in my hands. *I will not cry in the grocery store.* "He doesn't have anyone else, Lucy."

"That's his own damn fault. Listen, I'm not stupid, Daphne. I know that the reason why you aren't dealing with any of the logistical stuff like putting the house on the market—or at least moving him out, for God's sake—is because you're not ready to let him go. But given what he did to you? Well, it's just not good. Not good at all."

"Yes, but..." I know she's right.

"Where is he now?"

"In Texas, at her funeral. He left this morning."

"Where are you?"

"Food shopping."

"Mm," she says, purely passive aggressive.

I look at the contents of my cart. It is deplorable—as pitiful as the lovelorn single-girl groceries I've been buying the past few weeks (container of hummus, container of ice cream, wine, a nostalgic box of Double Stuf Oreos, the comfort food of my teenaged years).

"What are you going to do?" she says. "Nurse him back into loving you?"

I stand up straight and push the cart away like it's infected. "You're right," I say. "Okay, okay. You're absolutely right."


Twenty minutes later, I am on my way to Nana's, a restaurant where I'm meeting Andrew for a drink. When I called him from the grocery store parking lot, he happened to be on his way out. *And I happen to need a diversion*, I told myself as I put the keys in the ignition. *I deserve this.*

Even if the circumstances were different and there was no Owen, it was a horrible workday by anyone's measure, my worst day in a long time. My first patient stormed out of the office when I suggested that her constant stomach trouble might not in fact be a gluten intolerance but an intolerance to her shitty diet, which she proudly said consists mainly of Lean Cuisine, energy bars, and diet soda. Oh, and her self-reported two glasses of wine each night, which, according to the never-fail formula that I learned in medical school, means that she's drinking double that.

Carol is on vacation, so I was working with Diana, the new nurse in the office who has the impressive ability to ask thousands of questions in a given hour. She is young, new at this, and obviously only trying to do a good job—and she is—but every time we had a break between patients, she hovered around me, asking deep-thought let's-connect questions. *Why did you get into medicine? Do you think that the way we provide care is fair given that so many people can't afford it?* It's not that I'm opposed to her questions, it's just that I don't have any time for them when I'm strapped into my workday. I was about to say as much to her as we walked into an exam room, where our next patient promptly vomited at my feet. Ten minutes later, the results of her urine test confirmed that she has not gained ten pounds over the last two months because she'd been overzealous with the snacks but because she is pregnant with her fourth child. She is forty-eight and an exec at McKinney, the ad agency in town. When I told her the news, she burst into tears, and they were not happy ones. *You have no idea how fortunate you are*, I thought as I walked across the room to get her a tissue.

I'm pulling into the parking lot of the restaurant when it occurs to me that this is the intersection where Bridget had her accident. After I get out of the car, I scan the street, as if I might somehow gain some insight from the scene of regular people in regular cars crisscrossing past this everyday four-way stop. I feel a wave of anxiety wash over me. *Why am I nervous? Is it the circumstances of the past few weeks officially catching up with me?* I pull open the heavy wooden door and step into the restaurant. *It's just Andrew,*

I tell myself, taking a deep breath. *Nice, successful, blond-barnacle-attracting Andrew.*

Nana's is fine dining, a Durham institution. Like so many restaurants around here, it is unassuming, humble, and outstanding. There is a Subway sandwich shop behind it, a sketchy check-cashing place around the corner, a furniture liquidator across the street. The bar serves as a weeknight spot for a crowd of locals who look like money—mostly older professionals and residents of Hope Valley, the nearby country club neighborhood where Jack and Andrew grew up.

He is at the bar, in the corner. I watch the bartender slide his drink toward him.

"Hey!" he says when our eyes meet. He stands and pulls out the empty stool next to him for me to sit. "Good timing. That worked out well."

"Yes," I say, sitting down and running my hands over my skirt. "Meant to be, I guess." The small bar is quiet—too quiet. I feel like everyone in the room is listening to me.

"It's good to see you again," Andrew says. He has no idea, poor guy. No idea at all what the time bridging our night out to today has consisted of for me. *Do I tell him what's happening?* I want a drink.

I nod toward his glass, which is filled with a tawny liquid and has an artful sliver of orange peel christening the top. It looks like something I'm in the mood for. "What are you drinking?"

"A Sazerac."

"Okay," I say to the bartender, who is standing a polite distance from us, not wanting to interrupt but at the ready to take my order. "I'll have one of those."

"So how was your day?" he asks.

I tell Andrew about the patients from hell and then we chat politely about the restaurant, each of us leaning carefully—not too close—over the paper menu in front of us. I want to have a good time. I *need* to have a good time. But something about this feels like too big a risk. I should be at home, where it's safe. *And lonely*, I think. I need to stop wallowing.

I grab my glass off of the bar, take my first sip of my drink, and it burns. The next sip—I barely breathe between them—is more palatable.

"I've never had one of these before," I say.

"It's good, right? The official cocktail of New Orleans," he says.

"I love it there." There was a blurry spring break trip during my senior year of college, and I always wanted to go back and see it for real. We always said we would.

"I've spent some time there," he says.

"Oh, yeah?"

"I actually lived there for a few months."

"Just a few months?" I raise an eyebrow and smile. I hate how I'm faking it. I think of Owen in some hotel room in Texas, hanging up his funeral suit.

He smiles back, oblivious. "I was following an old girlfriend. It wasn't the healthiest relationship."

"Ah."

"I suppose we all have them."

The words hang in the air. Does he realize what he's just said to me? I slug a sip of my drink.

"You don't agree?" he asks.

"No, I do," I say. *Has Jack told him? Is this his way of trying to suss out some answers?*

His elbow knocks mine and I realize that I've been sitting here slumped against the bar like some old-timer in a smoky pub. I think of the song that my mother used to sing at dinner—*Daphne Mitchell, strong and able, get your elbows off the table.*

"Tell me more about her," I say.

"Isn't that breaking some dating rule?" he says. "Talking about former relationships?" His word choices may as well be tacked on the wall behind him and lined in neon: *Dating. Former.*

"Is this a date?"

"I don't know," he says, leaning in like it's good gossip.

I'm *married*, I think. *What am I doing?*

"New Orleans," I say, pointing at him with my pinky as I tip my glass to my mouth.

"Her name was Simone."

I roll my eyes. "Really?"

"Yep."

"How did you meet her?"

"In a bar, of all places. When I lived in L.A. after college. She was on vacation."

"Long distance?"

He shrugs. "I was twenty-four. She was exotic to me. I had no real job. New Orleans sounded fun."

"Was it?"

"Yes, actually," he says. "It was. I don't regret it."

"Whose fault was it?"

"Well it's always both people's, isn't it?" he says.

*Seriously?* I feel like my stool should drop into a hole in the floor. Someone should hit a drum cymbal. *Ta-dum-dum.*

"That's debatable."

"I'm sorry," he says. I look into his eyes, trying to decipher whether he knows. I should just ask him but I'm not sure that I want the answer. And I don't want to talk about it. I don't want to think about anything at all. His eyes are deep brown, like chocolate. The opposite of Owen's.

"Did it take you a long time to get over her?" I ask, not giving him a chance to elaborate.

"It took longer to get over New Orleans."

"So then you moved to San Francisco."

"No, first Sydney, then San Francisco."

"Sydney?"

He nods once.

"Another girl?" *Do I care? It actually doesn't matter what he says. This is about* fun, *not so much about talking.* I hear Lucy's voice in my head. *Go have fun. Fun! Is this fun?*

"It wasn't a girl," he laughs. "It was a job. Just for six months."

"A six-month job?"

"A friend from here set it up, actually. His father works with a big hotel chain there, they needed extra help with the lead-up to the Summer Olympics."

"That must have been an experience."

"Yeah. It's actually what got me interested in the hotel business."

"Simone must have become a quickly fading memory, what with all of the blondes. It's like a country full of Barbie dolls, yes?"

I feel myself relaxing, the warm relief from the whiskey kicking in, washing over me from my head to my feet, a welcome loosening.

"What are you suggesting?" he says. "Trust me, I'm no globe-trotting lothario."

I laugh and gasp simultaneously, my drink spraying.

"Well, maybe I am, then! If it's so unbelievable." He laughs, handing me his cocktail napkin.

"I'm sorry." I clear my throat. *"Globe-trotting lothario."* I want to ask about the woman at the farmers' market but I don't. "I'll stop with the inquisition."

"It's okay. I would rather talk about you anyway."

"Eh." I sigh.

He raises his eyebrows at me.

"Jack told you a few things?" I just go for it. Let's get it over with, deal with the disaster.

He shrugs. "He told me some."

"Great story, isn't it?" I grab my glass off of the bar and take another drink.

"Listen," he starts, angling himself toward me. "I'm really sorry."

I put my palm out. "You don't know the half of it."

I consider whether to elaborate, and I'm tempted, even though I really don't know him at all. I don't know his history, his hopes, his fears—I don't even know what his major was in college, whether he reads, what his family is like—but there is something about the way that he looks at me that makes me feel like I could tell him everything and it would be okay. Maybe (probably) it's just the alcohol, but the point is that I don't care what he knows, and that in and of itself is an improvement over the past few weeks.

"How about dinner?" he says, signaling to the bartender to bring us another round.

An hour earlier, I was in the harsh, commercial stink of the grocery store, clinging to an old habit. "That sounds wonderful," I say, pushing out the words and silently thanking my sister.

I kiss him. I don't mean to, but I kiss him. It is two hours later and we are standing next to my car and there is rain softly falling and, well, he leans toward me and I kiss him. It is strange, like I've never done it before, and wonderful, like I've never done it before, and the minute we pull away from each other, right after he brushes his thumb against my mouth and puts his hand on my back, pulling me gently toward him again, I feel guilty. The zing plummets like a dying radio signal. He must see this on my face, because when he pulls back, the first thing out of his mouth is that he's sorry.

"It's okay," I say.

"No, I shouldn't have—"

"Really, it's okay," I say. And it is. I *know* that it is. My heart is racing. I'm a married woman, a bona fide grown-up, kissing a man I barely know, but it's what had to happen. I'm certain of it.

"I had fun tonight," I say, and despite the fact that I can barely catch my breath—*Owen*—I mean it. I really do. Finally.

# CHAPTER NINETEEN

It is two days since my night out with Andrew, and Owen is asleep, collapsed on the couch in yesterday's clothes like he spent the night at a fraternity party. I'm sitting across from him, in the sagging armchair that I bought in a secondhand store when I first moved to Durham. I tuck my feet under myself and wait.

He got in around midnight—I was upstairs in bed, reading *The Woman in White* for Annie's book club. "It will scare the shit out of you," Annie said. "You'll be completely absorbed. It will be good for you."

I wasn't absorbed. I heard the door bang shut downstairs and I put the book down and listened. He turned on the television—*SportsCenter*—and in between the snapping commentary and the set-to-music game clips, I started to hear it again. Owen crying. Big gulping hiccups.

Blue got up and squeezed through the door, her claws *clack-clack*ing on the wood steps as she went to him. I did not. I picked up my book and tried to concentrate on the words but I just kept reading the same line over and over again. *Silence is safe. Silence is safe. Silence is safe.* The line seemed somehow prophetic, like that thing that people do where they pick up a Bible and lay their finger on a page and wherever it lands is the scripture you're meant to see.

∞

I watch him, the man whom I've loved for nearly half of my life. He is the soundest sleeper I've ever encountered—an inanimate dreamer.

We bought a king-sized bed a few years ago, even though it took up all but a moat of space around the perimeter of the small bedroom in our old apartment. It was something I insisted on after nagging about it for years. I wanted space, to lie in a lazy X across the mattress, to be able to roll over without having my face hit the space between his shoulder blades. Owen didn't agree, and even when he finally did and I managed to get him standing in front of the bleak sales guy in the dim, soupy light of the mattress store, he whispered to me that he still didn't want a new bed. "We'll never snuggle with all of that space," he joked into my ear. "We'll need separate zip codes."

And he was right. For the first few weeks, I scooched over to his side or he to mine, but before long, the invisible line separating our sides became more of a no-cross zone, and in the years since, it was the way that we preferred it, or so I thought. He came to bed much later, getting off work so late, and when he kissed me good night, *if* he kissed me good night, I wasn't awake to notice. I slept heavily, unconsciously. I took his presence for granted, and I hate myself for that now.

*I kissed someone else*, I think, watching him sleep. How would he react if I told him? Would he be angry? Or relieved because I'd evened the score in some way? Would it feel good to see the surprise on his face? Deep down, I know it wouldn't, even if there's a part of me that likes having my little secret. My mind can rest in that moment. For those few minutes in the parking lot, I was just Daphne—not Daphne the betrayed wife, Daphne with the messed-up marriage.

I get up and walk across the room to the kitchen to make coffee. At first, I'm careful as I unfurl the top of the bag of grounds, easy as I slide the machine across the countertop, but then I can't take it. I open the cabinets and slam them shut, find a couple of mugs and clink them on to the countertop. I call for Blue from fifteen feet, clapping my hands. "Come on, girl!"

I want to know about Texas, if it helped him. The anticipation is killing me.

He turns onto his back and I watch from behind the kitchen island. We wanted one big great room, one big kitchen and living space, and so we tore down the wall between the two. The contractor let us take turns with the sledgehammer. *The room will be great for parties*, we said (as if we ever entertained more than the thought of entertaining), *and good for kids.*

His eyes adjust to the light and he realizes where he fell asleep. He throws an arm over his face, curls up into himself.

"Hey," I say.

He startles and sits up. "I didn't know you were standing there."

I rap my fingernails against one of the empty mugs. "Do you want some coffee? It's almost ready."

He nods and runs his hands through his hair. When he gets up and walks toward me, it's not like before, the "good mornings" that always included a quick kiss, an idle three-second back scratch, a squeeze of my shoulder, and I've missed it, no matter how perfunctory those gestures might have been. It's like missing the box of tissues on your table, the scissors in the drawer, a can opener. These mundane everyday things that don't even register until you need them. How did I push Owen into that category? I miss so many things.

He pulls out one of the kitchen stools, sits down at the island, and rubs his eyes with the knuckles of his index fingers.

"How was it?" I venture.

He doesn't say anything at first. I watch him trace his finger along the countertop in an infinity sign.

"It was difficult," he says.

Our eyes meet for just a fleeting second.

"There were a lot of people there. Hundreds."

I turn to fill our coffee cups. Owen likes his light and sweet, what people call a *regular* in Massachusetts. I pass it to him across the counter. "Thank you," he says, not looking at me.

"Does she have a big family?" I ask, handing him the half-and-half.

He nods. "Two brothers. They all live there, and all of the aunts and uncles and cousins. And I think that with her being so young…I'd thought that there might be a lot of people, but I was still surprised at the turnout. I think it probably helped her parents, seeing all of the support."

I nod but he doesn't look at me and doesn't see it.

"A couple of former patients came."

"That's nice," I say. I think back to that newspaper article I found on the Internet, about the teenaged boy in New Jersey whom she counseled. I wonder if he is still alive. I bet he would have made the trip.

"It was strange for me to go," he says, rubbing his eyes.

"Why?"

"Nobody knew." He glances at me. "About the two of us. There was Christine, her roommate here. She knew. And I'd met her parents here at the hospital. But even one of her brothers, when I introduced myself, assumed that I was her boss. He told me that it was nice of me to make the trip for a coworker."

I'm glad to finally know but I wonder why he's telling me

this—does he feel badly about it, that she didn't share the details of her romantic life with her family? Or does he mean for it to make me feel better somehow, to try to minimize the depth of their relationship? So I ask: *Why are you telling me this?*

Our eyes meet then. "I don't know." He scratches the crown of his head. It's a gesture that he makes when he's uncomfortable, like when he first met my father. I've seen him do it a thousand times.

He rubs his hands together like he's cold.

*She had a roommate. What did she think about all of this? Does she know who I am? Has she seen me out—having dinner with Annie, buying groceries—and whispered to a friend that I'm the one, the one whose husband Bridget is seeing?*

I pour my coffee down the drain, even though the mug is nearly full. It suddenly tastes too bitter. "I'm sorry that you're dealing with this, Owen," I say. What else do you do? There's no Hallmark card for it. *So sorry for the loss of the woman you cheated on me with.*

"Thank you."

When I arrive at the office an hour later, I boot up my laptop, turning tiny semicircles in my desk chair as I wait for it. My screensaver appears—a photo of Blue on the day we moved into the house. One of the movers had left one of those huge cardboard wardrobe boxes lying sideways on the front porch, and with all of the commotion, she'd crawled inside to get some escape, her huge black blocky head poking out of one side to keep an eye on things.

I get online and find the website for the *Austin American-Statesman*. I click on the obituaries and type in Bridget's name.

It's just three short paragraphs, no photo.

*Bridget Batton, 26, of Austin, was laid to rest on April 18 at St. Michael's Episcopal Church. She is survived by her parents, Dr. Aaron Batton and Mrs. Luanne Batton, both of Austin, and brothers Brian Batton, of Dallas, and William Batton, of Austin. Ms. Batton was a graduate of McCallum High School and the University of Texas. She received a master's degree in social work from Columbia University.*

*Spirited and loving, Ms. Batton loved camping, singing and dancing, and spending time with her many friends, who say that she was often the first person to call when something wonderful or tragic happened. She was famous for her blueberry corn muffins, her karaoke rendition of "Jolene," and her abiding love for the Texas Longhorns football team. A skilled athlete herself, Ms. Batton was a Junior Olympic swimmer and often competed in charity triathlons.*

*Most recently, she was a social worker at Duke University Medical Center in Durham, North Carolina, where she counseled pediatric cancer patients and their families. Her life's work was helping others, giving hope when there often was none, and encouraging faith at the most difficult crossroads of a family's journey. In lieu of flowers, the family asks that donations be given to the St. Baldrick's Foundation, a pediatric cancer charity to which Ms. Batton often donated her time.*

I read it over and over again. She sounded lovely. Under different circumstances, we might have been friends. I wipe my tears, take a deep breath, and then, knowing that I only have a few minutes before I need to go over my schedule for the day, I find the website for St. Baldrick's and make an anonymous $100 donation in her memory.

∞

My phone rings just as I'm turning away from the computer. The area code is 415—San Francisco. "Good morning, Dr. Mitchell," Andrew says.

"Good morning," I say, trying to sound light.

"How are you today?"

I laugh a little. What other option is there?

"What?" He chuckles in response.

"Oh, it's nothing," I say.

"Listen, I was calling to see if you have plans tonight."

*Plans tonight.* Do I have plans tonight? I think of Owen at the kitchen counter. He needs me, but is it the best thing? For me?

"I do not," I say. I gulp it out. I force the words out of my mouth the way you'd remove a marble from the inside of a toddler's cheek with one crooked finger. "I'm free."

"Great! I thought maybe you could come for dinner."

"I can," I say. I close my eyes. I think of Lucy the other day. *Remember what he did to you!* I think of that kiss. I think of everyone who's imploring me to move on. *Go ahead, dive.* "What time and what can I bring?"

# CHAPTER TWENTY

Andrew's cousin is an archeology professor at Duke who's on sabbatical for the semester, and Andrew is staying at her loft downtown while she's somewhere overseas on a dig. The apartment is in a renovated textile mill near the minor league baseball park, right over the railroad tracks that cross through town. I hear a train roaring by as I'm waiting for the elevator to take me up to his place. It does nothing to drown out the way my heart is pounding in my chest.

I can hear music softly playing behind the door when I knock, and when he answers, the scent of rosemary wafts into the hallway. He must see on my face how this pleases me, because as he kisses my cheek, sweetly, discreetly, and takes the bottle of wine that I've brought, the first thing that he says is that he hopes I like roasted chicken.

I do, of course. I told him when we went out to that concert, when we were doing our best not to let our conversation turn into a job interview–like litany of questions: *How many siblings do you have? Where did you go to school?* Roast chicken is my favorite meal. My mother made it every Sunday night when we were growing up, and the smell—the indelible, homey, heartwarming smell— there's nothing better.

"Smooth move," I joke, because I can't help it. "It smells delicious."

"Good," he says. "But I have to warn you—I've never done this before. I almost cheated and stuck a rotisserie chicken from the grocery store in the oven but my mother assured me that I could handle it."

"Your mother?" I tease.

"What?" He smiles, handing me a glass of wine from the bottle that's open on the counter. "Can you think of a better reason for a man—even a forty-one-year-old man—to ask his mother for advice than when it's before making a woman dinner for the first time?"

"I suppose that's true," I say, wondering again why he's single. I can feel my face relaxing, my shoulders dropping. My mother used to physically push my shoulders down, as a joke that I never thought was all that funny. *Relax, Daphne. Take it easy.*

"I also needed to borrow her roasting pan," Andrew says.

"Oh, I see." I laugh.

"And her meat thermometer."

"I thought you said that you like to cook."

"When did I say that?" he says, leading me onto the patio.

"The other night at Nana's." It feels illicit to bring up the night that we kissed, and silly to feel that way—aren't we adults, after all? "You mentioned something about how the gnocchi reminded you of a recipe."

"Well, yes, I can boil some pasta," he says, leading me outside. "And I own a skillet, so I can do eggs. And stir-fries."

"And grill?" I ask, pointing to the Weber in the corner.

"Obviously," he says. "I do have a Y chromosome."

"Har-har." *Is this how I flirt? Sarcastic banter?* "I actually make a great grilled ribeye. And grilled salmon—I'm good at that, too." *Owen loves it,* I think. *No, he* loved *it.*

"Is that so?" He smiles. He always seems to be smiling, and I'm starting to believe that it's an unforced, completely natural thing for him. "Well, I'll have to take you up on that offer then."

"That was an offer?" I say.

"I hope so."


The dinner is delicious.

"Your chicken is almost as good as my mother's," I say, putting down my fork. I think of Owen eating a bowl of cereal at our kitchen table in the dark, and maybe it should maybe make me happy that he's paying his penance, but it just makes me sad.

"Almost as good as your mother's is a compliment I'll take," Andrew says. There is no furniture on the patio but we decided to eat outside anyway because it's such a beautiful night. He found a blanket in the linen closet—a blue, batik print one that reminds me of the kind of thing that my friends and I hung on the walls of our dorm rooms in college.

"So tell me about your cousin," I say. "Where is this dig she's directing?"

"She's in the south of France, in the Perigord region."

"I don't know it."

"It's an area known mainly for its foie gras and truffles."

"She's excavating truffles?"

He laughs. "There's some cave there. I'm not exactly sure."

Her apartment looks like what I would imagine an archeology professor's would—lots of printed wall hangings, statues, lithographs, oddly shaped rocks displayed as art. I'm sure it's all significant but, to my untrained eye, it doesn't look much different than a Pier 1 Imports showroom.

"What's your place like in San Francisco?" I ask.

"Well," he starts, stacking our plates and setting them to the side so that he can settle in closer to me. I let him. I lean back against the wall and admire the sunset, orange and pink, casting a delicate glow over everything. "The cost of living is a bit different out there."

"I am aware," I say. I swirl my wine in my glass.

"I'm in Marin County, just north of the city. My place was originally an old barn but the architect who owned it before I did turned it into a three bedroom."

"I bet it's amazing."

"It's not bad," he says.

"You can tell so much about a person by how they live." I think of my mother and her chaos, my reflexive obsessive neatness.

"That's true," he says. "Jack says your place is pretty great."

"Yes," I manage. "Do you miss being there? It's a bit more glamorous…"

"Than Durham? Nah." He smiles. "I love it here."

"I do, too." I look out at the skyline of former tobacco warehouses and mills, the water tower with the Lucky Strike logo, the brick smokestack, the trees beyond—the home I've come to love. *Could I leave now?* I wonder, permitting myself to fantasize a bit. *Could I take off for Northern California, find work in a little practice with a view of the Golden Gate Bridge, tour wineries on the weekends?*

"So how is it going…here?" I venture. I want to ask how much longer he plans to be in town but I don't want to seem too forward.

He looks at me before he speaks. "Actually, it's been pretty tough." He presses his lips together and squints at some deepdown thought. "Dad's doing much better but it's still not great," he confesses.

"I'm so sorry."

He tells me how he visits his father at the rehabilitation center for several hours each day, where he meets with the speech therapists and sits in on physical therapy sessions.

"I'm glad I've been able to be here to help out my mother," he says. "And meeting you has been an unexpected plus."

"It has," I say. I feel myself blush. "So what do you do when you're back home?" I ask, partly because I really want to know and partly because I'm too scared of what will happen if we wade into a conversation about us.

He reaches for the wine bottle and refills my glass. "I see movies, I go out to dinner, I work. The usual stuff. But I travel so much, to be honest, that I feel like I have to relearn how to just be at home every time I return from a trip."

I laugh.

"What?"

"It's just such a contrast from what I'm used to. My life is so predictable." *Was* so predictable, I think. "I can practically tell you what time I brush my teeth each night."

"That can't be true," he says.

"*I don't know*," I say in a singsongy voice. "Your life sounds pretty fabulous, I have to tell you. I think that most people I know would trade places with you."

"It's not bad," he says, winking.

I look at him for a moment, trying to decide whether to ask the question that's been on my mind. "Okay, I hope you won't be offended, but I have to ask," I say, taking a courage-building sip of my wine before I continue. "Why are you single?"

He laughs and tips his head back against the wall. "You sound like my mother."

I shrug. "It's a valid question, I think. I know that we don't know each other *that* well, but you seem relatively sane."

He laughs. "Relatively?"

"Well, like I said, we don't know each other that well," I joke.

He shifts his weight on the patio floor, and I can't tell if he's physically uncomfortable or if my question's made him that way. "I was in a relationship for a long time. It ended a couple of years ago," he says. "Are you sure you want the whole sordid story?" He smiles at me but for the first time it looks strained.

"Only if you're sure you don't mind telling me," I say.

"I don't mind," he says, and when our eyes meet, he holds my gaze for a moment before he begins. "So, I met her out there, through one of my business partners, and we were just good friends for a long time. She also travels a lot for her job, so it started out slowly, with one of us calling the other whenever we got back into town from wherever we'd been. We had a convenient kinship—we'd meet for dinner, lament about jet lag, quiz each other about which airports have the best frequent flyer lounges."

"What does she do?"

"She's a photojournalist. She started out at the *Chronicle* doing city politics but she's on her own now. She covers a lot of big headline stories—natural disasters, that sort of thing."

"That has to be intense."

"Yeah," he says. "And it requires a lot of spontaneity. You have to be okay with packing a suitcase and taking off at a moment's notice. My job isn't quite like that but we got each other, you know?"

I nod, thinking of how impulsiveness isn't something that's ever applied to me. "So what happened?"

"Well," he says. "I was in Chicago. We had just started scoping out that old bank for our next property, the one that Jack mentioned? And I was planning to surprise her. I'd schemed with one of her editors to concoct a fake business meeting on the East Coast, and the plan was to show up at the airport and whisk her off to Paris." He pauses and swirls the wine in his glass. "And, well, I was going to propose. But when I got there, ring in my front coat pocket and everything, she wasn't there. I waited for hours, tried every way I could think of to get in touch with her—I was worried that something had happened to her—but she had essentially vanished into thin air. When I eventually made it home, I found a letter from her explaining that the editor friend had slipped and told her. Turns out, she'd been secretly seeing another photographer she'd met years ago in Asia. They'd been rendezvousing during each other's assignments for years."

"Oh, Andrew," I say, putting my hand on his arm. "I'm so sorry."

"Yeah," he says. "It was pretty tough. I guess I've been a little gun-shy ever since."

"I can understand," I say. Our eyes meet and this time when he smiles at me, I'm sure it's sincere.

"I know you can." He squeezes my hand.

"How did you get through it?" I ask, wanting to know his secret.

"Hmm," he says. "Time, I guess? You know the old saying, *Time heals all wounds.*" He shrugs. "But I don't know, I wish whoever had said that could have been more specific. It's been two years for me and..." He laughs and shrugs again. "It does get easier. It really does."

I nod.

"I'm so sorry about what happened to you," he says.

"Thanks. It's been something." I shake my head. "You don't even know the whole story."

"Do you want to tell me?" He nudges closer to me and puts his hand over mine.

"I do," I say, realizing as I say it how much I mean it. I take a deep breath. "I guess the first thing is that he moved back in." As soon as the words are out of my mouth, I regret them. *Why did I start with that?* I feel the slightest jerk in his shoulder, in his leg next to mine, the unconscious tensing of his body in reaction to what I've said, and my heart starts to beat faster. "That sounds worse than I meant it...or maybe not worse, but different. Let me start over."

"It's okay, take your time."

I nod, and then I tell him everything, every last detail.

"So I don't know where this is going to go exactly," I finish, drowning the last bit of my wine. I feel a bit like my mouth has run off ahead of me, but I can't stop myself. "Despite everything he's done, I feel an obligation to help him through this. We're married, and he was—" I stop again. "He was everything." *Shit.*

When I finally get up the nerve to look at him, I expect to see disappointment in his eyes.

"I think it's honorable," he says, surprising me.

"Listen, I've loved spending time with you," I say, intent on steering the conversation toward something positive.

"Hey, Daphne, it's okay," he says, taking both my hands in his and looking into my eyes. "I get it. I really, really do."

I turn to him and search his face for signs that this has shifted things. Maybe he's as sincere as he sounds. Or maybe, who knows? Maybe he doesn't even really care that much. I still don't know what his relationship is to that woman at the farmers' market, despite the wedding ring I noticed on her finger. For all I know, I am one in a stable of many, solely a way to pass the time. I realize that it's paranoid of me to think this way, and something in my gut tells me that he's as genuine as he seems, but given how faulty my instincts have proven to be, I can't count anything out.

What I do know is that I need this one good thing in my life, whatever this one good thing is. I can't let what's happened with Owen's life spill over mine like water on paper. That's *his* life, not ours—something I need to remember. I need to lean away from him, as scary as the first steps might be. I *need* to. And for that very reason, before Andrew can give me any indication otherwise, I lean in and I kiss him, in a way that will show him how much I am here—or *trying* to be here. And I know, putting my hand to the nape of his neck, that I am doing it to convince myself of it, too.

# CHAPTER TWENTY-ONE

Annie is ignoring me. She made me vow to come to our book club meeting this month, and as I stand with a couple of women from her neighborhood, twenty minutes into a mind-numbing conversation about breastfeeding, I am shooting dirty looks at her that she is pretending not to see. Our book club (which, like much of my social life, is really Annie's) is a lovely mix of women from several corners of her life—they are other mothers, med school people she met at UNC, women who grew up with Jack or married people who did—and every time I attend one of their monthly meetings, which is probably quarterly, there are usually at least two or three women whom I enjoy chatting with, and I always end up telling myself on the drive home that I ought to make an effort to go more often.

I told Annie why I didn't want to come. It's my first social outing in Durham since everything happened and I have zero desire to spend the evening answering questions about my sad and sordid personal life. My biggest fear is that I'll feel marked—as if what Owen did to me is somehow contagious—but I mustered the courage to risk becoming "that poor woman" because I know I need to get out more. Being around Andrew has revealed, in full relief, just how quiet I've let my life become, and while a book club, of all things, is not exactly jumping out of an airplane, it's a step in the right direction.

That said, now that I am forehead-deep in a dissertation on nursing, I'm not sure that this is actually better than being at home, even if home means tiptoeing around Owen. I spot a plate of some sort of bruschetta-type thing on our host's kitchen table and make my exit, telling the two women, neither of whom hears me, that I'm starved.

"This looks delicious," I say to the person next to me, who is wiggling out of a windbreaker. When she turns to face me, we both startle—it's the woman from the farmers' market. I'll admit, she has the sort of aesthetic that I admire most in other women, in that she is wearing a button-down shirt that could have come from the boys' department with jeans and five-and-dime flip-flops, and she somehow looks more refined than any other woman in the room.

"Hey," I say. "We met—"

"The farmers' market," she says. I notice the way her eyes graze over me, assessing. "With Andrew." She doesn't say *Andy* this time.

"Yes," I say, trying to maneuver the messy piece of bruschetta I've just picked up. "Don't mind me," I joke, doing my best to be friendly.

"I brought those," she says.

*Of course you did.* "They look delicious."

"They are but I can't take any credit, I just followed my friend's recipe. Lots of garlic, just warning you." She grabs a cocktail napkin off of the table for me as I take a bite. She seems more relaxed than when I met her that morning. Maybe she's just one of those women who's different around men, like my sister.

"I am unapologetic about my love for garlic," I say, wiping my mouth with the napkin. "And I'm going to need this recipe. I'm Daphne, by the way."

"I remember," she says. "I'm Anson."

"Anson?"

"Yep," she says. "Named after my father."

"I bet you're tired of explaining that," I say. "But I like it."

"Thanks," she says. "I have a four-year-old. Her name is Jane."

"Ah," I say, laughing. *So she has a family?* "That's refreshing, actually."

"Do you have kids?" she asks.

"No, no, I don't," I say, skipping past it. Since I arrived here tonight, I've managed to deflect every personal question lobbed at me with vague answers and white lies. "But it's amazing what people name their children these days."

"Tell me about it." She laughs. "There's a child in my daughter's preschool class named Moniker."

*"Moniker?"* I cringe.

"You got it," she says. "I guess her parents thought they were being clever."

I raise my eyebrows. "They were being something."

"So what's your connection to this crowd?" she says, tucking her hair behind her ears.

"Annie Ridley," I say, pointing across the room to the couch where Annie's sitting with Nancy, her next-door neighbor who's one of those exasperating women who can't take a bite of food without lamenting about how fat it's making her.

"Oh, right, I knew that," she says. "Y'all are close?"

"We are," I say. "We work together."

"Have you seen much of Andrew?" she says, peering down at me.

*Ah, okay, so now that she's been friendly for a few minutes, she's ready to go in for the kill.* "Actually, I had dinner with him last night," I say, happy to have some material. She tries to hide it but the look on her face is like I've just smacked her. "You two know each other well?"

She rears back a little bit, laughing as she does. "Yes."

I can tell when she says it what it's code for: They have a history. I wonder how recent.

"We went to school together from kindergarten on up," she says. "I actually grew up around the corner from Jack. We did a lot of frog catching in the creek behind his house in the summers, a lot of kick-the-can in my front yard. My husband and I just moved back to the area. He teaches—he got a job at UNC. He was at Stanford."

"Oh, that's right. You were in California, too," I say, as if I'd forgotten. *She has a husband.*

"Yes, we were, but I rarely saw Andrew, with the way he's always running around." The way she says it feels like a warning.

"He's a lovely guy," I say, refusing to play along. "It's awful about his dad."

"He has a wonderful family," she says.

"You know them?"

"Well, you *knooow*," she says, drawing out the last syllable. "Andrew and I were high school sweethearts. And then we dated off and on in college during summer breaks. We reconnected, in the way that you do, and after college we drifted apart. I met my husband just after graduation and Andrew met some girl and moved to... where was it?"

*New Orleans,* I think.

"New Orleans," she says. "I guess we grew out of each other."

I can tell by the way that she's looking me over that that might not be the case, at least on her end.

"So... are you? Is it serious between you two?" she asks. "I'm sorry, is that too forward?" She puts her hand on my arm. Annie has lamented several times over the years—when her mother-in-law comes to the office unannounced, say, or when we're sitting in a restaurant and run into one of Jack's soccer pals—that Durham is too small. I feel this now.

"Andrew and me? Oh, I don't know," I say, leaving it at that.

"Really?" she says, cocking her head in a perplexed way that makes me wonder what he's told her.

"Really," I say. When we smile at each other, it's obvious how forced it is on both our parts—our grins are rubbery, threatening to snap.

"I wonder how long Andrew will stick around," she says, picking a piece of tomato off the top of one of the bruschetta and popping it into her mouth. "I saw Lorraine, his mother, yesterday and she mentioned that Andrew's dad will be released from his rehab center soon."

"Oh, really?" I say, doing my best to seem indifferent to the way that she's obviously trying to provoke me.

"I'm sure Andrew will be heading back to California any day now," she says.

I smile at her and look away. *I wonder why he didn't say anything last night.* The host is starting to gather the group in the family room for the discussion portion of the evening.

"I guess we should go sit," I say, catching Annie's eye so that she'll save me a spot next to her.

"Yes, we should," she says. She smiles at me, but it's one of those disingenuous Southern girl *bless-your-heart* smiles that is really telling you to go to hell. "It's *so* nice to see you again."


Several hours later, I wake up in the middle of the night and the room is spinning. I stumble to the bathroom, nauseous and sweating, and vomit into the toilet. *Food poisoning*, I think, remembering Anson and her bruschetta, the spinach dip I indulged in later, the brownie, the wine. After the retching subsides, I sit back against the wall, taking deep breaths, but as soon as I think it's over, it starts up again. My stomach convulses, my eyes water, my throat is raw. *Oh God, what did I eat?*

I am lying with my cheek against the cool tile floor when there's a gentle tap on the door. "Daph?" Owen's voice is scratchy. I woke him.

"I'm sick."

"You okay?"

I nudge the door open a crack with my foot and he steps in. He's wearing boxers and a gray Sox T-shirt. He never sleeps in a shirt, and it stings to know that he must have put it on before he came in here like I'm a stranger, somebody who hasn't seen him bare-chested hundreds of times.

He puts his hand on my shoulder. The room begins to rock. "Oh God, Owen. I'm going to throw up again." I crawl toward the toilet. "Get out."

He takes a step back as bitter yellow bile comes up, since there's nothing left in my stomach—and then he kneels behind me and rubs the space between my shoulder blades while my head hangs over the bowl. I realize, feeling his hand warm on my back, that it's the first time since everything happened that he's tried to touch me.

"What did you eat?" he says, once it's stopped.

"I can't even think about it." I pull a piece of toilet paper from the wall dispenser and wipe my nose. "Owen, go back to bed. I'll be fine."

He gets up but a few seconds later I hear the water running, and then he brings me a glass. I take it from him and place it on the floor next to me.

He sits beside me.

"Go to bed," I say again.

"It's okay," he says. "I wasn't really sleeping anyway."

The moonlight pours in from the window above us. Blue is just outside the threshold, watching us.

My stomach contracts and spasms, threatening to lurch. I take a few deep breaths and the feeling passes. "What time is it?" I ask. Owen always wears a watch, even when he sleeps.

"Almost four."

I wince. I have a full day ahead, including an early morning appointment with Mary Elizabeth.

"Think you'll make it in?" he says.

"I have to."

"Are you sure it's food poisoning? Anything else going around?"

"Not that I've seen," I say. "I'll text Annie later. I might not be the only one. Really, Owen, you should go to bed."

He shakes his head. "I'm fine here."

"It's just food poisoning. You need to be at work in a few hours."

"I know," he says. "I'm fine here."

We're both quiet. Blue snores next to us, sniffing and grunting. I try to concentrate on breathing through the nausea, perhaps also because it's easier than thinking about how awkward this is to be sitting here with him, on the square tiles we laid one weekend last November, both of us wearing earphones and listening to our individual podcasts, not bothering to talk to each other.

"What do you have today?" I ask.

"A twelve-year-old from South Carolina. New patient."

I wonder what it's like for him now, tending to people whose lives hang in the balance while he's mourning someone. "You've become a really good doctor, Owen," I say.

"Thank you," he says. "You have, too."

I glance at him. There have been many times over the course of our relationship when I accused him, silently, of not taking my work seriously compared to his own. I never said anything about it—maybe out of pride, maybe even out of competition—but I sensed it in the way that he sometimes talked to me about his work, hammering out detailed explanations of things that I of course understand, and also in the distracted way that he'd act when I recounted stories from my workday, as if the way that I care for patients couldn't possibly be as interesting, or as important, as what he does.

"Can I get you some crackers or something?" he says.

"I'm fine."

We sit there, the moonlight spilling over us. As strange as this is, and as rotten as I feel, something about being here together feels good. He leans forward to pat the top of Blue's head and I watch how her eyelids grow heavy as he starts to scratch behind her ears. There is a question that has been haunting me. I haven't asked it because I wasn't sure I wanted to know the answer. Maybe it's the circumstances of our unexpected comfortable silence, or maybe it's the psychological fog that comes in the middle of the night, and how it can make everything seem surreal, without consequence somehow, but I suddenly want to ask him.

He leans back against the wall.

"What if she were still alive?" I say.

He doesn't say anything. He shifts his feet on the tile, lining them up side by side.

"What if she were still alive, Owen?" I say again.

He puts his hand over mine on the cold floor and I let it stay there. "She's not, Daph." His fingers curl tight around my palm.

"But what if?"

He rests his head against the wall. "She's not here."

"And what does that *mean*?"

"It means that she's not here, Daph," he says, more forcefully this time.

I turn to look at him. His eyes are closed and his mouth is

pinched like he's the one who's sick. The taste in the back of my throat is metallic and sharp. I swallow against it.

"That's all you can tell me?" I say. "Nothing more?"

"I don't know that what-ifs will get us anywhere," he says. It is so typically him, so logical and reasonable. He was never one for speculating, and it drove so many of our arguments, how he could never just guess at a thing.

"You should go to bed," I say after a while.

"You should, too." He stands and puts his hand out, to help me off of the floor.

"Do you feel better?" he asks, as we step over Blue and into the bedroom.

*Do I?*

I don't give him an answer because I don't have one. I get into bed, my back to him, and listen as he walks down the hall and closes the door, the click of the latch behind him sounding final.


There are things that I remember from my childhood for no apparent reason. For instance, February 27 is Laura Ross's birthday. Laura Ross and I used to make Swiss Miss hot chocolate—the kind with the tiny, freeze-dried marshmallows—in her kitchen every day after school. Actually, we'd usually just pry the lid off the canister of powdered mix and pick out the marshmallows with our fingers. We'd sit on the counter, licking our fingertips and laughing at the handmade signs that her older sister had taped to the refrigerator, like "97 LBS!!!" in big blue bubble letters. In sixth grade, Laura's aunt took us to a Donna Summer concert, where we sang "Bad Girls" with such enthusiasm that you would think that we actually knew what the song was about. I haven't spoken to Laura since seventh grade, when her family moved out of our cul-de-sac and back to Indiana, and I wouldn't recognize her now if she showed up on my front stoop, but every February 27, I remember: Laura Ross's birthday.

I remember the time that my second-grade class made paper after studying colonial America. I remember the pulpy smell of it, and the soft, puppy-ear feel of it once it dried, and how much it annoyed me that my marker bled all over the bumpy surface when I tried to write my name.

I remember a summer afternoon at the community center pool when I was six, when I stood against the chain-link fence, my feet making wet-brown spots on the concrete, and watched my sixteen-year-old cousin do a flip off the diving board. It was the most amazing thing I'd ever seen in my life.

The memories are insignificant little nothings, throwaways, meant to be forgotten, which makes it odd that I recall them with such absolute precision compared to the milestone moments in my life—the day that I went away to college, how it felt when Owen and I moved in together, my first day of work as an M.D., losing my virginity, getting the keys to my first place, even our wedding day. These days—these important, formative, defining moments—are murky. It takes work to conjure up the details.

Add to that list: Owen's birthday, the night when he told me that he'd cheated.

I lie in bed, wracking my brain, trying to recall exactly what happened. Maybe it's that the shock hasn't worn off, some sort of PTSD, the cortisol clouding my neurologic well-being, but I feel like I can hardly remember it now. I remember how I felt. I remember being awake all night, the crying. I remember how I felt sick and scared, but I don't remember what he said or how I replied. I don't remember him walking out the door, or what I did immediately after. And I never thought I'd say this, but I now wish that every second of it was seared into me, because it might give me a little clarity.

# CHAPTER TWENTY-TWO

I make it to work the next morning even though I threw up again just before sunrise, and then again after a misguided attempt at some toast, and one final time just after I arrived at the office, where the smell of the coffee that someone had brewed sent me sprinting for the ladies' room. Annie says that as far as she knows, none of the other women got sick. I have irrationally decided to blame Anson's bruschetta, though at this point, I wonder whether the residual nausea this morning is actually my body's way of telling me that enough is enough: It won't take the emotional roller coaster anymore.

Owen was already gone when I came downstairs. He left a note on the kitchen counter, on the back of a crumpled receipt. *Hope you feel better*, it said in his familiar handwriting, all sharp angles and arrowheads. *Call if you need me.* I turned the receipt over. It was from a burger place downtown, two months ago. Fourteen dollars. Is lunch for one fourteen dollars? Does it matter anymore?

The only reason I'm at work is Mary Elizabeth's appointment—and thank God, she's here, now sitting across from me, in a T-shirt, pink twill shorts, flip-flops, her hair still wet from her shower. She looks like a kid.

"Do you love your job?" she asks out of nowhere as I look over the vitals that Carol took at the beginning of the appointment.

"I do," I say, glancing up from the notes. "How's your sugar today?"

"Excellent," she says.

Our eyes meet.

"Seriously," she says. "It's fine."

I scroll through the numbers. Her blood pressure is up slightly. Maybe she's nervous, as she should be after our last visit.

"I hate my job," she says.

"From what I can gather, you're lucky to still have it," I say, putting the laptop down and walking to the sink in the corner of the room to wash my hands.

She scowls at me. "Fair enough," she says. "But still, it sucks. When you're the youngest one at the law firm, you get the grunt work. I spent twelve hours yesterday in a room full of documents—stacks and stacks of boxes, some as high as the ceiling. Do you know what I had to do?"

"Tell me."

"Go through the pages one by one and circle the last name of the plaintiff in a case that the firm is handling. Thousands of pages. In twelve hours, I made it through two stacks."

"Well, like you said, youngest one at the firm, you get the grunt work. It will get better."

"It must be great, doing what you do, way more interesting to help fuck-ups like me," she says as I walk toward her.

"Is that how you define yourself, Mary Elizabeth?" I say, pulling my ophthalmoscope out to examine her eyes.

"Pretty much. It's accurate, no?"

"I guess so."

"I can't believe you just said that!" she shrieks.

"What?"

"Called me a fuck-up."

"You called yourself that." I probably shouldn't be so snippy with her but I'm fed up—with everything—including her inability to get herself straight despite the very best medical care from a team of specialists that thousands of families would kill to have watching over their privileged addict daughters. And, okay, maybe I'm displacing some of my own stuff onto her—up all night, Owen sitting next to me in the bathroom, his nonanswer when I asked him whether things might be different between us if Bridget was alive. *I don't know if the what-ifs will get us anywhere.* Really? *Says who?*

"So did you always want to be a doctor?" Mary Elizabeth says.

"Did you always want to be a fuck-up?" I reply, my fingers on her neck, checking her pulse.

Her jaw drops. And then she laughs, thank goodness. I smile at her.

"What have you been doing besides drinking? What other drugs?" I ask, crossing my hands over my chest and leaning my hip against the exam table.

She looks down at her knees. "Can't you talk to Denise about this?"

"What you guys discuss during your therapy sessions is between the two of you. You know that."

"Denise is kind of a freak, don't you think?" she jokes, trying to deflect my question.

"Mary Elizabeth, come on." The thing is, she's right. While I'm fully aware that the amount of therapy I probably need to deal with my stuff could easily pay for a vacation home, I guess I'm a stereotypical physician in that I think most shrinks are a little bit off, what with all of those hours spent wading through other people's problems. Denise is a kind woman who seems to be good at what she does, but she's also one of those adults who never outgrew Disney. Her office is blanketed in little Mickey and Minnie figurines, the plastic kind like what comes in a Happy Meal, and she and her husband, who don't have children, take several Disney vacations each year. Annie jokes that she's probably a freak in bed.

"What else besides drinking?" I ask again.

She shrugs. "I smoked some weed in school. Not for years now, though. Sometimes some Xanax, Klonopin."

"While you're drinking?"

"As opposed to?"

"And you're drinking all day?"

"Let me repeat: I spent twelve hours yesterday circling the name *Ferguson*."

"Nothing else? Not snorting anything? No other pills?"

"Honestly, no."

"How do you feel about inpatient?"

"*Finally*," she says. "I was wondering when you'd get to it."

"And?"

"I guess I should. Do I have a choice?"

"You're a grown woman."

"Tell that to my mother." She looks up at the ceiling, where the state-of-the-art LED system is subtly shifting the light from blue to green and then blue again. I wonder whether it actually relaxes people the way that it's supposed to. "When I went to the eating disorders place, I was the sanest one by a mile so I suppose going to rehab would be a good confidence boost. And the stories—I bet that the addicts have better stories than the ED girls. They were big whiners."

"Not you, though?" I say.

She cocks an eyebrow at me.

"Are you sober right now?"

"I am," she says.

I believe her, actually. I'm standing close enough to smell her breath and her speech is sharp, her eyes are clear.

"So you never wanted to be anything but a doctor?" she says. "You always knew? That's so lucky."

"I guess it is," I say, thinking how the last way I'd describe my life right now is *lucky*. "So you'll need to take a leave from work. Do you think that will be a problem?"

"My bosses will probably welcome the excuse to get rid of me."

"Denise is going to talk to you about the particulars," I say. "But we're going to stay in touch so that I can monitor you physically and make sure you're staying healthy."

Out of nowhere, she starts to cry.

"Hey, it's going to be all right," I say, patting her arm. "This can change everything for you."

When she looks up, she rolls her eyes at me. "We'll see," she says.

"Oh, come on." I hand her a tissue.

She yawns. A deep, thick had-enough sort of yawn. "I feel like something happened to me after high school."

"*Did* something happen?" I check my watch. She has an appointment with Denise after ours.

She shrugs. "No, not really. But all of the sudden, I don't know...I just keep making mistakes. I thought law school, becoming a lawyer—you know, finding a respectable profession— would make everything work out. How are you so together?"

I laugh.

"What? Look at you," she says. "I feel like I don't have any control over my life. I could never be like you."

"You don't know what you're talking about."

"Why are you so defensive?" she says. "I keep complimenting you and you act like I'm poking you in the ribs with a pencil."

"I'm not defensive," I say, realizing that I am. "I just prefer not to talk about my personal life in the office."

"Excuse me," she says, hopping off of the table.

"Denise is going to be waiting for you," I say. "I'll talk to her after your appointment."

She starts toward the door, waving the back of her hand at me like she doesn't need to hear anything else.

"Hey, Mary Elizabeth, listen: This is going to be good for you."

Suddenly, she turns and hugs me. "Thanks," she says, sniffling into the side of my neck. "I really hope you're right."

After she leaves, I close the door to the exam room and sit down at the little desk in the corner. I tell myself I'm just wiped out from throwing up all night, but it's the conversation with Mary Elizabeth that has me rattled. Was it inane of me to think that life was as simple as clicking together a few puzzle pieces? *College, doctor, marriage, kids, done.* I have always been so careful with my decisions, and maybe the error was in trying to plot it out, to predict everything—an equation that, it turns out, doesn't hold. Now that everything's fallen apart, what would it be like to chuck the compass? To check out for a bit? *Could I?*

I know how silly it is to look at Mary Elizabeth, who's so troubled, and covet her recklessness a little bit. There's obviously nothing I should envy, but in some way, the idea of living without thinking about the consequences—even the bad ones—seems so freeing, I'm sure because it's something I've never done. Her life is like bodysurfing in the ocean as a kid and that unexpected wave knocking you down, pulling you under, that instant when you're spinning, questioning—just for a second—if you'll ever come up for air. All chaos, no straight lines.

My mind starts spinning in its typical way—*What about the house and the mortgage? What would leaving the practice mean for my career?* I get up and, just as I'm turning into the hallway, nearly run smack into Dr. Billings.

"Excuse me!" I yelp. "I'm so sorry. I wasn't watching where I was going."

"Hello, Dr. Mitchell," he says in his even drone. "I just saw your patient."

"Yes," I say. "I think we've finally convinced her to try a treatment program. At long last."

"Well, that's great news," he says, nodding. "Good work."

"Thanks." I smile. *Good work.* It's only two words but it's the biggest compliment he's given me in months.

"Keep it up," he says, walking off.

Buoyed by my interaction with my boss and Mary Elizabeth's progress, I resolve on my drive home that whether Owen thinks the what-ifs matter or not, it's time to start making some decisions. I can't live in limbo anymore.

I walk in the house and his crap is everywhere—newspaper sections strewn across the kitchen table, dirty dishes piled in the sink, lights on that he neglected to turn off before he left for work. His stuff needs to go. I don't know what's going to happen with our marriage, and I don't know whether I can afford the house on my own if it comes to that, but I know for sure that he needs to be out of here. At least for now.

I'm picking up a pair of his shoes off the floor when I hear the door open behind me.

"Hey," Owen says, dropping his keys on the table. "You feeling better?"

I nod, barely glancing at him as I put the shoes on the bottom of the stairs and start collecting the newspapers. I don't have to say anything—he knows what I'm thinking because he's heard it before: *Look at this mess. Can't you pick up after yourself? You're a grown man. I'm not your mother.* Our phantom arguments worm their way back to me and I feel the telltale tightening in my chest that is always there now, lying latent.

"So I've been thinking that we need to start dealing with some logistics," I finally say, shoving the pile of newspapers into the recycling bin.

He stops and stares at me for a beat, then rubs his hands over his face like the very thought exhausts him. "Okay."

"I know it was well past midnight and I was throwing up, but last night I deserved a better answer than the one you gave me."

"About Bridget?"

I nod.

"I know."

"I realize that—" I have to stop myself before I can say it. "I realize—" I stop again. "I know that you're grieving, Owen, but you also need to understand that it's crazy for us to be living here together as if nothing's happened."

He nods. "I've been thinking about that, too."

"You have?"

He nods again.

"I can't move forward like this. We've barely even spoken about anything. We're in this house together every night avoiding each other, avoiding everything!" I rub the heels of my hands over my eyes. "I don't know how much longer I can just go with the flow. It's not right."

"I understand," he says. "So you want me to move out?"

I look at him, leaning across the kitchen counter from me. *Of course I don't want you to move out. I want you to not have cheated on me. I want our marriage, pure and true, the way that I thought it was.* "I need to move forward," I say.

He looks at me for a lingering moment and nods.

I turn away. "Maybe we need to start thinking about selling the house," I say, walking to the pantry for the broom.

"Really?" he says, surprised. It's irritating that he's surprised. Does he not realize the magnitude of what's happened?

"Yes, maybe," I snap. "It's not what I want, Owen, but then again, not much is these days."

He scratches the back of his head. He seems anxious and impatient. "I definitely don't want to sell the house."

"Listen, I don't want to give it up any more than you do, not after all of the work we put into it," I say, shaking my head. "But I can't handle the mortgage on my own and you can't either." I start sweeping, my eyes following the lines in the hardwood planks.

"No, Daphne, I don't want us to sell the house because I want us to work this out. I don't want to split up."

I stop sweeping.

"I want to come back. I want to move forward. Together."

"I don't..." I shake my head. "I don't know, Owen." I grip the broom handle.

"Do you think it's possible?" he asks. "Does any part of you want to try?"

"I think that for the first time in my life, I don't trust my own thoughts." Our eyes meet for just an instant before I look away.

"Daph, I understand. But I think that what happened, all of it—and all of it my fault, I own it—was just a symptom of a larger problem. A larger, *solvable* problem."

"Which is?"

"That we took each other for granted."

"I agree with you," I concede. "We didn't prioritize our relationship at all. But what about Bridget, Owen? You still haven't answered me. What if she were still here?"

He turns away and looks out the window.

"I know how much you cared about her." I gulp the words out. "And I think this could be a reaction to her death, Owen. You feel alone. You're mourning her loss. You can't—" My mouth's gone dry. "I can't let you make me your fallback because she's gone now."

He turns back to me. "She was never going to replace you, Daphne," he says. "I cared about her, that's true, and I can't believe that she's gone. But what happened between her and me was never going anywhere. That sounds like a disrespectful thing to say now, I know. But it's the truth, Daphne. I said as much in that email I sent to you."

I think of the line from the email: *I am drowning in regret over the decision I made.*

"I meant every word of it, Daphne," he says, walking to me. "I regretted everything, and I *know* that you don't need to hear this, and I'm ashamed to admit it, but once she was in the accident, I didn't feel like I had a choice but to stick it out." He shakes his head. "I know how selfish it sounds, but I already felt like scum for what I did to you, and the thought of then doing that to her when she was going through what she was going through...I knew I'd made a big mistake. I *knew it*. I *promise* that this isn't just a reaction to what's happened. When you told me to stay away after Bridget called you, it decimated me. You were so angry, and rightfully so. I knew that what I'd done had cost me our marriage."

"Why the hell did you let her call me anyway?" I ask. "That was so bizarre."

"I didn't know she was going to. I left her room to get a coffee and when I came back, she was already dialing your number. She got it off my phone."

I turn and go back to the pantry for the dustpan, if only because I can't stand to look at him. My skin feels like it's on fire. I feel awful and I'm certain it has nothing to do with whatever hit me last night. "I don't know how to move on together, Owen," I say as I walk back into the room.

"You really don't?" he says.

"I don't know how to trust you again," I say. "I still don't know what your relationship with her really was. You told me that it was sex and that it was just the one time but that obviously wasn't the case."

He scratches the back of his head and nods. "You're right."

"So what was it?"

He pauses, taking in a big gulp of air. "It was a friendship," he finally says.

"A *friendship*?" I blink back the tears that are starting to well up in my eyes. "Owen, you owe me more than that."

He runs his hands through his hair and leans against the island. "It was a flirtation at first but it grew into a deeper friendship. And then one day soon after New Year's, after we came back from Virginia, she asked me to have a drink with her."

"And you'd missed her, over the holidays?" I ask.

He bites his lip. "It's not important now."

"It is, though," I say.

"I had missed her."

I nod. "It wasn't just the one time, was it?"

His eyes meet mine for a split second before he looks away. "It was a few times," he says. "And after the last time, I knew that she and I were starting to head down a road that we couldn't, and that's when I told you. I needed to sort out what I was feeling and why I was doing something that I never thought I was capable of. I felt like shit for what I'd done. I never wanted to hurt you. I needed the time on my own to figure out why I'd done it, Daph, not to continue sleeping with her. That was over. I swear." He wipes his nose and I realize that he's starting to cry, too. "I'll do anything, Daphne. I know I don't deserve it but I want another chance."

I glance around the kitchen, the heart of the home that we built together. I am now the only obstacle keeping us from moving forward, and if I just say it—*Let's try again*—I can have everything the way that I always intended it to be. I think of our vows: *For better or for worse. Till death do us part.*

"Does any part of you still love me?" he asks. *To love, honor, and cherish.*

I rest my forehead against the broom, my hands clasped over the handle, and close my eyes. "I love the you that I thought you were," I say.

"Daphne, I'm still that person."

"Owen," I say, finally letting myself really look at him. "You have no idea how badly I want to believe you."

I can see the disappointment come over his face. "So where do we go from here?" he says, his voice barely audible.

"I don't know," I say, resting the broom against the counter. "But I think you should move out, at least for a while."

"You need time," he says.

I nod. "I do."

# CHAPTER TWENTY-THREE

I feel crazy. I can't make a decision. Every time I look at him, I see her. Every time he looks at me, I see yearning. And so rather than be at home, where this thing is a monster, forcing me to examine it, I distract myself with Andrew. My personal board of advisors—Annie, Lucy, and my mother—agree that this is the best option.

We go out to dinner. We see an action movie. We stroll through Duke Gardens, Andrew pointing at various clumps of blooms as we walk and asking me to name them. We meet at a brewery downtown for beers. There's a bit more kissing—occasional, not serious, nothing more. I don't talk about Owen and he doesn't ask.

We get to know each other, and I find myself talking about things I haven't thought about in years. I tell him about my misguided attempt at cheerleading tryouts during my senior year of high school, when I decided, for a few weeks, that I wanted to be a bit more like Lucy. We talk about our college experiences and how different they were—mine, a small liberal arts school in New England not unlike the one that Owen went to, and his, a behemoth football-obsessed state school in the South. We connect over small, silly things: our mutual love for *Saturday Night Live*'s early years, our mutual disgust for sour cream. He grew up climbing trees, loves baseball. He didn't go to summer camp. Being with him makes me feel happy, even light, like his company is slowly rubbing off the tarnish of what happened to me.

Annie and I meet for a drink at Six Plates, a cozy wine bar with velvet furniture and soft lighting that is perfect for this unusually chilly night and my pensive mood.

"The fact that Owen wants to start over should make me feel better," I say, finally confessing some of the thoughts that have been buzzing between my ears. "It's what I should want to hear, isn't it?"

"Daphne," she says, plucking a sliver of cheese off the slate slab between us. "You know that the last thing I'm going to tell you is to trust a word out of his mouth. That's what my mother did—made promise after promise and broke every one."

"But why would he say the things he has if he didn't mean them?" I ask.

She laughs. "If I had the answer to that, I could've saved myself thousands of dollars in therapy. Listen, I speak from experience: You cannot trust him."

"But he's my husband."

"And my mother was *my mother*."

I nod, slowly spinning my wineglass by its stem.

"Is he moving out?"

"I told him that I thought it would be a good idea, for now at least. He's supposed to go look at some rentals next week."

"Do you feel good about that?"

I shake my head and shrug. "I don't know."

"It will probably help," she says.

"We'll see," I say. "What I really need is a break from all of this. I need to get out of town. I need a spa trip, an ashram retreat, wide-open space, anything. I want to be like *that*," I say, nodding toward a table of what I assume to be a certain type of Duke graduate student—they look wealthy, worldly, and far more sophisticated than I was at twenty-two. There are many, many bottles of wine on the table between them, plates and plates of food. They are laughing loud, celebrating something. "If I could just stop thinking," I say.

"Well, I won't argue with that," Annie says. "You don't have to scrutinize every little thing."

I make a face like I'm offended. "Right, because that's easy for me." I stick out my hand as if to introduce myself. "Daphne Mitchell, nice to meet you."

She chuckles. "Why don't you call Andrew?"

"I should," I say. "I owe him a call."

She nods once and pushes my phone toward me. "You need more therapeutic kissing," she says, wiggling her eyebrows.

"Right." I confessed to her last week. "By the way, did I tell you that Owen brought me flowers two days ago? Daffodils and daisies, left on the kitchen counter for me to find after work."

"Was there a card attached? *Sorry for ruining our marriage?*" she says.

"No, there wasn't," I say. "But he's trying."

"He called a florist, Daphne."

I tick-tock my head back and forth, considering it. "Yeah. I know."

She leans toward me. "You're too smart to let yourself get duped by him."

"Evidence would suggest otherwise." I take another sip of my wine. "Anyway, Andrew. Do you know what he said the other night?"

"What?"

"He said that doing his job well means enabling people to

have the fantasy that we all want when we stay in a hotel—to be coddled, to escape real life. It occurred to me when he said it that that's exactly what he's doing for me. Do you think he realizes it?"

She shrugs. "Does it matter?"

I grab my phone and hop off the barstool. "I'll be right back."


I walk outside intending to call Andrew but once I'm there, standing out on the bar's patio, I find that what I really want is a few moments to myself, away from Annie's well-intentioned, but nevertheless relentless, advice. I put my phone in my pocket and wrap my sweater tightly around myself, breathing in the cool, crisp air. It is torture to have this decision be my singular burden to carry. I don't want any action I take toward Owen to be a reaction to what he's said. I'll admit that there is a component to this that is about him earning it. He needs to understand that I can't forget. And even if it happens as simply as it could—I ask him back, snap my fingers, marriage resumes—there is work to do. We need to figure out how this happened. We need to fix things so that it doesn't happen again. I need to know that a hundred horrific thoughts won't ping into my brain every time he works late or takes a call in another room or walks out the door on his own.

I don't know, which is not a comfortable place for me to be. It never has been.

The other night, I was sitting in the backyard, my toes in the grass, sipping my wine, when I watched a plane carve a gentle arc across the sky in the far distance. It reminded me of my mother, who can't get on a plane unless she's heavily medicated, and a neighbor we had growing up who was a pilot. At a neighborhood Christmas party one year, I overheard him tell her that if she's on a plane and there's turbulence, she should ask for something to drink, put it on the tray table, and watch. The liquid will hardly move, which should calm her because it will prove that the bumps she feels aren't actually that bad. What Owen did to me is unquestionably abysmal, but I asked myself, watching the plane become a fading dot and then disappear, Does it have to destroy me from the inside out? Is it really unforgivable, or is this—the jolting terror that *seems* like the end—actually what we've needed to right ourselves? Maybe it's nothing to be scared of? A blessing, even.

I don't know how to say this to Owen yet. I want to figure out the exact right words. And so, following one of my father's many idiosyncratic life rules, I've decided to wait out this dilemma and hope that an answer comes to me. Or, as Dad would say, *When in doubt, don't.*

The fact is, Owen wants us back. And that tiny confirmation is enough to hold me bobbing, head above water, for the time being.

# CHAPTER TWENTY-FOUR

I have spent my entire Saturday morning cleaning. I have fluffed the throw pillows on the couch. I have folded the dish towel next to the sink into a precise rectangle. There is a new bottle of hand soap in the powder room.

Owen is going to be at the hospital for most of the weekend. None of the rentals he's seen has panned out yet but I'm hopeful that this will be the week. And thankful that work will keep him out of the house in the meantime.

I go to my closet, put on a pair of heels, and then halfway down the stairs, I take them off. Who wears their nice shoes around the house?

When Andrew arrives, I open the door before he has a chance to ring the bell. Blue, one step behind me, sniffs up and down his legs. He bends to scratch the top of her head.

"This is Blue," I say, gently tugging her away by her collar so that she'll give him a break.

"Blue?" he says. "What's the significance?"

"Like the Joni Mitchell album."

"Are you a Joni Mitchell fan?" he says.

"Nope. I actually can't stand her," I say, waving him in. I've never said it out loud before.

"A Case of You" was on the jukebox on the day Owen and I

reunited with each other at the start of residency. It's a song that I loathe, *always* loathed, but when it came on in the bar where we ended up for drinks, it was in the hazy, dopey hour when we realized that this was going to lead somewhere. *"What are the chances that the two of us, out of all of the people in the world, would find each other again?"* we marveled over our beers. *"That we would both choose to become doctors! And then both pick the same place for residency! And then both decide on the same afternoon, at the same time, to pick up a sandwich at the same restaurant!"* One month later, on the one-month anniversary we were young and sappy enough to celebrate, Owen played the song when he surprised me with a candlelit picnic, replete with sandwiches from the place, and I didn't have it in me to tell him how much I hate Joni Mitchell. I decided that I'd hold my secret, even years later, when his eyes lit up as he suggested it for our new puppy's name. I figured that at least we weren't naming her Joni. I could pretend that the Blue stood for something else—the ocean, the sky, the pond at his grandparents' house. It didn't matter, what was important was what it stood for, which was our history, which was unshakable at the time, to me.

"Your house is amazing," Andrew says, walking slowly down the hall, taking in the wall of windows at the back, the original moldings, the oak floors now so clean they shine.

"Come on in," I say, walking ahead of him.

"So this is the kitchen." I wave my hands around like I'm on one of those home makeover shows.

"Ohhhhh, a *kitchen*," he jokes.

"I guess it's obvious," I say.

He leans on the countertop, and something about the gesture, so casual and meaningless, suddenly makes me uncomfortable about having him here. It feels out of context in an alarming way, like I've cut-out collaged one part of my life and pasted him where he doesn't belong. Even though I know that Owen won't be home until very late tonight, I can't help but feel on edge, like I'm doing something dishonest and dangerous and I'm going to get caught.

*I am not doing anything wrong*, I remind myself.

I flitter into the living area. "Here's the living room," I say. "Do you say den? Family room? People say different things."

"Den, I think," he says, grinning at me, amused.

"And, out there—that's the back porch."

"Your green thumb is in evidence," he says, peeking through the glass-paned door at the herb garden I planted in large terra cotta pots by the steps.

"Yeah," I look around the first floor. "I guess you don't need to see the laundry room. The bathroom is over there," I point.

He takes a step toward me. "This is weird for you, isn't it?"

"No, no," I say, my voice high and completely unconvincing.

He raises an eyebrow. "You sure?"

I bite my lip. "It's a little weird. I never imagined that I'd have someone here."

"Someone *else*," he says, scrunching his nose.

"Yeah." I take a deep breath and pull away just as he's about to put his arm around me. I don't want his arm around me. Not now. Not here. "It doesn't make any sense, I know. I'm sorry."

"No, it's okay."

I walk back toward the kitchen. "You know what? Forget it. Forget that I said anything. Do you want something to drink? A beer?" I say, opening the door. I realize that my hands are shaking.

"I'm okay," he says. "In a little while."

"Let's go out back," I say. "To the patio." *Maybe if we go outside…*

"You got it," he says.

"I'm not taking you outside because it's too weird to be inside, just for the record," I say, smiling.

"I know," he laughs. "Daphne, it's fine."

"You know what?" I say, my hand on the doorknob, one foot halfway out the door. "Forget it. Let's stay in here." *I know how crazy I seem, it's just...settle down,* I tell myself.

"Okay." He laughs, less surely now, walking backward as he says it. I wouldn't blame him if he continued right out the front door and into his car.

"Let me show you the rest of the house." I walk to the stairs. Actually, it's more like marching. "Come on," I say, waving him toward me.

He follows behind. I can't tell whether he's entertained by the way I'm acting or alarmed.

"This is the guest room," I say once we're upstairs, walking past Owen's room, the door halfway open, the floor littered with his laundry. "Excuse the mess, I have a guest," I say over my shoulder, attempting a laugh. He fortunately laughs with me.

"This is my office," I say, walking into the center of the room and slicing my arms through the air.

"It's great," he says. "Love the windows." He points to the view of the rolling hills outside.

"Who's this?" he says, picking up a framed photo of Lucy on my bookshelf. "Your sister?"

"That's the one."

"She looks about like I thought she would," he says. In the picture, from college, she is posing like a magazine cover girl, turned three-quarters toward the camera with her hands on her hips. "You see much of her?"

"Some."

I think of the text that she sent me this morning, after I told her that I'd invited Andrew over: Sleep with him, please.

I start to walk out of the room and Andrew stops me, touching me gently on my upper arm.

"Hey," he says. "It's okay, Daph, for this to be weird for you."
*Daph.*

"I'm fine. It's fine, really." I pull away from him.

"I can tell that you're not fine," he says. "I can tell that this is upsetting you."

"It's not, it's fine," I say, more insistent. "Come on, I need to show you the rest of the house."

"You need to or you want to?" he says.

I stop and look up at the ceiling.

"Answer the question, Daphne." He says it sincerely. He couldn't be nicer about it. Still, it pisses me off.

"I *want* to," I say, and the minute it's out of my mouth, I know that it's a lie. "Come on."

I tug his sleeve and start to pull him toward the hallway. I smile, trying to recover from my performance. He follows behind but I can tell he's reluctant. Something's changed and we both feel it. I walk silently down the hall. His boots (suede, stylish, evidence of his city life and the kind of thing that I used to try to get Owen to buy) squeak on the floor behind me—the original floor that we refinished and stained ourselves. Owen, he's everywhere, haunting everything, glooming over us.

"And this is our bedroom," I say, my hand on the jangly glass doorknob. The moment it's out of my mouth, I realize what I've said. I stop where I'm standing and close my eyes. *Fuck.*

He doesn't say anything. I turn slowly, hitching, like the tiny, twirling mechanical ballerina on the jewelry box that I had as a girl.

"*My* bedroom," I correct myself. I put my palms over my eyes.

"I think maybe it's too soon for me to be here," he says softly.

"I really wanted you to see my house," I say.

"You wanted to get this over with," he says.

"That's not—" I start.

"Daphne, it's okay," he says, smiling. "I understand. I *really* do."

"I'm sorry."

"I don't want to make you uncomfortable," he says.

"You're not," I say. "This is all me."

We both stand there, in the bedroom where I imagined that Owen and I would soothe our babies to sleep, worry over our teenagers when they missed their curfews, fight over the thermostat as we got older.

"Daphne, I think I should go," Andrew says.

"No, please don't," I say. "We can have lunch out in the backyard. I'm really fine."

"It's okay," he says, taking a step toward me and pulling me in for a hug. It doesn't help me feel better. "Please don't feel bad."

"Okay," I say, letting go of him. I want to go back and revise this whole incident now. Let us linger in the living room and browse the bookshelves, sit together on the swing outside. Rewind. Make this *nice*.

"I'll call you later," he tells me.

"Okay," I answer, not sure I believe him.

"You'll show me out?"


I close the door carefully behind him and then I walk the long hallway back into the house. It's like walking a plank. This *damn house*. It is almost as if it is a living, breathing thing, its tentacles slipping around me. I start to feel flushed, like my body temperature has shot up twenty degrees, and the room goes blurry, an out-of-nowhere dizzying anxiety that I've never experienced before. I slowly make my way into the living room, holding the walls as I go, and then I drop to the ground and press my palms to the floor to try to steady myself. *I must be having a panic attack.*

I try to take deep breaths but they won't come. I feel stuck, like I'm trapped on the inside of some horrific collector's item snow globe. *I feel lost in my own home.* I squeeze my eyes shut and keep breathing, willing the sensations to go away.

I don't know how long it is before I peel myself up off the floor—it feels agonizing, like I'll be stuck in the moment forever—but when I finally do, I wobble on unsteady feet toward the cabinet against the wall. I don't know why I suddenly want to torture myself in the way that I'm about to, but I can't help it. I need to look. I pull the silver album from the shelf and hold it in my lap for a moment before I open it. Our wedding day was idyllic, it really was. There was rain in the morning and Mom was freaking out so much that I forced her to have a glass of champagne with breakfast. Thirty minutes before the ceremony was to start, the clouds parted just enough to hold it outside, under the grand oak tree that Owen climbed when he was a kid. It was *perfect.* I touch the photos with my fingertips as I turn the pages. Lucy and my grandmother. Owen's parents toasting us. Walking down the makeshift aisle with my father. Leaving the ceremony with wide smiles, our hands clasped together and raised above over our heads. Owen, looking into my eyes as he put the ring on my finger. *He meant it*, I think, leaning closer to the page to study his face.

# CHAPTER TWENTY-FIVE

The hail is what wakes me. It pops against the roof, a mad staccato, and the wind howls and howls. *I don't remember hearing anything about a storm,* I think, jumping out of bed as another sharp crack of thunder hits. I go to the window, tentative because it's so awful outside. The windows are so old that I wouldn't be surprised if the storm shatters them. I jump away as another blaze of lightning strikes and illuminates the yard in erratic flashes.

The thunder booms and shakes the floorboards as I walk quickly down the hall to the guest room, Blue following close behind me. Storms have never bothered me before, but this one is different.

The sky earlier was as clear as could be. I'd spent the evening outside, walking the perimeter of the flower beds, which were so well tended at this point (victims of my obsessive, misplaced anxiety) that there was hardly a weed to pluck or a yellow leaf to inspect. I was turning on one of the sprinklers from the spigot on the side of the house when I heard Owen through the open window above, talking on the phone to his mother, I knew, because he asked something about her algebra students. I could only make out snippets, a word here and there, but I heard him say *Texas* and *funeral.* There was murmuring, an *I don't know*, and then I heard him say *mistake*.


I knock before I push the door open. He is sitting up in bed propped up on his elbows. He's just woken.

"Crazy," he says, combing a hand through his hair.

I nod and take a couple of steps into the room. It smells sour and warm, like sleep. "Surely it can't last with it being so strong," I say, hearing my mother in my voice. She always said this to Lucy and me when we got stuck sitting in the parking lot at the pool during sudden summer storms. Blue hops up onto the bed and Owen curls an arm around her.

Owen and I have hardly spoken in almost two weeks, just perfunctory hellos and good-byes. And then yesterday, as he filled his travel mug with the coffee I'd brewed, he mentioned that he'd finally found a promising rental and asked if I'd read the email he sent about the house. He'd called our real estate agent about the possibility of putting it on the market.

"I scanned it," I said, motioning for him to hand me the pot. The truth was that I couldn't bring myself to read it, even though I was the one who asked him to get in touch with her in the first place.

"We should talk about it," he said, jamming a stack of files into his bag.

"We should." I turned to get more sugar out of the cupboard. The door clicked closed behind me.


He sits up and pats the side of the bed. "Come sit down." It's only four steps from the threshold to the edge of the mattress but the walk feels agonizing. He shifts his feet under the covers to make room for me to sit and I do, tentatively. This is the first bed we ever slept in together, my bed, the one that my parents took me to buy at a warehouse store just before medical school. The linens are the ones that we put on our wedding registry. Owen's mother bought them for us.

The branches of an old oak tree are swaying violently just outside the window. The hail pops against the roof. There's a boom and the lamp on the nightstand flickers, and then the room goes dark. *Of course.*

"I'll go get a flashlight," he says.

"They're in the cabinet above the washing machine." I'd put them there the week after we moved in, along with a book of matches and a first aid kit. I'd labeled the shelf "Emergency" with my label maker, which I knew when I was doing it was a little silly. It seems asinine now.


Moments later I see a cylinder of light bob down the hallway and then Owen, holding a flashlight and my phone, which is ringing. He hands it to me.

Mary Elizabeth. *It's one o'clock in the morning.*

"Sorry," she says when I answer. I can barely hear her for the noise outside. I press my fingertip to my other ear.

"Sorry, what?" I say. "What is it?"

Owen catches my eye. "What?" he mouths.

"Patient," I mouth back.

He nods and sits down next to me and then flops backward onto the bed. He points the flashlight up to the ceiling, casting a canopy of light over the room.

"I'm sorry, Dr. Mitchell," she says. "Can't do it."

*Shit.* Her voice is all lazy hissing.

"Mary Elizabeth, where are you?"

"Why?" she says.

"Where are you?" I can hear the faint trill of music and laughter in the background.

"Birthday party downtown," she slurs. "Some friend of a friend. I don't know. Anyway. Anywaaay."

"Mary Elizabeth, why did you call me?"

"I'm not going to Caron or whatever it's called. The treatment place. I don't need it."

"You *clearly* need it." Owen sits up. The light from the flashlight bounces on the wall. "Who's with you?"

"Some old friends, some new friends..." Her voice trails off.

"Where are you exactly?"

I glance at Owen. He furrows his brow at me.

"Parrish Street, I think? Some new cocktail place. Yeah, Parrish. Parrish."

She's not just a little drunk. She sounds like a mess. A dangerous mess.

"Can you put someone on the phone? Someone who's with you?"

I hear a fumbling and then nothing.

"Mary Elizabeth? Are you there?"

"Yeah, yeah," she says. "What?"

"Mary Elizabeth? Is anyone with you?"

She sighs heavily into the phone. "Treatment. I don't need treatment," she mumbles.

"Listen. Stay where you are, okay? Just stay there!"

I stand up and race down the dark hall to my room to throw on some clothes, all the while listening to her mumble. Owen follows behind and watches me from the threshold.

"What are you doing?" he says.

I hold the phone away from my face. "I'm going to get her. She's a disaster."

"But you can't—"

"I know it's unorthodox, Owen, but I really think she's in trouble. I need to do something. She's confused—she's hardly making any sense. She's been drinking and God knows what else and she's diabetic. I'm worried she'll go into a coma."

He looks out the window. The rain might be pouring even harder now.

"Daph, you shouldn't risk this. What if something goes wrong? We could call the bar, couldn't we? Call 911? Send an ambulance? It's bad out there."

I know he's right, but something in my gut tells me I need to do this. I need to get her to a hospital, where her parents will be forced to see her like this, and I think if I have the support of some other doctors—more troops—then she might be convinced to get the help she needs.

He knows what I'm thinking without my having to say it. "I'll come with you," he says. He hurries down the hall to get his clothes and shoes.

Mary Elizabeth is droning into the phone, practically incoherent.

"You don't have to come," I say, sprinting past him and down the stairs.

"No, no," he says, wiggling one foot into his shoe. "I'll drive. You stay on the phone."


I know I'm doing the right thing when we get downtown and I see her slumped underneath the awning of an old shoe repair shop. She has waited for me, which means that even if she won't admit it, she wants my help. She knows how low she's sunk.

It's half the battle, maybe more.

The temperature outside is probably in the sixties but she is

shivering and clammy, two signs that her blood sugar is danger-
ously low. Owen and I get her into the backseat of my car and she
tries to brace herself, her body wobbling despite the fact that we're
not moving yet.

*"Whooss he?"* she slurs, nodding her head toward Owen. *"Your
huss-bin?"*

Neither of us says anything.


We get to the hospital and Owen runs in to get a wheelchair. As
we're racing in, I give the providers her history, and within minutes, she receives a glucagon injection, which will quickly raise her
blood sugar level before she loses consciousness.

I call her parents after finding their number on her phone. As I
suspected, they look more irritated than relieved when they finally
arrive forty-five minutes later. As I shake her mother's hand, I notice that she either wears a full face of makeup to bed or she took
the time to apply it before coming here.

We talk again about the treatment center and they nod their
heads impassively as I speak. I may as well be reciting the Pledge of
Allegiance. I do my best not to notice the way that they look me
over—my rain-soaked hair and wrinkled clothes not giving off the
impression they expect from their family physicians, I'm sure—
but by the time Owen and I leave, I feel confident that they are
going to do the right thing. When I check on Mary Elizabeth before we go, she's sleeping soundly.


"That was something," Owen says as we're driving home.

I look out the window. The storm has passed but it's still
raining.

"Thanks for coming with me," I say.

"Of course," he says. "You were right. You did the right thing. She was a wreck."

"That she was," I say, stifling a yawn. The adrenaline's worn off and I'm officially exhausted.

"How old is she?"

"Twenty-seven." I notice his subtle grimace when I say it. She's about the same age as Bridget.

We're quiet for the rest of the drive. No matter what he says about what he wants for our marriage, I know he's mourning her. When I peek at him, I can see it all over his face. More to the point, I can feel it.

I reach out and put my hand on his arm. "Are you okay?" I say.

"Yeah," he says bluntly. He presses his lips together and stares out at the road.

"Are you sure?" I ask. I don't know exactly what it is that I'm searching for. I suppose I want to know if he's being honest with me, and with himself.

He nods. "I'm okay."

"You did a good job tonight," he says once when we're back in the house. He locks the door behind him and flips on the outside light.

I walk to the kitchen for a glass of water and he follows behind me.

"I was really impressed seeing how you handled her," he continues. "I never thought of your work consisting of emergencies like that, I guess."

He means it as a compliment but it stings regardless. "Well, I'm glad you got to see that I do more than diagnose sinus infections," I say, taking a glass from the cabinet.

"Daph, that's not what I meant," he says.

"I know," I say, stifling another yawn. The last thing I'm interested in right now is a debate with Owen about whether he respects my work. "It's fine. Thanks for your help."

"I was happy to do it," he says, and then looks at his watch. "I should probably go to bed."

"Okay," I say, walking to the pantry. "I know I should, too, but for some reason, I'm starving."

"You know what?" he says, as I pull a box of crackers off of the shelf. "I'm kind of hungry, myself. Do you want a grilled cheese?"

Owen has made me thousands of grilled cheese sandwiches over the past decade. They are his specialty, if only because they are the only thing that he can cook.

I glance at the clock. It's almost four o'clock in the morning. "You know, that actually sounds pretty good."

"With tomato? Bacon?" he says, walking to the refrigerator.

"I don't think we have either."

"Just the classic then?"

"Yes," I say, walking into the living room. "Just the classic."


It feels like a long time before my eyes adjust and I realize that it's morning. The first thing I see is the uneaten sandwich on a plate on the coffee table in front of me. Bright white columns of early morning light are streaming through the windows across the room.

I am lying on the couch and Owen's arm is around my waist. He is asleep, breathing shallowly, his stomach rising and falling against my back.

Nothing has happened. I'm sure of that. I must have simply fallen asleep while he was cooking. And for whatever reason, he decided to snuggle in next to me.

I don't move. I don't *want* to. The familiar weight of his arm around me is a comfort. His breath on the back of my neck, a salve. Here, sleeping, we can be our old selves. I can fence in this moment and ignore everything else.

Maybe it's that I'm still in that hazy fog before consciousness, or maybe I know exactly what I'm doing, but I pull my fist from underneath my chin and uncoil my fingers, and carefully, or maybe carelessly, I rest my palm on top of his hand. It feels like it's where it belongs.

And I don't stop there. I realize that once this starts, there is no going back.

I lace my fingers into his and then I pull his hand up to my chest, holding him closer to me. He stirs and I pull him even closer, and then he wiggles his fingers away from mine—I can't tell whether he's awake yet, I don't want to know—and he moves his palm down to my torso. He pulls me closer, drawing me to him. He's awake.

I don't move at first. If I'm asleep—or pretending to be—I'm not responsible for anything. I snuggle back closer to him. He wraps his foot over mine. His nose nuzzles behind my ear. I keep my eyes closed.

This shouldn't be happening. I *want* this to happen.

He whispers my name and I don't respond, pressing my lips together as if to keep anything from pouring out. Yes. No. *I don't know.*

I want this.

I need this.

He kisses my neck, softly, tentatively.

His face stays there, pressed into the crook of my neck, and I know what he's feeling because I am feeling it, too. He is home now. We are home.

He kisses me again, a bit more insistently. His palm cups the dip of my waist, pulling me toward him. "Daphne," he whispers again. He might know that I'm awake, he probably does.

I stretch my chin up toward the ceiling—stirring, waking—and I open my eyes but the sun streaming in is so bright, I close them again and turn to Owen, *my* Owen, the only one, and I kiss him.

He kisses me back, eagerly, and at first I do the same because it is like our lives depend on it.

But then his hand is on my stomach and his mouth is pressing more deeply to mine and though I have been here a thousand times before with him, there are all of the times between now and then, not with me. I think of Bridget. I think of Andrew. I think of Owen, practically on top of me now, and I feel like I'm sinking. Disappearing, even.

I push away from him, both hands on his chest. "I can't do this. I'm sorry."

I close my eyes tight, willing the tears away, and he settles back onto the couch.

He doesn't say anything so I finally look at him, and the expression on his face isn't one of disappointment or frustration. He just looks sad. So very, very sad.

It's then that I realize that he may feel even more lost than I do.

There isn't a thing I can think to say, it's all too cloudy, and so I don't. I untangle myself from the blanket he must have put over us—a quilt, a wedding gift from his aunt—and I go upstairs to my room, where I sit on my bed. I wait for a decision to come to mind, a point of action, but it doesn't. I wait for him to come up here, like I think I want him to, but he doesn't. I wait for a long, long time.

# CHAPTER TWENTY-SIX

I arrive at Annie's house as she's pulling a bag of groceries from her trunk. I never stop by without calling first but when I left the house, I didn't have a destination in mind. I just needed to get out.

She peers at me, perplexed, and I'm reminded of the way that she looked at me when she came into my office on the morning after Owen told me he was leaving. "What's going on?" she calls to me as I march up the driveway.

I grab the two gallons of milk out of the trunk. "I made a big mistake," I say.

"Uh-oh," she says, hoisting three bags of groceries into her hands. "Come on. Come inside."

I follow behind her, past the soccer ball in the driveway, the scooter left on the front walk. I wait at the door while she fumbles with her keys and then she starts inside, holding the screen door open with her foot until I can catch it with my elbow.

She pushes a stack of library books out of the way and puts the bags down on the kitchen counter. Molly and Luke weave through, shouting hello to me as they run past. "What did you do?" she says, looking behind her to make sure that they're gone.

"I fell asleep on the couch with Owen."

Her eyes burrow into mine. "What does 'fell asleep' mean?"

"Nothing happened. Not after a few minutes. I stopped it."

She puts her hands to her head. "Daphne, what were you thinking?"

"I don't know," I say. "That's kind of the crux of this whole thing."

"What?"

"Not thinking."

Samantha, her eight-year-old, appears in the doorway and skates through the kitchen in her socks. Luke, her oldest, rambles back in. I can smell him across the room—like sweat even though he's not sweating. He's all boy, just like his dad. "Mom, I'm hungry," he says.

"There are hundreds of thousands of snacks in the pantry," she says, shaking her head at me.

"But I don't want any of that stuff," he whines, shooting his basketball on to the banquette window seat that lines one end of her kitchen table. "Yes!" he shouts to the room, pumping his fist. "Do we have any frozen pizza?" he says.

"Luke," Annie says. "You're ten years old. Where would you guess we keep the frozen pizzas? Also, it's not even eleven yet. How about you take your sisters outside."

He rolls his eyes but follows orders.

Annie turns to me. "You need to get Owen out of your house immediately," she says.

I tell her about last night and Mary Elizabeth. She pulls a carton of strawberries out of the grocery bag as I talk, then a bottle of lemonade. "Want some of this?" she asks, holding it up.

I shake my head. "My stomach hurts."

"I bet it does," she says, getting herself a glass. "Just look at what you're doing to yourself."

"You know, maybe I should go," I say.

"Why?" She comes back to the counter and twists open the jug of lemonade.

"Because I didn't come here for a lecture," I say.

She raises her eyebrows. "Excuse me?"

I shake my head. "I'm sorry, but you act like you're some marriage expert, like I'm an idiot for not seeing things your way. Let me tell you, Annie, being in this situation isn't actually that simple."

"I know it's not."

"No, you don't! That's the thing—you keep spouting off all of your opinions and you have *no idea* what it's actually like." I didn't come here intending to fight with her but I can't help myself. I'm so tired of her opinions. I'm so tired of all of this.

"Could you lower your voice?" she says, turning to glance out the window to the backyard.

"I'm sorry," I say, putting my hand out. "But you *don't* know what this is like."

"I have a little bit of an idea," she says.

"With all due respect, I think it is totally different than what happened with your mom," I say. "But if you're so sure, then tell me: If Jack left you and then came back, begging for forgiveness, what would you do?"

"I don't know." She shakes her head. "That's impossible to imagine. It would never—"

"Exactly," I say, slamming my hand down on the counter. "*It would never happen.* Don't you get that a few months ago, I would have said the exact same thing?"

"I totally get that, which is even more reason to cut him out of your life. What he did to you is unforgivable."

"But, *dammit*, don't you see, Annie? He is still my husband and he is still the love of my life." The words seem to reverberate once they're out of my mouth. We both freeze, staring at each other. "Well, there it is then," I say. "I know it's the worst thing you could hear me say, but there it is. I'm in love with my husband, despite everything."

She puts her hands over her mouth and shakes her head.

"I guess I'm just not..." I shake my head. "I'm not as tough as I apparently need to be. Because my feelings for him haven't totally changed."

She doesn't say anything, although I am sure she wants to.

"Annie, I know that you don't agree with me but I don't know how to get over this and, more to the point, I don't know that I want to."

She nods.

"That ridiculous thing that people say? How they *just can't live without someone*? I always thought that was swoony bullshit, daytime drama stuff, but it's true, Annie. I don't think I can live without him. Think about it—if Jack did what Owen did. How long have you guys been married again?" I ask.

"Fourteen years."

"We've been together for ten."

"Well." She rubs the back of her neck. It's a gesture that I've seen her make with her kids, Jack, and occasionally, our coworkers. She's irritated.

"What is it, Annie? What do you want to say?"

"Daphne, please don't get so defensive," she says. "I'm only trying to talk to you about this. I'm worried about you."

"Why on earth are you worried?"

"Because you've put yourself in a terrible situation! Look, I understand that it's going to take a while for you to get used to life without him, but I think that what you're doing—letting him stay at the house, falling asleep with him on the couch for God's sake, and what all of that entails. You're playing with fire."

"Yes, but—" I shake my head. "You're forgetting that he is my Jack. Imagine it, Annie. *Really* imagine it."

She throws her hands into the air.

"What?"

"He's *not* Jack," she says. "Jack didn't start a relationship with another woman, Daphne. Owen did. And now, because he doesn't have anyone else, he's using you because he knows that he can."

"It's not like that, Annie," I say, my voice low.

"Are you sure? Daphne, somebody needs to be the voice of reason here. You're not taking care of yourself. I see it in the way that you're acting and in the way that you're letting Owen trample all over you. What he's been through doesn't mean that you should be the person cleaning up the mess for him, especially given that it's at the expense of your self-respect, not to mention your future."

"Annie, I am handling myself just fine," I say. "It's not perfect, but it's my marriage, and I still love him. I still love him so, so much." My voice breaks and then I feel the tears start falling. Before I can stop it, my shoulders start to shake and the sobs start rolling out from deep in my gut. I ball my fists and squeeze them to my eyes. God help me if one of her kids walks in right now.

"Daphne, honey." She circles around the island and wraps her arms around me, shushing my gulping sobs as if I were one of the children. "You're going to be fine."

"I just want things to be the way that they were."

"That's just it, though. The way things *were* weren't actually the way things *were*."

I take a deep breath and then I say the thought that's been lurking in the back of my mind for weeks now—my skeleton thought, the thing I can't shake. "I want it anyway. I want it back, what I knew, even if it was a lie."

"You don't really mean that, Daphne. It just *seems* easier to go back to him, but it's not."

"Even so," I say, plucking a napkin off of the stack on the counter and blowing my nose. "I want to give him another chance. And it's what he wants, too."

"You're sure?"

"Yes. He's never stopped loving me. And not only do I believe him, I feel the same way."

"Despite everything?"

"We can work through it. It wouldn't be the craziest thing in the world. Lots of people stay together after an affair."

"Right, but it's not as if his ended because the relationship went sour or because he came to his senses. It ended because she—"

I put my palm out. "Annie, stop. I know you're just trying to help but I've been over all of this in my head. And remember that email that I showed you? He wasn't in love with Bridget. He said it then. It was over before it even started."

"Okay," she says, throwing her hands up in the air. "I guess you have some decisions to make."

I can see how much she hates this. "I guess I do."

"What about Andrew?" she asks.

"Andrew?"

She nods.

"There's nothing to explain. He knows my situation. He doesn't have any expectations."

"Okay," she mutters. She picks up the bottle of lemonade and walks it to the refrigerator.

"I didn't mean to blow up at you," I say. "I know that you only want what's best for me."

She nods.

"Andrew's a really good guy but he's not my husband. And he lives in California."

"You could, too."

"I could do anything."

"That's why I wish you wouldn't do what you're doing."

"The weirdest thing of all is that it feels like the only thing I can do, Annie."

"You're certain?"

I nod.


For a long time after I leave her house, I just drive. I fiddle with the radio and eventually turn it off. The phone rings—Andrew—and I send it straight to voicemail.

I drive south, past Chapel Hill, past the gas station near Pittsboro that we tracked down after reading that it had the best ham biscuits in the state, and then I keep going for almost another hour. I don't take any turns, I don't even change lanes, I just go, hands at ten and two, for a long, long time. I eventually turn around, take a familiar left, and then another one, and without needing to think about it—not anymore—I drive myself home.


Owen pops up from the couch when I arrive. There is a baseball game on the television, a bag of tortilla chips on the coffee table, and the sight of it all, this familiar tableau, sets my mind right.

My mother's voice rings in my ears. *Don't overthink it.*

And so I don't.

Owen circles around from the couch and meets me in the kitchen before I've had a chance to put down my keys. "Daph, listen—about earlier."

"It's okay." I smile at him. Owen. *My* Owen. Every curve on his face is familiar, every freckle, every line.

"No, I should've woken you when you fell asleep. I shouldn't have taken advantage and lay down with you."

"Stop it, Owen."

"I'm sorry. I know that this is so bizarre. I'm fucking things up by being here."

"Owen, stop," I say. And before he can say anything more, I

kiss him. I press my hands to either side of his face and I kiss him. And when he doesn't stop me, I just keep kissing him. I'm tired of dwelling in the past, as murky and disastrous as it has become, and I'm tired of thinking through the details. I just want the two of us, here, now.

When I wake up, it's nearly dusk. Owen is still asleep. His forearm is crossed over his face and he's snoring softly. For a long time, I just watch him.

It was not some soap opera scene, what happened today. We didn't softly moan each other's names, rediscovering each other, and I didn't cry into his chest once it was done. We didn't linger over each other's bodies, there were no romantic declarations. More than anything, it felt like something I needed to get past and now that it's done—we've slept together, in our bed—I feel sure that this is right.

I thought of her, as much as I kept trying not to. I wondered if he sensed it. He must have been thinking of her, at least in some under the surface way, or maybe it's only my insecurity. *Don't overthink it.*

Finally, he wakes up. Our eyes meet and we both smile but neither of us says anything. He runs his hand across my shoulder and along my arm, and then he stretches an arm around me, pulling me in close. "Hey," he says.

I gulp against the lump in my throat. This is where we're supposed to be.

"I love you," he says, pulling me closer.

"I know, Owen," I say. I wonder when the time will come when that phrase, coming out of his mouth, stops feeling like an apology. "I love you, too."

# CHAPTER TWENTY-SEVEN

I'm walking out of the office one night, trying to dig my keys out of the bottom of my bag, when I look up to see Andrew leaning against my car.

"So what's the worst thing for me to say in this situation?" he says as I wave and walk toward him. "I just happened to be in the neighborhood?"

I shake my head and laugh, relieved to see that he's not angry with me.

He's left three messages since his disastrous visit to the house. I haven't returned any of them. Annie said earlier today, in the condescending way she's been speaking to me all week, that I'm acting like a thirteen-year-old for avoiding him the way that I have. She said all of this offhand, over her shoulder, as she was walking into her office, and so partly because I wanted to stick it to her (screw her for being so judgmental), I shoved myself right inside the threshold of her door and told her that I'd decided, because I *had* actually thought about it, that I was going to call Andrew after work today and tell him that I'm giving my marriage another try. I turned and left before she could reply.

∞

*My marriage.*

It should feel monumental that we're trying again but the truth is that it doesn't. There is no falling-in-love silliness, no dreamy reuniting, it mostly feels like the way that things always were. I fell asleep reading last night, and when Owen came into our room later and kissed me just softly enough on my cheek that it woke me, I blinked open my eyes to see that he was in bed with his back already turned to me. When my alarm went off this morning, he had left for the day. The mirror in the bathroom was still fogged over. There were lathery bubbles on the bar of soap in the shower. I made the bed, folding the flat sheet over itself and pulling it taut. I fluffed the pillows and put the undershirt that he left on the floor in the hamper. I turned on the dishwasher before I left the house.

"What are you doing here?" I say to Andrew in the parking lot, reaching to give him a quick hug.

"I guess this sort of behavior is bordering on creepy?" he says. "Do you want to borrow my phone to call in the restraining order?" he jokes, pretending to hand it to me.

"No, not at all." I laugh. "I'm so sorry that I haven't been in touch. It's just been..." I search for the right word.

"Complicated?" he says.

"Yes," I say. "I'm sorry."

I stand there with my hands in my pockets, unsure whether I should launch into the grand explanation I'd devised about how I'm giving my marriage another go. *Does he even want to hear it?* He is so kind, I think, and a week ago, he was the only bright spot in my life. It's unsettling how quickly my convictions keep shifting under me, as if I'm not actually the one in control. *I shouldn't have been so rude.*

"I'm sorry to stop by like this," he says.

"It's okay," I say. "I'm glad you did."

He narrows his eyes, pressing his lips together like he's trying to decide whether to say something. I feel a nervous flutter deep in my stomach.

"What is it?"

"I actually came to say good-bye," he says. "I'm leaving town first thing tomorrow."

*"Tomorrow?"* I'm surprised by how immediately it saddens me—and how suddenly remorseful I feel. "Leaving? Really?"

"Yeah," he says. "I need to attend to something at work. I hate to leave my parents but I'm telling myself that it will be good for them to get into a routine, and I frankly need to get back to my life, too. My partners are kind of losing it having me gone for so long."

"That makes sense," I say. "I'm sorry to hear it, though."

"I wanted to say good-bye in person," he says, locking eyes with me. "It doesn't need to be good-bye, of course."

"No, of course not." It's the easier thing to say. *Will I ever see him again? In what context would it be?*

"I'll likely be back before too long," he says. "I'm not sure exactly when, though. I'm going on an exploratory trip for the company—two weeks visiting hotels throughout the Mediterranean."

"Now, that sounds terrible," I say. "I'm sure it will be treacherous."

He grins and nods.

"I'd like to try to make a stop here on the way back," he says.

*I should tell him.* "I've loved getting to know you," I say, almost stuttering. "It's been so much fun."

"I thought so, too," he says. "It was such a nice surprise. I hope everything works out for you, however you want it."

"Thank you," I say. "And, listen." I look down at my feet. "I'm so sorry about the other day, at my house. That was so awkward."

He laughs. "It's honestly fine," he says. "You've been through a lot. You're a wonderful person, Daphne. You deserve the best."

"Thank you." I'm startled by the way that I already miss him. *Is it strange to be nostalgic for what could've happened?*

"If you're ever in San Francisco?" he says.

I nod. "I'm going to miss your smile," I say after a moment. I don't want to forget him and what he did for me, intentionally or not.

"Come here." He waves me over.

We hug for a long time, and I close my eyes to savor the moment. I know I'll never see him again, certainly not like this.

He kisses the top of my head, and just as I tip my head up to return the affection, a car pulls through the parking lot. I quickly let go—God forbid one of my coworkers sees me standing out here like some teenager parked behind the high school.

When I look, the car is already careening away, as if it were just cutting through to make a U-turn.

"I always loved those old Wagoneers," Andrew says, his hand skimming my back.

My heart pounds, watching it speed away.

# CHAPTER TWENTY-EIGHT

Owen has never once been to my office. Not when I first got the job—my *dream* job—and gushed about the beautifully appointed waiting room, the state-of-the-art treatment rooms, the legendary boss. Not for a single annual holiday party, because he either couldn't leave his office or needed to attend his own. Not even when Annie threw a surprise lunch for me on my birthday last year and he didn't show up because he said he got called into an emergency at the office.

"I didn't know you were seeing someone," he says when I get home and walk out to the backyard, where he's tossing a tennis ball to Blue. Actually, he's hurling it toward her. She speeds after it, oblivious to his mood.

I remember this feeling now, coming home ready for a fight.

"I didn't know you were, either," I say, holding his gaze until he finally looks away, shaking his head.

"What? Was that a low blow?" I say, walking toward him. "Or just the truth?"

"When were you going to tell me?" he says.

"Tell you what?" I say, playing dumb to piss him off. It feels good, frankly. *How dare he accuse me of this, after everything?*

"When were you going to tell me about the guy I just saw you *embracing* in the parking lot of your office?" he shouts, overenunciating each word to make his point. "I assume, given that he knows where you work, that you haven't just met."

*Embracing?* I ignore him. I walk to one of the pots of herbs that I planted a few weeks ago, and press my fingers to the soil to see if it needs water. I remember how I felt when I planted these, so hopeless and lost that a pot of basil and oregano depressed me. *Who is even going to use this stuff?* I'd thought. I wanted so badly for this to feel like a home again, where people live and cook and say simple, wonderful things like *How was your day?* That's the way it should be now. If anything, we should be overcompensating, piling on the kindnesses to make up for the past few months.

"Are you going to answer me?" he says to the back of my head.

I take a deep breath before I turn and face him. I have no energy for a fight. I haven't done anything wrong and he doesn't get to be angry at me—not for this. "I don't owe you anything."

"Okay, well, let me know when you decide to stop punishing me so that we can have a mature conversation," he says. "All I'm asking for is information. You could have at least told me that there was somebody else. I have no right to tell you not to see anyone, honestly. But I guess I'm just surprised, considering everything that's transpired over the last few days. I have a right to know."

"You have a *right to know*?" I think of what Lucy said a few weeks ago. *If he did it before, he'll do it again.* I feel the adrenaline start to course through my veins. *How dare he throw this in my face?* "How about when we bought this house last fall and spent every day renovating it, talking about the family we were going to have here? How about last Christmas at my parents' house, when we sat around the dining room table with both of our families and you happened to be thinking about the coworker you were about to sleep with? Did I not have *a right to know* about what was going on in your life? About how you were seeing someone else? About how you were giving up on our marriage? How about that, Owen, did I not have a right to know about any of it?"

"Fine," he says, throwing his hands up. He starts to walk away and I chase after him.

"Wait a second," I say. "Don't you dare walk away from me in the middle of this."

He turns and looks at me. The spot in his jaw that pulses when he gets mad is beating like its own little heartbeat.

"You don't have any right to tell me what to do with my life now," I say, angry tears stinging my eyes.

"Just explain to me what I'm doing here," he says, his hand moving back between the two of us, the *here* signifying *us*.

An angry laugh bursts from my mouth. "Oh, Owen, seriously? You want *me* to answer that question? You're the one who got us here." I mimic the hand motion he's just made. "For the record, his name is Andrew and he's a friend of Annie and Jack's."

He nods.

"I just met him. There is no *history*. We went out for the first time right after you moved out." *On the night that Bridget died*, I almost say, but I bite my tongue. "We are just friends, nothing more, and he knows all about what's happened, so I'm sorry to disappoint you but you remain the only adulterer in this relation- ship."

He stands before me, his jaw pulsing. "Who are we kidding, Daph?" he says, his eyes piercing mine. "*What* relationship?"

I freeze. "How could you say that?" I shake my head at him, willing myself not to cry. I could tell him about the kissing. I could tell him about how Andrew has been kinder and more attentive to me than he's been in years.

He takes a step toward me. "For the record, I was coming to your office to surprise you, Daph. I wanted to take you out tonight. And at dinner, I wanted to tell you everything I should have been saying for the past ten years. Specifically, how I've loved you since the day I met you, when we were kids at camp and you sat across from me in that canoe. And how I don't deserve you— I've *never* deserved you—but I plan on spending the rest of my life proving myself to you and giving you the love that you should have been getting all along. I don't know, maybe it's not worth it, if you don't think I deserve a chance anyway."

"Owen." I don't know what to say to him. He stands before me, arms at his sides, and he looks tired, more than anything. Burned out. I feel the same way.

"I guess it was naïve of me," I say, tears beginning to roll down my cheeks. "But I didn't expect us to fight, Owen, not now, when we both say we want to fix what's happened. I know that there's a lot of work to do but I didn't expect it to be like this. I want to look forward, not back. I *can't* look back anymore."

We stand there looking at each other, Blue turning circles around us.

"Come here," he says.

I step toward him and he folds his arms around me.

"I'm sorry about the way that I reacted," he says. "I was taken by surprise."

I hook my fingers behind his back. "Of course you were," I say. "And I'm sorry about that." *Am I sorry?* "I guess this is going to take a while."

A couple of hours later, Owen is out picking up takeout for our dinner when Lucy calls.

"So listen, I got invited to go to this thing," she says.

"What kind of thing?" I ask, picking up an armful of folded socks from the laundry stack on the bed.

"It's a restaurant opening—David Arrupe's new place."

"Who?"

"Oh, Jesus, Daphne. He's only one of the most celebrated chefs in the world."

"Uh-huh. So?"

"So the restaurant just happens to open next week—on the night before my big sister's birthday. I thought you might like to come?"

My sister has never in our adult lives invited me anywhere.

"Hello?" she says, when I don't squeal in response.

"I guess I can't believe what I'm hearing," I say, walking to my closet.

She sighs. "Do you want to come or not?"

"It's in New York?"

"Yes. New York, New York, where I've lived since I graduated college."

"And you want me to be your date?" I say, pretending that I can't grasp what she's saying just to annoy her.

"Yes. For your birthday. It's not that complicated."

I carry the wrinkled pants that I want to wear to work tomorrow to the bathroom, hang them on the shower rod, turn the hot water on full blast, and close the door. "You must really feel sorry for me," I say. *I wonder what Owen has scheduled next weekend, whether he's working.* I haven't filled her in and I don't dare tell her now.

"You can come up on Thursday, take Friday off. The party's Friday night and then we'll enjoy the weekend."

"I don't know, Luce. I can't exactly just take off."

"For one day? When's the last time you went on vacation?"

I think back. Aside from the holidays and the recent Friday that I took off to go to Virginia, it was last summer. We went to Wrightsville Beach for Fourth of July weekend. We had margaritas at a bar next to the ocean on Saturday afternoon and talked about getting pregnant, and it became one of the many times that Owen said he wasn't ready and we ended up in a fight. We're going to have to revisit all of those old arguments and talk about how the past few months have changed what we want—or don't.

"I guess it's been a while since I've been anywhere," I say.

"Just say yes, Daph."

*Maybe some time away from each other would be good for us.*

"Okay," I say. "Let me double-check with my office in the morning, but yes—I'm leaning yes."

"Get out!" she says. "I can't believe you're actually going to come. Bobby will be pissed—he thought for sure that he had your spot."

"And are you disappointed, too? Was asking me just your good deed for the day?"

"Sis, come on."

"Sis? You haven't called me that since we were kids."

"*Sis*, give me a little credit. I want you to come. And I'll expect your call in the morning."

We hang up. I put the last bit of laundry away and am closing one of my dresser drawers when I pause. I open the top drawer, reach toward the back, and fumble at the bottom for my rings. I've worn them for five years, through *almost* everything. I didn't take them off when I did the dishes, went running, not even when I worked in the yard, so I'm surprised by how, after just a few weeks, they can feel so awkward on my finger when I slip them back on.


When I get downstairs, the takeout bag is on the kitchen counter. Owen is hunched over his laptop. He barely glances up at me as I start pulling containers out of the bag.

"Hey," I say.

"Sorry, I just need to answer this one thing," he says, typing. He glances up at me, his smile so quick I barely catch it. My mind drifts back to that beach weekend. I remember the tense silence when we left the restaurant and walked to the car. I remember how I sat on the beach the next day, trying to read, but my eyes kept wandering to the young families I saw making sandcastles next to the shoreline. He was oblivious, lying sound asleep on his stomach on his towel, and it made me so angry that I was the only one feeling that yearning, watching those kids play.

"I just talked to Lucy," I say.

"Oh, yeah? How's she doing?" he says, his eyes scanning his computer. He taps on the keys.

I get out two plates, two forks. I consider whether to make his plate for him. I decide to get a glass of wine.

"She's good," I say. "Really good." *She also hates you*, I think. She'd emailed a few days earlier to say that her department won a National Magazine Award for a story that she directed about sun damage and skin cancer. *It's like the Oscars of magazines*, she explained. *The best of the best.* I start to tell Owen about it but then I change my mind. He's still tapping away.

"Is she still with Billy?"

"Bobby," I say. *They've been together for three years now—how can he not remember his name?* I take a sip of my wine.

*Does he even remember that weekend at the beach?* I think, looking at him in his Bruins T-shirt, the original taxicab yellow faded to a mellower mustard shade, his eyes shifting back and forth across his computer screen.

I walk over to him. "She asked me to go to New York for my birthday. For a party."

"Who?" he says, finally standing. He laces his hands behind his head and sticks his chest out, stretching.

"My sister?" I say.

"Right." He shakes his head as if to wake himself up. "Sorry. These patient records—I feel like I can't get caught up lately. But New York? Great! Are you going to go?"

"I think so," I say. "But it's my birthday. You wouldn't mind?"

"Oh, oh," he says, realizing. *Just now realizing*, I think. "No, of course not. You should go." He smiles and nods at me and it is so unnatural, like I'm staring at a wooden marionette doll.

"I'm definitely considering going," I say. "But it's kind of last minute. I still need to check with work."

"But that shouldn't be a big deal, right?" he says. "Can't someone else handle your appointments?"

"I guess so," I say, trying not to let the comment annoy me. *Sure, my patients can just get shifted to another doctor, one of the faceless drones. After all, we're not* real *doctors, like you.*

He leans down and starts typing again. I pull out the chair next to him and sit, watching the bones in his fingers move like piano keys—up, down, up, down. "A trip would be nice. I could certainly use a vacation," I say. I wait for him to acknowledge what I've said but he doesn't. "And there's some big party for a restaurant opening." I wrack my brain, trying to think of the chef's name.

"Well, it's hardly surprising that Lucy would have a party to go to," he jokes.

"Yup," I say, the word plunking out of my mouth. "And like I said, I could use the vacation."

He looks up at me and his Adam's apple rises and falls as he swallows. "It sounds like it will be a lot of fun," he says flatly. "You should go."

I get up and walk back over to the kitchen counter. "We should eat," I say, opening the takeout containers. "The food's getting cold."

# CHAPTER TWENTY-NINE

I'm convinced that there is something in the New York City water that brainwashes its residents. My sister spends $3,000 a month on rent, which is almost double my monthly mortgage payment. I have no idea how she does it, especially given the amount of money she spends on restaurants and her wardrobe, but I have a sneaking suspicion that Bobby helps to fund her lifestyle. Her apartment is about the size of one of my exam rooms and has a kitchen no bigger than a shower stall. When we climbed the rickety five flights to her door, she said something about how the "charming" old stairs in the building's brownstone mean that she never feels guilty about ordering dessert. "And the view, well..." she said, the two of us standing on the landing that was barely big enough for a doormat. "That's worth it alone."

A few minutes later, she stood tippy-toed in her stilettos as she pointed out the thin window in her living room. "See? I have a view of the Statue of Liberty." I peered over her shoulder. Just barely, past the building across the street blocking three-quarters of the view, you could eke out the tiniest sliver of a glimpse of the tip of the iconic statue's crown.

She's been in this apartment for less than six months, and according to her, it really pissed off Bobby that she decided to get her own place instead of moving into his loft on Greene Street.

"But I like my four hundred square feet," she said. "I think that even when we finally make it official, I'll keep my own place. I like my little pied-à-terre," she said, winking to me as she walked four steps across the room to the crowded metal clothing rack shoved in the corner next to her kitchen sink. It occurred to me, watching her flip through the hangers, that it feels incredibly strange to witness how the people closest to you choose to live their daily lives, particularly when you make such different choices.

For dinner last night, she took me out for sushi at a hole in the wall in her neighborhood. There was a line of people waiting to get in. "The *Times* just wrote about it," she explained as she walked past the crowd and caught the hostess's attention, who rushed to kiss Lucy on the cheek like they were family before leading us to a table in the corner. She ordered for us and I let her, soaking up the opportunity to be pampered. The waiter brought two short glasses of sake and I launched into my update on what's happened with Owen, hoping that the fact that we were in public, in one of *her* places, would keep her from screaming at me.

And it worked. Maybe she was going easy on me because she finally realizes what I've been through, or maybe (more likely) she's past the point of caring all that much, but when I finally finished talking, saying for probably the tenth time that I take marriage seriously and that I need to give it a shot, she looked up at me and said, "I guess you need to do what you need to do, and I respect that. If there's anyone who can appreciate needing to handle things in your own, individual way, it's me."

"So you support me then?" I asked, dragging my fork over the seaweed salad that she insisted we order even though I told her I've never been able to develop a taste for it. (She was right, of course—I still thought it tasted mostly like dirty dishwater, but it was the best dishwater I'd ever had.)

"I don't know that I'd say I support the decision, but I always support you," she said. "It's not what I'd choose for you."

"I know," I said.

"Just be careful," she said. And then she raised her hand to get the waiter's attention and launched into a story about her noisy upstairs neighbors.

*Could I live here?* I ask myself the next night, one hour into the party. I have just consumed two glasses of the most delicious champagne that I have ever tasted in my life, and that might be all that it is, but as I stand on the penthouse floor of a beautifully renovated building in the West Village, staring out a wide wall of windows at the twinkling lights below me, the sweet tree-lined streets, the deep black glimmer of the Hudson River in the distance, I feel like the city's elusive magic is taking hold of me. I always preferred Boston and its sturdy history, the robust austerity of the locals, but I don't know, maybe there's something.

Lucy says you get used to the noise, as if it's natural to have a constant din of traffic and construction and people in the back of your ear while you run to the grocery store or shop for a birthday present. I never understood the constant marching from point A to point B all day long, the defensive trudging through a mass of people and cars and mess. I said as much to her as we were walking to the hotel for the party and waiting on a crowded corner to cross the street. "You have to live here to understand it," she said. "Forget the big picture. Look at the little things." She pointed to two elderly women crossing on the other side of the street—twins—with matching hats, the same burgundy lipstick,

evening gloves, dark sunglasses. They were holding hands and gig-
gling. "See?" Lucy said, elbowing me.

The lights out the window shimmer, incandescent, giving everything a smeary, romantic glow.

"It's a lovely evening, isn't it?" a voice just over my left shoulder
says.

"It is," I say, turning. He's sipping a glass of wine that he holds
cupped in his palm, the stem slipped between his fingers like it
was designed for his hand.

The people at the party are Lucy people, fashion people. This
guy is maybe fifty. His navy suit looks custom made, his tortoise-
shell frames are like artwork. His accent, of course, is Italian.

The restaurant is on the top floor of a new boutique hotel in
an old renovated watch factory, the history of which is reflected
in the large, gilded gears on the walls. I of course immediately
thought of Andrew when I saw it and even started to take my
phone out of my bag to text a photo to him but I stopped myself.
He surely already knows about this place. I zipped my bag closed
and stood at the edge of the party while Lucy kissed hellos. The
room looks like it has been bathed in gold, from the starkly shaped
brassy dining chairs, to the elegant tables with legs as thin as pins,
to the sleek bar that looks as if it's floating in the corner of the
room.

I had brought a simple black dress to wear, which Lucy quickly
vetoed, handing me a melon-colored sheath that she said shows
off my shoulders and is the "color of the moment." Half of the
women and men in the room are wearing some variation of the
shade.

"Are you in food?" the man says, taking a step forward so that
we're now side by side and staring out the window together.

"Excuse me?"

"The food business? Are you in it?"

"Oh," I say, putting my fingertips to my brow. "No, no I'm not. I'm here with my sister. She's a magazine editor."

"A food magazine?"

"Actually, no. That doesn't really explain anything, does it? She's a beauty editor. To be honest, I'm not sure how she got invited. How about you? You're in food?" I say.

"Wine," he says, holding up his glass.

"Ah," I say. "Do you know this one?" I hold up my flute.

"I know it well." He smiles. "My ex-wife's family has been producing it for decades."

"Oh," I say, sorting the details. "Your ex-wife's family...so that's how you got into wine?"

"Mm." He smirks. "It was part of us, yes. But no, I was in the wine business long before I met her. Anyhow," he says, nodding at my glass. "Great wine." He leans slightly sideways toward me and mock whispers, "Not-so-great wife."

"Got it," I say, wondering if she cheated. Maybe he did. *How long am I going to mark every breakup I hear about with that label?* "So what brought you here?"

"I helped David assemble his wine list."

"The chef."

"Yes, he's a dear friend."

"Ah," I say. "So I know that the wine is French, which means that your ex is French. But you—I know you're not French."

"I'm from Parma. Italy."

"Yes, I know it," I say. Annie and Jack went a few years ago, for their anniversary, and smuggled back a textbook-sized hunk of prosciutto in their suitcase for us.

"You've been there?"

"I have friends who have."

"It's a wonderful place," he says. "Not too many tourists. You should go."

We *should* go, I think. We should start doing all of the things we always said we would do. *Would he take the time off?* "Do you still live there? Are you visiting?"

"No, I live here. Almost ten years, actually."

"I don't understand how people do it." I shake my head. "My sister, too."

"I think it takes a year to get used to it, but after that, you're stuck. I've met so many people who say that they're planning to stay for just a year or two and then years later, I run into them walking out of a deli with the *Times* tucked under their arms. It's hard to live anywhere else once it's under your skin."

"Is that what happened to you?" I say.

"Maybe." He raises his eyebrow.

"The ex?"

"I moved here right after my divorce. A fresh start."

"Ah," I say, thinking of my own "fresh start" with Owen.

"And you?" he says.

"I'm visiting. I live in North Carolina."

"I've never been there."

"I'm not surprised," I say.

"What does that mean?"

"I don't know." I shrug. *What do I mean?* "Maybe you seem like your travel would take you to more exotic destinations."

"North Carolina isn't exciting?"

"I don't know that that's the adjective that the state tourist's bureau would use. Beautiful, yes, and peaceful, but maybe not exciting."

"Do you like it?"

"I did," I say, savoring the last sip from my glass. "I do."

"You don't sound very certain."

"I liked it very much until recently," I say. I lean into him. "Not-so-great husband."

"I see," he says. "So you're divorced?"

"No," I say, looking down at the rings on my hand. "It's complicated."

I stare out the window. One thing I've always noticed during my visits here is that you never see the stars at night. All of the light from the skyscrapers clouds them out.

"You've been together a long time?" he asks.

"Ten years. Married just over five."

"But he's not so great?"

"It's a long story."

"Maybe he's your New York," he says.

"What?" I turn to him.

"Maybe you just got used to him."

I laugh, if only to recover from the sudden pang that his comment brought on.

He examines me, a mixture of delight and confusion on his face.

"I shouldn't say he's not so great," I say. "That might not be fair." *Is it, though?*

"What do you mean?"

I look at him. He has a gentle face and the sort of deep caramel skin tone that suggests a lot of good vacations. "I'm trying to figure it out."

He asks about my work, and I am explaining the structure of our practice to him when my sister arrives, stepping between us and putting an arm around each of our shoulders. "So, dear sister, I see you've met Paolo."

"You're Lucy's sister!" he exclaims, and then takes a step back, looking me up and down like I'm a store mannequin. "Yes, yes! Now I can see the resemblance."

A single "Ha!" pops like a bubble from my mouth. I may be

wearing my sister's dress, but there is no resemblance. Lucy is dressed in a white tank dress that looks like it's made from the medical gauze that I use at work and gold heels that match the restaurant's décor. "So how do you know each other?" I say.

They look at each other and burst into intimate, mellifluous laughter.

"Oh," I say. "No need to elaborate."

"We met a long time ago," Lucy says.

"Seems like it was yesterday to me," he responds.

They explain, their voices weaving over each other's, that David, the chef, arrived in New York from an Arizona trailer park ten years ago. The legendary story is that his first "food job" was slinging $1.50 hot dogs at Gray's Papaya, an open-24-hours place on the Upper West Side, and late one night, one of the city's most acclaimed restaurateurs stopped in for a chili dog. He'd had a bit to drink, as he is known to do, they started talking, and the next thing David knew, he was working as a line cook in one of the man's restaurants. Within six months, he was head chef, and now, with backing from a superstar Brooklyn hip-hop artist and the Upper East Side family who owns the hotel we're standing in, he's opening his first place.

"In the two months that the hotel's been open, the bar down-stairs has become one of the hottest places in the city," Paolo says. I'd noticed the library-like bar off to the left of the lobby when we walked in—dark, warm, with leather club chairs and Persian rugs. It seemed much more my style than this sleek upstairs space.

Lucy and Paolo begin to subtly point out the celebrated guests—the restaurant critic for the *Times*, the hip-hop mogul and his family, the up-and-coming indie movie darling and her rocker boyfriend, the fashion designers. Before long, the lights are dimmed and we all make our way to seats at the sleek tables dotting the room, everyone fumbling and trying to look graceful despite the fact that it's darker than it would be if this were a movie screening and the curtain had just gone down.


The next thing I know, I hear the beginning notes of "Moonlight Mile" by the Rolling Stones. It is one of my favorite songs—Owen's, too. Mick Jagger's voice begins to pump through the sound system, and for a moment, I think he might actually be here, but instead, a gleaming spotlight illuminates each table, and in front of each of us is a plate of food that looks like a carefully engineered photo on the cover of a food magazine. There is a spindly, ruffly salad, some sort of spiky candied orange thing, a golden-seared scallop, a broth the color of a Caribbean sunset. Lucy digs right in. Paolo, to my right, nearly buries his sophisticated Roman nose into his plate and uses his hand to wave the aroma toward his face, inhaling the scent as if he wants to slurp the whole lot of it right into his lungs. When he finally rises up and looks at me, the lenses of his avant-garde eyewear have fogged over. We both begin to laugh, and then I proceed to eat the most delectable meal I have ever tasted in my life.


Six courses later, I observe—because this feels like an out-of-body experience—that I haven't had this much fun in years. Paolo has tutored me on each glass of wine I've consumed. The food was more art than sustenance, and I relished every bite, as evidenced by the way that Lucy's dress is pulling tightly over my happy potbelly. Seated across the table from Paolo and Lucy and me is an architect and her partner, who is a banker and a fellow Massachusetts native, and a Web mogul and his sculptor girlfriend. The company has been interesting and wonderful, maybe in part because I had no expectation that I would enjoy anyone whom I met tonight. I assumed that they would be pretentious, snooty, too self-absorbed to bother with basic courtesy. I realize, once again, that I need to stop making assumptions about my sister and the world that she inhabits.

And so, when people stand and start milling around and giving each other good-bye air kisses, I suggest that we all go downstairs to the bar.

"How much wine did my sister drink, Paolo?" Lucy leans across me to joke, grasping his leg just above the knee.

"Can you blame her?" he says, squeezing his hand over hers. "Did you taste that Viognier? Have you ever had anything better?"

"Maybe once or twice," Lucy says, winking at him.

"Oh, Jesus. Please." I say, extracting their hands from each other's. "Let's go downstairs."


The bar is crowded but Paolo is able to get us comfortably en-sconced at a table in the back of the room next to the fireplace. It's chilly, or perhaps I'm just cold because the silk dress that I'm wearing is no sturdier than a tissue. A bottle of champagne appears and Lucy hands me a glass, telling me that my birthday begins in exactly four minutes. She flashes her telephone to show me—11:56 p.m.—and for a moment, I feel despondent, that tumbling-backward sense of loss about the past few months. But then I raise my glass, and I take a small sip of the crisp, lovely champagne, and I vow to myself that I will get over it within the next four minutes. I will not let myself spend a second of my next year wallowing in what he did to me.


We get back to Lucy's around three, an hour I haven't seen purely for fun since my twenties. When she goes into the bathroom to get ready for bed, I call Owen. I know I shouldn't—he's most definitely asleep—but I'm a little drunk, it's my birthday, and he's my husband. I should be able to call him at three o'clock in the morning to tell him about dinner and "Moonlight Mile" and Paolo and the whole thing. The disappointment sinks deeper each time the phone rings and I realize that he's not going to pick up. I wonder if it's woken him—if he squinted at the caller ID, saw it was me, and decided not to answer. I wonder if he's home. "Hey," I say after the voicemail message. "Just me. Sorry to call late. Wanted to tell you about tonight. I'll try you in the morning." *He'll wish me a happy birthday tomorrow*, I think, holding my phone in my hand. *He'll call as soon as he's up.*

I lie back on the couch, looking up at the old tin ceiling tiles, and listen to the water running as Lucy performs what I'm sure is an overcomplicated beauty ritual that I will someday regret never doing.

I unfold the thick, soft throw on the end of the couch, place it over me, and click on the text message icon on my phone.

Have you heard of a new hotel in NY called the South Village Inn? I type. It's only midnight in California. He could be awake.

A message pops up on my screen almost immediately: You could say that.

So you do know it? I type. I thought you would. I went there tonight—for a party with my sister. Came up to NY for a visit yesterday.

No kidding! I can't believe that, he writes.

No, I'm not kidding, I type. I do get out of Durham every once in a while, smartass.

No—ha. It's not that, he writes. It's just that as of ten o'clock this morning, we own that place.

I read the message twice to make sure I read it correctly—*owns* the hotel?

You OWN the hotel?!

Yep! My partner is there—signed the papers this morning. It hasn't been announced yet. I can't believe you're there!

I sit up and read the line again. Wait, I type. But Lucy said some family owns this place. Didn't it just open?

Yes. Owners about to announce their divorce—decided to sell the hotel rather than fight over who gets to keep it. Didn't want to do Donald and Ivana, Part 2.

And they sold it to YOU? Amazing!

I know! US! The suckers. That's why I had to go back to California so abruptly, to work on our pitch.

Unbelievable! I write. You're even more big-time than I thought you were. I wish I'd known earlier tonight. Could've name-dropped—something the crowd I was with would have appreciated. It's absolutely gorgeous.

Thanks, he says. No big deal, though, really, for a big-time guy like me.

I laugh just as Lucy's coming out of the bathroom. "Who is it?" she asks, patting some sort of blue gel under her eyes with her ring fingers. "Owen?"

"No." I glance up at her as I type.

She stops and raises her eyebrows at me. "Annie?"

I shake my head as another message pops up on the screen. What are you visiting for? he asks.

"Ohhhh," Lucy says, looking over my shoulder before she leans down to plant a kiss on my cheek. "Well, don't text all night. We have a big day tomorrow."

I put the phone in my lap and look up at her. "Thanks for tonight," I say. "It was so much fun."

"Happy Birthday," she says, tousling my hair.

After she's closed the door to her bedroom, I pick up the phone.

I'm here to celebrate my birthday, I type.

When is it? Not today?

Today!

Damn! Never should have let my partner take this one. Would have loved to celebrate with you.

I hesitate for a minute, my thumbs hovering over the screen, and then type back: Me, too.

# CHAPTER THIRTY

When I open my eyes, it takes a second or two to realize where I am. The beigey pink curtains. The muffled whir of traffic outside the window. *Lucy's room.* My phone is ringing. I reach across the bed to the spot next to the windowsill where I put it to charge last night.

"Hello?" I clear my throat.

"Happy Birthday," Owen says.

"Thank you." *He remembered.* I snuggle back under the covers. Lucy must already be up.

"So you had a late night," he says.

"We had a lot of fun. I'm sorry I called so late. I couldn't resist. Or maybe the wine couldn't resist. Did I wake you?"

"Just briefly," he says. "I fell right back to sleep."

"Oh," I say. "Then why didn't you—" *Forget it—not worth it.* "Are you going to the hospital today?"

He laughs. "It's ten o'clock in the morning, Daph. I've been here for two hours."

"It's ten?"

"Ten."

"Wow." I sit up and notice the note on the nightstand. *Went out to grab bagels, sleepyhead. See you soon.*

"What do you two have planned for the day?" he asks.

"Lucy's out picking up breakfast. She's taking me to a spa later."

"Of course she is," he says. Something about his tone annoys me.

"It will be great," I say. "I just want to put on a fluffy robe, let a stranger rub my back for an hour, maybe drink some more champagne. Forget real life for a few hours, basically."

"Oh," he says. "Well, good."

*Well, good?* There's an awkward pause. *Is he going to say that he misses me? Is he going to comment on what I've said?* "You deserve to be pampered, Daphne. Go enjoy yourself! I wish I could be with you on your birthday but I'm so glad you're having a good time." When we were first together, we had a tradition of buying each other cheap, nostalgic birthday cakes—I made him a Funfetti cake from the boxed mix one year, he got me a Carvel ice cream cake the next. Last year, he brought home a box of chocolate and some flowers, and I remember thinking, as he presented it to me and I noticed the $7.99 price tag on the chocolate that he didn't bother to scrape off, that he probably got both from the hospital gift shop as he left work. I'm surprised there wasn't a little plastic "Get Well Soon" sign stuck in the bouquet.

"What will you do today?" I ask. "I hope you won't work all day on a Saturday."

"No. I'll probably work here for a while, maybe catch the baseball game later."

"Sounds good," I say. "No other plans?"

"Nope."

I wait a few seconds to see if he'll elaborate. He doesn't. The conversation is fading out (not that it ever really got started) and I suddenly want to escape it as quickly as possible. "Well, I should probably get up. Lucy may be waiting for me."

"All right. Have a good day, okay?"

"I will," I say.

"Okay, love you," he says.

"Love you, too." I hang up the phone and hold it to my chest. Why didn't he sound more animated, more excited, *happier*? There are a lot of things that he could have said. I don't know what exactly—I'm not sure what he did wrong. *Did I do something wrong?* The call felt edgy and weird. Uncomfortable. Bad.

I reach and pull the curtain from the window. It's overcast. There's a restaurant across the street where a crowd of people are standing outside, waiting for tables for brunch. I lie back down, pick up my phone, and start to reread last night's texts from Andrew, but a few seconds in, I stop myself. This probably shouldn't be the thing I use to make me feel better.

Later at the spa, Lucy and I are discussing the phone call with Owen and snacking on a fruit plate between treatments.

"It's not that I don't think he cares about my birthday, I know that he does, it's just that he always seems distracted, especially on the phone. He was at work, though," I say, leaning back into a lounge chair so soft and cushy that I've decided that the only thing that will get me out of it is the promise of more spa treatments.

"You're supposed to be relaxing," Lucy says. "Not thinking about Owen."

"You're right," I say. "It's just irritating."

"No offense," she says. "But I find it kind of funny, given recent events, that you say his quote-unquote *distractedness* is merely *irritating*."

I ignore her. I have just spent an hour under the expert hands of Matilda from Finland and I will not let anything bother me now. I close my eyes and take a deep breath. They must pump eucalyptus oil into the ventilation system. I get the occasional massage at work and have had maybe one or two "spa day" experiences during bachelorette weekends for girlfriends when I was younger, but I've never been anywhere like this. The spa is a jewel inhabiting the top floor of a nondescript building off of Second Avenue. I have yet to see another customer, but I can only imagine what it costs people who do not have Lucy's job title. Everything is white—the walls, the ceiling, the floors, the chairs, the towels, the robes. It's like a new age asylum, or heaven. I suppose I could use some of both.

"So," Lucy starts. That one syllable is all I need to hear to know that she's not done talking about this. "What about that Andrew?"

I pick a bright red raspberry from the plate between us, pop it in my mouth, and savor the sweetness. "Well, for starters, 'that Andrew' isn't my husband. Two, that's not how I think about him. Three, even if I was interested in moving on and meeting someone new, it's not that simple. My approach to men is not like deciding which chocolate to pick from the box."

"Maybe it should be," she says, stretching her legs out in front of her and wiggling her toes. "You know, I was thinking about this—" she starts.

"You were, were you?" I interrupt. "I should give you Annie's number. You two could talk for hours."

She gives me a look. "*Anyhow*, I was thinking: Remember that story about Grandma Jean and her emergency cigarette?"

"Yes, I remember." My grandmother was a relentless chain smoker for many, many years, and when she finally quit, she decided to keep one last cigarette in the drawer of the old secretary desk in her family room, just in case. My mother always checks to see if it's still there when she visits.

"I think Owen's your emergency cigarette," Lucy says.

I chuckle. "That doesn't make the tiniest bit of sense."

"I think it makes perfect sense, actually," she says. "You're hanging on to him *just in case*. You don't think you can be totally without him."

"Or maybe I *want* to be with him," I say. "And this entire experience is going to make our relationship worlds better than it would have been otherwise."

She leans over to inspect her just-painted toes—or to pretend to.

"Lucy, tell me what I'm doing wrong by wanting to build a life with the person I married."

The messy bun on the back of her head shakes back and forth. "I don't know."

"You don't know? Well, then, thanks for the talk."

"Daphne, I don't know what I'm talking about, okay?" she says, leaning back into her chair and turning to me. "All I know is that even before all of this happened with Owen, you've never seemed particularly enamored. He's great on paper, sure, but I never would have described the two of you as passionately in love."

"We've been together for a long time, Luce. What do you think marriage is like? It's not slow-dancing-in-the-kitchen, *Bridges of Madison County* bullshit."

She sneers at me, jokingly, and reaches for a piece of apricot. "As I said, I don't know what I'm talking about." She chews for a minute and then continues. "Listen, don't take this the wrong way, but you've carefully calculated every single thing that's ever happened in your life. You've achieved everything you've ever wanted, and you should be proud of that. You've worked hard."

"Uh-huh." I turn to face her, warily anticipating what's next.

"And what happened with Owen is awful and not at all your fault but I'll be honest with you, I don't think you were any better off before it all went down."

"You don't think my marriage was good, basically."

She puts her palm up and shrugs.

"You and I are just different, Lucy. We want different things. With all due respect, I don't want a life like yours. I don't want to cheat on my boyfriend with Italian wine distributors."

She laughs. "Wait. *Paolo?* Is that what you're talking about? I never slept with Paolo."

I raise my eyebrows.

"He's simply a massive flirt, Daphne. He's Italian, for God's sake."

"Seriously?"

"Seriously! I've never cheated on Bobby. And I can't believe you would think such a thing."

"On the occasion or two that I see you each year, and in every phone call or email I get from you, you're always talking about some person you're meeting for drinks or going to dinner with— I can't keep up with all of the names!"

"Daphne, those are business dinners half the time and social outings with Bobby the other half. Honestly, do you think I'd do that to him?"

I shrug. "Lucy, I don't know. Maybe I'm just drawing my own incorrect conclusions, but you and Bobby don't seem all that committed. It's a very different relationship than what I'm used to."

"Owen seems real committed," she says under her breath.

"Lucy, come on."

"Bobby and I couldn't be happier," she says. "We're absolutely serious about our relationship, but the difference is we don't treat it like work. We have *fun* together. We keep it light because there's enough heavy elsewhere. That's why I love him, Daphne. We have very separate work lives that are plenty stressful—I know you don't believe that my life could be demanding, but guess what? It's more than facials and road-testing mascaras. Do you know what's happened to the magazine industry over the past ten years? Circulation and advertising numbers have plummeted. It doesn't exactly make my job easy. Bobby is the place where I go to get a break from all of that. He is the good part, the positive part, the *real* part."

"Okay," I say. "I get it."

"Daphne." She shakes her head. "Let me ask you this: If you were told you had one week to live, would you be happy to spend it the way that you and Owen spent your time, before he dropped the bombshell on you?"

I shake my head at her, wracking my brain to come up with an example of the *real* and wonderful life that Owen and I had together. The truth is that I barely remember being together during those weeks leading up to his birthday, when he confessed. I can't remember one recent instance when we really laughed together, or shared a private and meaningful talk, or spent the kind of time together that left me feeling like there was no place I'd rather be. Maybe I have mistaken the way that we'd become for a "comfortable normal" when it was anything but. I feel that lurking suspicion rising to the surface—maybe we had lost each other long before he told me about Bridget.

"You're not answering me," Lucy says.

"We had a lot going on, Lucy," I stammer. "We were renovating a house together. We were on the verge of starting a family. We were building a life."

"Right, but were you doing those things together—*really* together? Or side by side like business partners? Or even—I know how those baby talks were going—as adversaries?"

The thing is, I know she's right. I look at her—my dear silly sister with her fluorescent nail polish and her hair piled on top of her head—and I think that she is far wiser than I give her credit for. She has me pinned. I take a sip of lemon water.

"Listen, I never had a relationship like yours, that lasted so many years and went through so many changes," Lucy says. "But

I think that the person whom you choose to devote your life to should excite you at least and should give you some sort of comfort. I know that it's not easy, but shouldn't marriage at least be a sort of relief from the rest of your life? Just look at Mom and Dad."

I think of my parents, who still go out for dinner every Friday night just like they did when we were growing up. Dad helps with Mom's cooking contests, taking every mini pot pie and bar cookie recipe to his coworkers for feedback. She gets the paper for him each morning, unfolding it at his place at the breakfast table so that it's ready to go when he comes down from his shower.

I don't know that it's possible for Owen and me to be that way now. We stopped cheering each other on years ago, if we ever really did it at all. When we began to drift apart, neither of us did anything about it. We were too busy with other things—other priorities—to stop it.

I remember something I learned years ago: The brain, despite all of the miraculous things that it can do, is actually incredibly inefficient, even lazy. It is attracted to things that it knows and even draws us toward what's already familiar. On average, you will typically pick the ice cream flavor you usually order, or buy a car that resembles one that's similar to the make and model you already have—and maybe even choose a partner based on your history instead of what's better for you in the long run.

Change, meanwhile, is terrifying—especially, I suppose, for a prudent type like myself.

"There might be something to what you're saying," I concede, readjusting my robe around me. "Maybe I'm idealizing the *before* a bit too much."

She leans across the table between us and pats my arm, and when she leaves her hand there, I put mine on top of hers and squeeze it.

"Maybe it's something worth thinking about," she says.

"Yeah," I say, but as I look into my sister's eyes, nodding to reassure her that she hasn't offended me with the suggestion, I realize that I might not need to think it over at all. Maybe I already know. Maybe I always have.

# CHAPTER THIRTY-ONE

Even though Lucy's apartment is all the way across town, and it's starting to drizzle, and we're both woozy from the high-dollar relaxation, I insist that we walk home. I'm feeling contemplative, quiet. A walk seems right.

There is plenty to look at as we pass each block but my mind is on the past, reeling back to moments from the last ten years, a flip book of my relationship—the fights, the moves, the meals, the jobs, all of it normal, none of it glaringly bad until recently. It is, in essence, a constant, low grade, just okay. I should have set the bar higher, I think, instead of just flipping to the next page in the playbook I'd set for my life. I should have worked for more.

Lucy chitchats. Do I want to go to a movie tonight? There are films playing that we won't get in North Carolina for a few more weeks, if at all. Or there's a cozy Italian place where we can gorge ourselves on spaghetti and cannoli. Or—it *is* my birthday—we could dress up and do something classic. Bemelmans Bar at the Carlyle. The 21 Club. "Or," she says, putting her hand on my back as we turn the corner toward her block, "we can order in and binge-watch some bad television. How about that?"

We pass by the Laundromat, where there is a heavily made-up woman sitting by the window reading a paperback romance. The smell of detergent wafts out of the open door. I look up the street toward Lucy's skinny brick building, a conspicuous bright green sliver in the middle of the elephant-gray block, and that's when I see him, sitting on the stoop, balancing a big box with a bow on his knees.

I stop.

"What is it?" Lucy says, following my gaze.

I open my mouth to answer but then Owen stands and looks from me to Lucy and then back again. He slumps to one side, like the gift he's now holding under his arm is suddenly weighing him down.

We walk toward him. Lucy marches slightly ahead of me, protecting me. I rush to meet her pace, worried what she might do.

"Happy Birthday," Owen says.

I feel like the wind's been knocked out of me. "What are you doing here?"

He says hello to Lucy and she nods at him.

"Why don't you go upstairs?" I say to Lucy.

Her eyes are on Owen as she walks up the stoop. "I'll be inside," she says to me. I know she'll race straight to her window to watch this.

The door latch closes behind her. "I assumed she would hit me or something," Owen says, trying to make a joke.

I shift my weight from one side to the other. The whole walk home, I've been thinking about what I will say and how I will explain it to him and now here he is, standing before me. *I need more time.*

"Surprise!" he says. It comes out almost like a question.

"That's for sure," I say. My heart is in my throat. "Why didn't you say anything about this when I talked to you this morning?"

"Well, it wouldn't have been a surprise then, would it?" he says. "I started to, actually. I wasn't sure whether this was the right thing to do. I thought Lucy might go apeshit." He pauses and takes a step toward me. "I needed to see you on your birthday." Something about the way he says it makes it sound rehearsed. "I was getting ready to go to the airport when I called."

I'm not sure what to do with this. He's swooped in, the timing's all wrong. "Thank you," I manage.

It is starting to legitimately rain. People on the street are opening their umbrellas. I look to Lucy's stoop, where there isn't enough of an awning to give us any cover. "What about there?" Owen says, pointing across the street to a café.

I nod.

It is mostly empty inside except for a couple of young women having coffee on the banquette in the front of the restaurant. We get a table by the window. Owen orders a beer. I ask for a cup of tea.

"I really wanted to surprise you," he says. "I hope you don't mind."

I see the nervous way he chews on the inside of his lip. I wonder how he thought I would react. Did he expect me to break into a sprint when I saw him and jump into his arms? "I looked up Lucy's address on the computer at home."

*At home.*

"I brought you something." He presents the gift to me. "You probably noticed."

"Thank you." I start to pull off the paper.

What kind of gift do you give the woman you were thinking about leaving just weeks ago? How do you apologize enough? I remember that man at the sports bar in Virginia and how he said he brought flowers to his wife every day, begging for her forgiveness. I remember how helpless I felt and how I wished at the time that I could call that woman and ask her advice. *Has she actually forgiven him despite all of the years?* I glance at Owen. *Does she still sometimes*

*look at her husband across the kitchen table and wonder whether he'd
do it again?*

I pull off the last bit of wrapping paper. His gift is a framed
photo of the lake at our summer camp—mountain peaks framing
the water, the L-shaped dock that I cannonballed off of so many
times, the cove behind the wall of maples where the canoes lay
stacked. You so rarely see it empty like it is in the photo. There
are no kids kicking up sand as they race across the little beach or
teenaged counselors lined up on the docks, twirling their lifeguard
whistles. It looks too placid, unreal.

"I can't live like this anymore," I blurt.

This day, this surprise, this week, these months—I can't do it.
A heaviness comes over my body, like a splintering, a giving out. I
just *can't.*

"Let's not then," he says, but he doesn't mean it the same way
that I do. "Let's not do this anymore, Daph. Let's move forward."

I study the photo. *How long ago*, I think. *Years, decades, life-
times.*

"This isn't who we are anymore," I say, tapping my finger
against the glass.

"Daphne," he says. "That's why I'm here. Let's start over, right
now." I feel the way he's studying me to gauge my reaction.

"Our whole relationship is about the past," I say.

"Daph."

"Owen, let's be honest for once. It's true. This…" I hold up
the picture. "It's a lovely gesture. Thank you."

He nods once.

"But this isn't us."

"Of course it is," he says. He reaches to put his hand over mine
and it isn't a comfort. It feels cold and stinging, all wrong. I pull
away. "This is part of our history, Daphne."

"All we are is our history, Owen. Don't you see that? There is nothing pulling us forward and there hasn't been for years. It's like our feet are cemented in this fable of what we were supposed to be." My voice rises as I realize the truth of it. *This is the problem, isn't it?* "The past is all we are, it's all we've been for a long time—maybe even before Bridget came into the picture." I look into my husband's eyes. "I don't know if it's enough anymore."

"Please," he says. His eyes are wet. "I know I fucked everything up but please give me the chance to show you how dedicated I am."

I place the photo on the table. "I've realized something, Owen," I say. "All of our goodness is there." I point at the glass again. "In the memories, in the *years-ago* memories. Even in the past month, when I was pining for you, I was yearning for what we were a long, long time ago, before we started pretending that everything was okay. We haven't made any good memories in years. You never would have done what you did if that wasn't true."

He shakes his head and then lowers it, looking at his lap.

There's a waiter nearby, unfolding white tablecloths for the dinner service. Another is placing votive candles on each table. Later, this room will be full; families out for Saturday dinners, couples on first dates, women in lipstick and perfume, celebrating. I get the same impatient feeling that I felt out on the street, like there's somewhere else I'm supposed to be.

I look across the table at Owen and our eyes meet. I realize that I stopped asking him to be my husband years ago. I haven't wanted anything from him—I haven't wanted him—until he left me. That means something.

"Please, Daphne."

"I can't." I say. "I can't cling to this any longer."

"I've changed, Daphne."

"What is it about us that you love, Owen? What is it that's so special?"

"I love you," he says. "I love this." He points to the picture. "You're my wife, Daphne."

"We're hardly even friends anymore."

"That's not true. *Please.*"

The thing is, I can hardly listen. I look out the window and watch a taxi stop down the block. A woman throws her shopping bags in the backseat and disappears inside. When they pass us, she's leaning forward, telling the driver where she needs to go.

"Daphne, I want another chance. Please."

"I can't."

"What about everything we talked about at home?"

"We didn't talk, though, Owen. We just fell right back into where we'd been."

"But—" He grabs my hand. "We were in love." A tear rolls down his cheek. "Please change your mind. I'll do anything. I want to fix this."

It would be easier. I could reach across the table and wipe his cheek and wrap my arms around him but it wouldn't be right. I need to walk away. The life I had could make me stay. The life that I want requires that I don't.

"Please," he says again.

I get up from the table and I wait for him to do the same and then I hug him hard, knowing it will be the last one.

"I have to go, Owen."

"Daphne, don't."

It doesn't feel good, walking out of the restaurant and across the street to Lucy's apartment. When I get to her stoop, I turn back. He's watching me through the window. Our eyes meet, and then I see the waiter bring him the bill. I press the buzzer on Lucy's building to be let in, and before she can answer it, I press it again.

# CHAPTER THIRTY-TWO

She's standing in her doorway when I get to her floor.

"What happened?" she asks.

I feel my face start to crumple. "It's over, Lucy. I ended it."

She guides me into the apartment and closes the door behind her.

"This isn't the way it was supposed to go," I moan. *Do I mean today? Do I mean everything?*

We sit on the couch. She cradles my head to her chest. I sob and she holds me tighter, telling me that everything's going to be okay.

The hours go by in a blur. At times, I talk for what seems like days, and at others, I can't talk at all. It's a roller coaster, an emotional detox, and my sister reassures me throughout that I'm doing the right thing. I know that I am, but I am hollowed out, sad and scared. The sun sets and I go into her bedroom and shut the door behind me. I lie on the bed and I close my eyes and I fall into a deep sleep without trouble, like it's been months.

When I wake up early the next morning, the weight in my bones still there, I don't cry. I watch my sister sleeping next to me, her eyes moving beneath her eyelids.

I walk out to the living room to check my phone. Owen left a voicemail just after ten p.m. He decided to rent a car in the city and drive up to his grandparents' farm. Blue is at the kennel where we always board her. His voice is even. I miss him. I could join him. We could glide on that lake and smooth over the facts and plan what's next. It would be easy and wrong.

I save the message despite myself, and then I shower. Lucy and I go to a diner for breakfast and then we kiss and hug good-bye on the street before she puts me in a cab for the airport. On the plane, I am seated beside a couple who look to be in their mid-sixties. The woman calls her daughter to tell her when the flight will get in. When she hangs up, they talk about stopping at the grocery store on the way home and the meeting that she has later that week. We start to take off and they hold each other's hands. I close my eyes.

This is life now, figuring things out, the way that it needs to be.

I pick up the dog and drive home. I touch the walls and run my hand over the counters and then I sit on the sofa for a long, long time after I should have turned on the light.


Days pass. I go to work in the morning and then the morning after that, and the morning after that, and so on. Owen doesn't call and I don't try to get in touch, though I wonder where he is and when he'll show up. When he finally calls one afternoon from Massachusetts, I answer. I'm surprised that he's stayed away from work this long, if not from me.

"I'm going to come home this weekend," he says. "But I have a conference next week, so I'll be leaving again on Tuesday."

"Okay," I say. *I can stay at Annie's.* I listen to him breathing, the sound of papers rustling in the background. "I'm so sorry, Owen."

He clears his throat. "Don't be," he says. "You didn't do anything wrong."

"We both did," I say.

"I'll call the agent about the house," he offers.

∞

During my lunch break one day, I call Mary Elizabeth at her treatment center. She makes angry jokes about her "dumb-shit druggie roommate" and confesses that she daydreams all day about fruity vacation drinks *("the umbrellas, the pineapple slices, the maraschino cherries")*. Predictably, she turns the tables midway through our conversation. "How are you doing?" she says. "Any addict fuckups take my place?"

"No one could take your place, Mary Elizabeth," I say. "And I'm not that great, actually. I'm dealing with some personal stuff."

When she doesn't respond, I know she is as surprised as I am by my candor.

"You'll be fine," she says. "Whatever it is that's happening."

"I will," I say. "And you will be, too."

The next evening, I drive home after work, stopping on the way to pick up a few flats of brightly colored annuals to plant before the open house that our real estate agent is holding that weekend. They are yellow and pink, red and orange, happy buy-this-house colors. I put my keys on the kitchen table after I come in the door and I kneel down to greet Blue, scratching her under her chin. I turn on the light and I stand at the counter, flipping through the mail. There, among the bills and catalogs and advertisements, is a postcard. It's a generic travel guide scene, crumbling old buildings with terra cotta roofs lining a harbor.

*This is Corsica*, it reads. The handwriting is messy, like a boy's.

*The sun? Too warm.*

*The food? Too good.*

*The hotel? Too luxurious.*

*Come! Help! Save me!*

And I decide in that moment, almost without thinking about it, that I will.

# QUESTIONS FOR FURTHER DISCUSSION

1. The epigraph at the beginning of the novel is a quote from Nora Ephron: "You can never know the truth of anyone's marriage, including your own." Do you agree?

2. How much do you think that Owen and Daphne's similar careers helped or hurt them? Do you think that Owen and Daphne would have fallen in love if they hadn't shared a childhood history?

3. Daphne bristles when her dad tells her that she's "always been so good at figuring things out." Why do you think this upsets her? Is her carefully controlled nature ultimately a positive or a negative trait?

4. Do you believe that Owen would have wanted his marriage back, as he claimed to, had Bridget lived?

5. When Daphne is grappling with whether to take Owen back, she remembers the traditional marriage vows she made at her wedding: *For better or worse, till death do us part.* Do you believe that the vow is an absolute or are there exceptions? Do you believe that an affair should always end a relationship? If you were in Daphne's shoes, could you have forgiven him?

6.  After an appointment with Mary Elizabeth, Daphne reflects that she irrationally envies her patient's ability to act without thinking of the consequences. When, if ever, is that an admirable quality?

7.  Was Annie's reaction to Daphne's situation appropriate? Was she simply a concerned friend or do you think she let her personal history affect her opinions about what Daphne should do? What advice would you have given her?

8.  When considering the possibilities with Andrew, Daphne says that she can't just jump from one relationship to the next. Could you? If you received a postcard like the one that Daphne receives at the end of the story, would you go?

9.  At the end of the novel, Lucy tells Daphne that she thinks marriage should be the part of a person's life that's "easy and fun," where you go to receive comfort from the rest of the world. Do you agree?

10. Where do you see Daphne, Andrew, and Owen five years from now?

# ACKNOWLEDGMENTS

I am so grateful to have had the pleasure to work on another book with the expert help of my agent, Katherine Fausset, who provided valuable insight from the story's earliest stages, and my editor, Emily Griffin, whose astute feedback and judgment was essential to making the book everything it could be. Thanks to both of you for once again making this work so enjoyable.

Thanks to my go-to medical experts, Dr. Matthew Crowley and Lindsay Wojciechowski, FNP-C, who provided the behind-the-curtain info I needed to understand how medical practices work and also helped me devise plausible ailments for my characters. Tremendous thanks also to everyone at Grand Central, particularly Claire Brown, who designed the gorgeous cover.

I simply could not do my job without the help of women like Ana Bray, Lili Wang, and Tiffany Yellock, who kept my kids happy and entertained while I wrote. I am so lucky to have the endless support of my parents and my brother, whose enthusiastic emails make this whole thing more fun.

Finally, allow me to clarify that the man I married bears zero responsibility for inspiring the poor husband behavior in this story. To Jay and the girls: Words can't express how grateful I am for the gift of our family, and Jay, for your friendship, encouragement, and tireless optimism. Thanks for making each day all roses and stems.

# ABOUT THE AUTHOR

Kristyn Kusek Lewis is the author of *How Lucky You Are* (Grand Central, 2012). A former magazine editor, her writing has appeared in many publications including the *New York Times*, *O: The Oprah Magazine*, *Real Simple*, and *Glamour*. She is a graduate of the MFA program at the Vermont College of Fine Arts and lives in North Carolina with her family.